Mediev.

K. M. Ashman lives in ...   ...es with his wife and dog.

Mainly concentrating on historical fiction books, especially in the Roman and Medieval eras, he found significant success with the India Summers Mysteries, a series of books about a librarian and her Special Forces partner, who delve deep into history to solve modern-day problems.

Also by K. M. Ashman

The India Summers Mysteries

The Roman Chronicles

The Medieval Sagas

The Road to Hastings

MEDIEVAL III

Sword of Liberty

K. M. ASHMAN

CANELO

First published in the United Kingdom in 2013 by K. M. Ashman

This edition published in the United Kingdom in 2022 by

Canelo
Unit 9, 5th Floor
Cargo Works, 1–2 Hatfields
London, SE1 9PG
United Kingdom

A CIP catalogue record for this book is available from the British Library.

Print ISBN 978 1 80032 447 3
Ebook ISBN 978 1 80032 446 6

This book is a work of fiction. Names, characters, businesses, organizations, places and events are either the product of the author's imagination or are used fictitiously. Any resemblance to actual persons, living or dead, events or locales is entirely coincidental.

Cover design by Black Sheep

Cover images © Depositphotos

Look for more great books at www.canelo.co

Printed and bound in Great Britain by Clays Ltd, Elcograf S.p.A.

1

MIX
Paper from
responsible sources
FSC® C018072

Foreword

Medieval III – Sword of Liberty is the third book in the Medieval series and though it can be read as a stand-alone novel, it is recommended that you first read the other two books, *Medieval I – Blood of the Cross* and *Medieval II – In Shadows of Kings* to get a feel for the backstory of the main characters.

The storyline is obviously a work of fiction but like all my books, it is set against the backdrop of real events at the time.

Foreword

Prologue

In 1274, Edward the First, also known as Longshanks, ruled England having inherited the crown from his father, Henry the Third. Across the border to the west, the smaller country of Wales was ruled by Prince Llewellyn ap Gruffydd, a direct descendant of Llewellyn the Great.

Tensions were strained between the two countries and minor conflicts were commonplace between the lesser nobles, but when Edward found out about Llewellyn's proposed marriage to Eleanor du Montfort, the daughter of his deceased father's greatest enemy, he was incensed and in 1275 arranged for her ship to be intercepted as she travelled from France to be with the Welsh prince. Eleanor was imprisoned causing the relationship between Edward and Llewellyn to deteriorate even further and in 1276, war broke out between the two countries.

In 1277, Edward led a huge army into Wales and captured the Welsh harvest on the island of Ynys Mon, forcing the Welsh prince to surrender before any major battle was fought. Later that year, the two men signed the treaty of Aberconwy, where Llewellyn surrendered control of most of the country in return for keeping the lands of Gwynedd and the title, Prince of Wales. Edward was satisfied and released Eleanor from prison to fulfil her marriage vows to Llewellyn and for the next few years, an uneasy peace existed between the two monarchs.

Despite the treaty, the people of Wales were still unhappy being ruled by an English monarch, and especially about the construction of English castles at Flint, Rhuddlan, Builth Wells and Aberystwyth. Subsequently an undercurrent of resistance steadily grew until in 1282, a full-scale rebellion against Edward's rule forced the English king to invade Wales once more, only this time with full scale conquest as a goal.

Despite some initial setbacks, Edward's army was ultimately victorious and after several battles throughout Wales, Prince Llewellyn was killed at the battle of Orewen Bridge. Edward finally realised the threat the Welsh posed and embarked on an unprecedented building programme in the north of the country, constructing enormous castles at Caernarfon, Conwy and Harlech, not just as bastions of military strength but also as a signal to the Welsh about the futility of opposing his might.

These castles formed the backbone of his defences in Wales, an unassailable system of fortresses, each designed to support each other against any threat from the Welsh.

They were a symbol of his power, a system of invincible fortifications and in effect as impregnable as a ring of steel, unassailable by any living man.

...or so he thought...

Chapter One

The village of Mynydd Du, mid-Wales – 1294

The windowless back room of the ramshackle tavern was bitterly cold and smelled of damp dogs. The darkness was broken by a dozen flickering candles spread around the walls, each fighting its own battle against the howling gale outside as it sent its icy fingers through the gaps in the aged stone walls.

Three men sat around a rough table, each nursing a tankard of sweet tasting ale and though they were there for the same reason, nobody spoke, they just sat in the gloom alone with their thoughts.

The Pilgrim's Rest was a small tavern in the village of Mynydd Du and well known amongst all Welsh nationalists as a haunt for patriots who held one cause close to their hearts, the defeat of King Edward's army and the return of self-governance to the land of their fathers.

Until the death of Llewellyn twelve years earlier, the tavern was also a well-known recruiting house for any man wishing to join the Prince in his cause but after he died, the subsequent occupation of the country by Edward's forces meant it had become a more subdued establishment where men planned unlikely revolts over tankards of cheap ale, only to forget their drunken plans when they woke the following morn. Most nights, frustrations were shared between men quick with plans but light of resolve and many years passed without change, but tonight was different – for tonight, rebellion was in the air.

–

The door to the back room opened and a figure bent to enter before taking his place at the end of the table. Meirion ap Rees was a landowner from north Wales and though he made a modest living, was better known as a fixer, a man who knew everyone and carried secret messages between the nobles of Wales, coordinating the resistance against the English.

Meirion undid the leather ties of his cloak and looked around the room, judging the reliability of the men should their support be counted upon. Within moments he knew he worried needlessly for two of the men had proven themselves time and time again against the forces of Edward. Though the days of battle had long gone, each had made the English king pay for his occupation on a daily basis, harassing his supply lines and causing disruption whenever they had the chance.

On one side was Cynan ap Maredudd, a welsh noble who once held huge swathes of land throughout Mid Wales. The defeat of Llewellyn meant much of his land was forfeited to Edward and though he still held sway over three full Cantrefs, his grudge against Longshanks ran deep and he dreamed of the day when the King's men would once more be on the receiving end of Welsh steel.

Opposite him sat another well-known figure, Morgan ap Maredudd, a Welsh lord from Glamorgan in the south and though his motives were not as noble as his title, his ambition and patriotism made him a valued ally in the continued struggle against the English.

Finally at the far end of the table sat a man with the hood of his cloak still raised, hiding his face from the others. Though it was disconcerting, Meirion knew it was a man who could be trusted. He had no title and owned not a square yard of land. His dwelling place was unknown and his only ambition lay in obtaining the next purse for himself and his comrades. This was a member of the Blaidd, the roaming band of mercenaries that had gained notoriety throughout the country for their ruthless skills in battle and fierce loyalty to any man who paid their price. The Blaidd were named after the wolves that once roamed the forests of Mid Wales and were made up of any man, outlawed or not, who had proved themselves in conflict and though not regarded as brigands by their own people, they were wanted by the crown for their constant raids on English interests.

'Gentlemen,' said Meirion taking his seat, 'thank you for coming. My apologies for the poorness of the location but Edward's men have been particularly active these past few weeks and it is the best I could do.'

'The location matters not,' said Cynan, 'the business of the day outweighs minor discomfort.'

'Agreed,' said Meirion, 'then we will begin.'

'Wait,' said Morgan, 'first I would know the name of the stranger.'

All eyes turned to the man at the end of the table.

'All you need to know is that I am here on behalf of the Blaidd?' said the man.

'Are you the leader?' asked Morgan.

'He is not,' interrupted Cynan. 'The leader is a man called Goddeff. I have had opportunity to share ale with him on many occasions.'

'Goddeff is dead,' said the man, 'and I have taken his place.'

'Dead,' gasped Cynan, 'surely he was not bettered by any man?'

'He was not. He snapped a leg while hunting boar and the infection killed him. It was not a good death.'

'So you say you are the new leader?' said Meirion. 'How do we know this is true?'

'You don't,' said the man, 'but if you doubt my word, I am happy to leave you to your business.'

'No,' said Meirion eventually. 'If what I have to say comes to pass, we will need the Blaidd riding alongside us as brothers.' He looked at the other two men. 'Are you content we continue?'

Both men nodded before Cynan spoke up.

'I suppose we have no choice,' he said, 'but at least do us the courtesy of introducing yourself, stranger, for if we are to do business, I would at least know the name of the man who lightens my purse.'

The man removed his hood and stared down the table.

'I am indeed the leader of the Blaidd,' he said, 'and my name is Garyn ap Thomas.'

Chapter Two

The island of Ynys Mon

The bearded swordsman looked down at the man at his feet. His victim stared defiantly back, looking past the sword resting upon his throat as if daring his assailant to press home the killing thrust. A trickle of sweat ran down the fallen man's forehead and silence reigned, broken only by the sound of both men straining to re-gather their breath.

The conflict had been hard fought and for a while the outcome could have gone either way, but the experience of the older man had proved too much and he pressed home an unexpected advantage before tripping his assailant and pressing his sword against his victim's throat.

They stared at each other before the fallen man spoke. 'Well?'

The victor paused before finally moving his sword to one side and extending his free arm. The fallen man grabbed the offered hand and pulled himself to his feet.

'You were lucky this time,' said Madog. 'I slipped on the wet floor.'

'Perhaps so,' said Geraint, 'but wet floors are commonplace on all battlefields and have to be taken into account.'

'Fair point,' said Madog bending to retrieve his sword.

'Another bout?' asked Geraint.

'Not this time,' said Madog. 'I have guests to host at the manor. Edward has sent messengers with documents that need signing. Perhaps you would like to join us?'

'You have my thanks but I must decline,' said Geraint. 'I respect your duties as a host but would find the company less than engaging. Please, accept my apologies.'

'No need to apologise,' said Madog, sheathing his sword. 'Your view of the English is no secret and though I share your worries, politics demand I treat my visitors with courtesy.'

'Granted,' said Geraint, 'I just ache for the day when the men of Wales unite to return our land to the people.'

'Well, when that day comes, perhaps we will stand side by side with swords drawn but for now, I will leave you to enjoy your minor victory.'

Both men laughed and Geraint watched his friend walk back across the field to the doors of his manor.

Geraint had been born in Brycheniog in the south, many years earlier and after a life of service as a soldier, fate had seen him come north to fulfil a promise and see through a commitment to his country.

Following a quest to find a man of royal lineage to unite the warring factions of Wales, fortune had revealed a boy of ten years old called Madog ap Llewellyn of Ynys Mon. Madog was the proven grandson of Madoc ap Gruffydd and thus enjoyed direct lineage from both Owain Gwynedd, King of Wales and Henry the first, William the Conqueror's son, thus having both a Welsh and English route to the throne.

Despite this royal lineage, Geraint had been astonished to find that the boy was unaware of his unique place in

Welsh nobility as his mother had kept the identity of his grandfather to herself in an effort to keep him away from the lethal politics that wracked the country at the time.

When Geraint had confronted her with the knowledge ten years ago, she had made him swear he would not tell the boy until he was at least twenty-one years old and able to defend himself against any would-be assassin. Geraint had accepted on condition he was appointed the boy's protector to see him safely to manhood. Subsequently, for the past ten years Geraint had held a position in the household's guard and was tasked with the personal safety of the young prince as he watched the boy turn into a respected young man.

Subsequently it fell to Geraint to teach Madog the art of conflict and all things military and though the boy's skills were as good as any man, he was yet to face an opponent in real combat, a weakness that worried Geraint on a daily basis.

—

Madog disappeared into the house and Geraint made his way over toward the annexe that housed the estate's men at arms, but before he reached the door, a page ran up to him.

'My lord, there is a visitor to see you in the eating hall.'

'Thank you,' said Geraint. 'Does this visitor have a name?'

'Not really,' started the boy, 'but I'm not sure.'

'What do you mean, not sure? Did he give you his name or not?'

'All he said, my lord, was that the shield of the poor demands audience.'

Geraint's face split into a wide grin and after almost knocking the boy to the floor with an encouraging slap to the back, he strode purposely toward the eating hall. He burst into the room and stared at the back of a man with white hair hanging down his back.

'Tarian,' he shouted, 'you old devil, can it be true?'

The man answered without turning.

'Geraint ap Thomas, I knew it was you before you spoke. Only you would make such a common entrance.' He stood up and turned to face Geraint and for a few moments, both men stared at each other without speaking. Finally Geraint strode over and gave his old mentor a manly hug.

'Careful,' groaned Tarian, 'my bones are not what they used to be.'

'Nonsense,' said Geraint releasing him, 'they are yet as strong as Mandan Ironwood.'

'Perhaps a few years ago,' laughed Tarian, 'but alas no more.'

Geraint looked at the man the people once called the Shield of the Poor. The once giant of a man was slightly stooped and the hair that once fell jet black below his shoulders was no less long, but now whiter than the driven snow.

'My appearance has caught you off guard,' said Tarian.

'I admit it has,' said Geraint, 'but I still sense the spirit that once led us into the unknown.'

'The spirit is as strong as ever, Geraint, but alas the body is tired and aches for eternal rest.'

'Nonsense,' said Geraint. 'Come, we will sit in the warmth of the kitchens and threaten a venison steak out of the estate's cook.'

'Sounds good,' said Tarian and walked alongside Geraint through into the kitchens.

Within half an hour they were seated at a small table in the corner of the busy kitchen, eating choice venison steaks and a side plate of roasted vegetables fresh from the cook's ovens. A large jug of ale stood half empty before them and they talked freely, reliving the adventures they had shared many years ago on Tarian's ambitious quest. Eventually the laughter eased, the stories tailed off and silence fell between them. Geraint filled up the tankards once more and stared at his old friend.

'So, Tarian,' he said, 'as good as it is to have you here, I suspect this is not a trip for reminiscence.'

'Astute as ever, Geraint,' said Tarian. 'There is indeed business to be discussed and I am here to put in place the final piece of a puzzle that has been many years in the making.'

'I assume you are talking about the coming of age of a certain young man?'

'His birthday is indeed known to me but is a coincidence for I would still be here even if he was five years younger.'

'What do you mean?'

'The time is upon us, Geraint, the day we dreamed of for so many years has come to pass. The mood of the country is one of rebellion and men whisper in dark corners, each making plans against the shadow of Longshanks.'

'Men have plotted so since he returned from the Holy land but nothing ever transpires. Even those brave enough to chance their arm are soon betrayed by those loyal to Longshanks and it has been said there are so many Welsh heads displayed on the walls of Worcester, the crows grow fat from eyes alone.'

'And it is that sort of sentiment which stirs the beast into action,' said Tarian. 'Our people have had enough, Geraint, they are taxed to a standstill, yet see those in the pay of Longshanks grow fat while our children starve. Taverns are raided by his soldiers and our churches are stripped of their relics in a bid to raise funds for his next war. Our farms are going untended as the young men are coerced into joining his army and it is said he intends to sail against the French in a matter of months.'

'So why exactly are you here?'

'You know why I am here, Geraint, I am here to fulfil the pact we made all those years ago. We have nobles in the south waiting to rise against the English and it is all I can do to hold them from attacking immediately. Our numbers are strong, the swords are sharpened and the young men chomp at the bit to strike against their oppressors.'

'Then why do they wait?'

'Geraint, as you have already said, there have been many such uprisings since Llewellyn fell and all were doomed to fail. Not because the men lacked heart but because they set forth about their task in isolation while the rest of the country slept. Would we send lone riders out to confront the enemy on a battlefield? No, we would not, but that is exactly what those men did, took on the might of the crown by attacking in isolation. They were doomed to failure from the start and it was the actions of desperate men.'

'So what has changed?'

'This time we are organised. For the last few years, men of note have been coordinating the resistance and there are ten thousand men at arms waiting for the signal.'

'Ten thousand?' said Geraint raising his eyebrows in surprise.

'And more,' said Tarian. 'That number does not count those who will be caught up in the fervour. We estimate we can double that number within weeks of showing our hand.'

'And what is it that stops you taking that next step?'

'We need a spark, Geraint. A beacon to lead us back to freedom. I know it has been a long time but we always knew this day would come. From the very first time we talked on the forecastle of the *Coronet*; we shared a dream that would eventually bring us to this point. It has taken far longer than any of us would have liked but that has not been a bad thing. The time is right, the mood of a nation is behind us and all we need is a figurehead. The time is now, Geraint, you have to tell Madog of his destiny and charge him with leading this country back into freedom.'

Across the courtyard, Madog walked into the banqueting hall of the manor. His mother, Angelique, was at his side and they took their place at the head of the table running across the width of the hall. The two runs of tables stretching away from them were populated by nobles from across Ynys Mon, as well as minor officials from Cantrefs across north Wales. Though the occasion was not great in itself, it was always prudent to receive any delegation from Longshanks with due ceremony and displays of wealth.

Their guests were already there, two men granted the honour of sharing the top table and each stood behind a chair to either side of those reserved for Madog and Angelique. Everyone nodded slightly as Madog entered for though he was not royalty, he was the Lord of Ynys Mon and as such demanded respect.

'Please, be seated,' said Madog and as everyone took their place, Madog turned to the man sitting beside him.

'Simon of Kent,' he said, 'I trust you have travelled well.'

'Indeed we have, my lord,' answered Simon, 'and have been well looked after since we arrived. Your hospitality has not gone unnoticed and I will personally ensure Long-shanks hears about it.'

Madog nodded almost imperceptibly. It would not be good to indicate that he accepted any blessing from Edward but similarly, acknowledgement was expected in such matters. For the next two hours they enjoyed the best the manor kitchens could offer. The first course consisted of boiled ground beef in a spiced wine sauce and a side dish of onions with almonds and currants. Other courses followed including baby rabbits and curlew, but the finale was a fattened roast swan stuffed with tiny swallows and plums. The guests clapped in appreciation as Simon was invited to carve the bird and eventually the feast ended with a selection of fruits and wafers.

Once the meal was over, the servants produced a selection of the best wines from the continent and ales to slake the thirst of the driest of throats. Minstrels came next as well as tellers of tales and as the conversation flowed, Simon of Kent turned to Madog.

'You keep a magnificent table, my lord. Never have I eaten such splendour outside of the royal court.'

'I am pleased you think so, Simon,' said Madog. 'We may not be a rich people but we will not be found wanting when entertaining messengers of the King.'

'Indeed,' said Simon, 'which brings me onto the business of the day.'

'Will it not wait until the morrow?'

'Alas no. Your hospitality is second to none and I would love to stay for the merrymaking but we must be away before dawn for many more miles lay before us. Could I beg a few minutes of your time to share the purpose of our journey?'

'Can you not do it here?'

'A quieter atmosphere may be more conducive to such business,' said Simon with a forced smile.

'So be it,' said Madog and rose from his seat. For a few moments the noise in the hall quietened as the guests feared the evening was over but Madog soon put their minds at rest.

'Please,' he said, 'enjoy the hospitality to your heart's content. I will return as soon as certain matters are laid to rest.' Cheers echoed around the room and as he and Simon of Kent left the hall, the festivities resumed behind them.

The two men walked through the cold stone passages before heading into an antechamber warmed by a roaring log fire.

'Bring wine,' said Madog to one of the two servants standing by the door. He turned to Simon who was staring up at a magnificent portrait above the fireplace.

'Do you know him?' asked Madog joining the messenger before the fire.

'If I am not mistaken, it is Llewellyn ap Gruffydd.'

'You have the correct name but wrong generation,' said Madog. 'This man is Llewellyn ap Iorwerth, or Llewellyn the Great as he is known to us Welsh.'

'Hmmm,' said Simon, 'though the title depends on your viewpoint, I suppose.'

'Granted you see him in a different light,' said Madog, 'but to us he always was and always will be known as Llewellyn the Great.'

'We digress,' said Simon turning around, 'let's get down to business.' He opened a leather bag hanging at his side and retrieved a series of scrolls sealed with red wax.

'These are communiques from the King himself,' said Simon. 'They report the need to raise taxes for his coming war in France.'

'More taxes?' sighed Madog. 'Our people are already taxed to a standstill. They struggle to afford even bread.'

'We all need to tighten our belts, Madog. The King is about to set forth on a campaign against the French and it is in all our interests to ensure he is well resourced. A few extra pennies may not make a difference to a family while collectively they could ensure the security of our country.'

'I disagree,' said Madog. 'Those same few pennies could mean the difference between life and death to the hungry. He can't keep raising the tax burden, Simon, the people will only take so much.'

'On the contrary, Madog, the King can do as he sees fit and I would suggest you keep such exhortations of what he can or can't do to yourself.'

Madog stared at him, struggling to contain his ire.

'I can see you are upset, Madog,' continued Simon, 'so will leave you with your thoughts.' He threw the rest of the scrolls on the table. 'Within these you will find the King's expectations, men at arms, weapons, stores and horses. The list is detailed. The Constable of Caernarfon will arrange the collection within four weeks. In addition, every person will be taxed one third of all moveable possessions.'

'Moveable possessions? Are we not already taxed a quarter of all value?'

'And that will remain but in addition, there will be an extra tax on possessions. It's not hard to understand, if it moves, it's taxed. If a man has three carts, he must give one to the crown or the equivalent value in coin, such value to be determined by the Constable or his officers.'

'But that's unsustainable,' said Madog, 'the burden of tax will drive people to their graves.'

'War is an expensive pastime, Madog and there is a need for every man to share the burden.' He stood and sealed the bag containing the scrolls meant for the next manor. 'I will leave you to it; Madog for the road is hard before us. You will find everything is in order within the scrolls and I would encourage you to embrace this opportunity to support your monarch, after all, Edward is king of both England and Wales, you would do well to remember that.'

Without waiting for a reply, he turned and left the room. Madog stared after him before turning and throwing his tankard against the wall in a fit of rage.

Across the courtyard Tarian and Geraint were saying their goodbyes. Tarian was astride his charger while four other horsemen waited patiently for him to join them.

'Are you sure you won't stay?' asked Geraint. 'The barracks are humble but warm or I can arrange a room at the main house.'

'No, the fewer who know of my involvement the better. I have arranged lodgings at an old friend's place not three miles from here.' He paused. 'Speak to Madog, Geraint; make him see the value in joining our cause.'

'I will try, Tarian but cannot promise success.'

'Do what you can. In the meantime, try to judge the mood of Ynys Mon. We will need every blade in the field if this is going to succeed.'

'And what will you do?' asked Geraint handing up the reins.

'I have to meet other men such as myself to arrange a time to strike. It is important we act together otherwise we will fail as those before.'

'When do you anticipate such action?'

'We will wait for Edward to set sail and when his army is in France, we will sweep through our country, eradicating the English from our lands. By the time word of this reaches Longshanks, Wales will be free and in possession of a united army. Even if he returns to face us, which I doubt, he will find nought but Welsh steel waiting for him.'

'My heart races with the thought, Tarian; let's just hope the nation's heart beats with the same pace and fervour.'

'We will see, Geraint, we will see.'

With that he turned and galloped his horse out of the courtyard closely followed by his men at arms. Geraint

18

watched him go and turned back toward the barracks. Before he reached the door, a voice called out from the rear door of the manor kitchens.

'Geraint, come quickly.'

Geraint heard the urgency in the woman's voice and raced across the flagstones to find one of the housemaids wringing her hands with worry.

'Anne, what causes you such angst?' he asked.

'My lord, it is the master, he is wild with rage and threatens to have my John sent to the stocks.'

'For what reason?'

'Something to do with the English visitors, my lord. My John says he has never seen the master in such a state.'

'Where is he now?'

'In the room with the big picture.'

'Don't worry, Anne,' said Geraint, 'I will see what worries him so.' With that he crossed the kitchens and strode down the corridor to the family rooms. Within moments he saw the worried face of one of the servants outside a closed door.

'John,' he said, 'what is his mood.'

'Still sour, my lord. He says I will be in the stocks by dawn.'

'Fret not, John,' said Geraint, 'they are the words spoken in temper. Go back to Anne and ease her worry.'

'Thank you, my lord,' said John and ran down the corridor.

Geraint watched him go before opening the door and walking into the room. For a few seconds he could see no one but then realised Madog was seated in a large chair facing away from him.

'Get out,' roared Madog without standing up.

'My lord, it's me,' said Geraint quietly and walked over to the table to pour himself a tankard of wine.

'And what do you want, Geraint?' sneered Madog. 'Has my overbearing mother sent you here to calm my ire?'

'On the contrary, my lord, your mother does not know I am here.'

Madog fell silent as Geraint poured his drink and sat in the seat opposite him.

'Make yourself comfortable,' he said with a sneer.

'Is this a problem?' asked Geraint.

Madog stared into Geraint's eyes but soon lowered them as his older friend's steely gaze bettered him once again.

'No, I suppose not,' he said.

'Good,' said Geraint. 'So, why don't you tell me what this is all about?'

'Just venting my frustration, Geraint,' said Madog. 'Better within these four walls than in the gaze of my staff.'

'And since when have you taken out your anger on those whom you better?'

'I don't know what you mean?'

'Even as we speak there is a servant trembling in fear at the thought of a week in the stocks. Is this the action of a noble man?'

'Oh, that? Empty words, no more. I will make it up with him on the morrow.'

'See that you do,' said Geraint.

'You are very free with your demands, Geraint,' said Madog, 'but I am no longer a mere boy under your instruction, I am lord of this manor and will act as I please. You would do well to remember that.'

'Why, Madog?' asked Geraint leaning forward. 'What punishment do you have in store for me? Placed in the stocks, whipped in the village square or what about having me beaten by your men at arms? Feel free, Madog, I will not resist and when you are done and you feel less anger, perhaps we can discuss this thing as fellows.'

Madog stared once more, but this time did not lower his gaze.

'You have entered this room uninvited, drunk my wine and talked down to me as a mere boy, yet you know there will not be punishment for you are the only man I respect. The rest are but cattle at the feet of Longshanks.'

'You are wrong, Madog. There are many men who demand respect, not just in this country but across Christendom and in that I include Longshanks himself as well as many of his nobles.'

'What treason is this?' gasped Madog. 'How can you sit here and lavish praise on someone who has brought our country to its knees?'

'I lavish no praise, Madog, but respect him as a strong enemy for make no mistake, that is exactly what he is.'

'He is a tyrant.'

'He is a king who keeps his enemies at bay on three fronts, Scotland, Wales and France. Any man who can do that while maintaining an iron grip on his own country has to be respected.'

'You are quick with your praise, Geraint yet know nothing of politics. What ruler taxes his people to breaking point then pushes them further for his own aims, knowing full well that many will starve as a result of his edicts?'

'Your meaning escapes me,' said Geraint.

Madog leaned forward and pushed the scrolls toward him.

'Read the latest from this man you so admire, Geraint, see the esteem in which he holds your countrymen.'

Geraint picked up the scrolls and for a few minutes the room was silent as he digested the contents. Finally he replaced the scrolls and sat back in the chair, sipping at his tankard of wine.

'Well?' said Madog.

'Well what?'

'What do you think about these latest demands?'

'I think they will be crippling,' said Geraint.

'As do I,' said Madog. 'I fear not for myself or family, for we have enough lands to make sure we survive, but what about those who look to me for leadership. I can't feed every mouth from my treasury or soon we would be as destitute as those who serve us.'

'And you are angered by this?'

'Of course I am angered,' shouted Madog, 'but I am getting more incensed by your failure to understand the seriousness of the situation. Do you not care?'

'I care, my lord, but do not exhibit my frustration as I am more interested in your reaction.'

'My reaction? Why on earth does that concern you?'

'Because there are things afoot that may have a bearing on the situation and depending on whether your feelings are genuine or just a fleeting reaction, you may well have a great say in the outcome.'

'You speak in riddles, Geraint. Explain yourself or leave me to vent my anger in my own way.'

Geraint paused and stared at Madog for what seemed an age.

22

'Well?' demanded Madog.

'You are right,' said Geraint, 'you deserve an explanation. I was waiting for the right time but things are happening fast and perhaps we can't afford to wait.'

'You are making no sense!'

'Regain your seat, my lord, and fill your tankard, for I have a tale that will be hours in the telling. When I am done, you will see things from a different perspective and you will have a decision to make that will decide the future of Wales. All I ask is that you listen to everything I have to say without interruption and when I am done, I will leave you with your thoughts.'

'Well, I am now intrigued, Geraint,' said Madog sarcastically, 'so spin this tale of mystery. At the very least I will be entertained before I face the real world once more.'

'Then so be it,' said Geraint. 'My tale starts over a hundred years ago and starts with Madog ap Llewellyn.'

'I have heard of him,' said Madog, 'he was a great seaman who left to discover new lands across the seas.'

'Indeed he was, my lord, but not only was he a renowned mariner, he was also your direct ancestor.'

Chapter Three

Bristol Castle

'Open the gates,' roared Nicholas Fermbaud, Castellan of Bristol Castle, 'our monarch approaches.'

Men ran to their stations and the huge oaken doors swung slowly inward away from the raised portcullis. Along the battlements, men at arms took to their stations between the castellations and in the courtyard below, pages lined up ready to take care of the horses, while servants lined the passageways of the impressive keep.

The visit of the King had been anticipated for weeks and Nicholas had spared no expense to ensure everything was ready. Quarters had been prepared and the kitchens stocked with fresh provisions in anticipation. Despite the preparations, Nicholas was nervous. The King was known to have exacting demands and did not suffer poor standards. The Castellan walked over to stand on the steps of the great hall as he waited for the column to arrive.

Within moments the sound of horses echoed around the courtyard as they thundered over the wooden bridge spanning the moat and men threw themselves out of the way as the King's outriders galloped through the gate. Fifty knights reined in their destriers and formed an outward-facing perimeter, forcing those loitering in the courtyard back toward the perimeter walls. Each knight displayed their coat of arms on their shields and it was plain to see they came from many of the great families of England.

Nicholas knew these men were battle hardened with many having bloodied their lances in both the Welsh and Scottish wars. He also knew this was a display for his benefit, designed to remind him of the strength of Edward. Since the second war of the barons almost thirty years earlier, Edward ensured he reminded his nobles of his authority at every opportunity.

Within moments another fifty horses rode across the bridge, though this time every knight carried shields emblazoned with three golden lions on a red background, the coat of arms of Edward. These were the King's personal guard and they formed two lines facing inward, each holding their lances upright as a guard of honour. Finally the King himself arrived and as he passed, every knight raised his visor in salute.

Nicholas knew this pomp and ceremony was purely for effect but despite this, he had to admit it was an impressive entrance and would have a huge impact on all who witnessed it.

Edward rode up to the steps of the keep and waited as Nicholas bowed.

'Welcome to your castle, my lord,' he said.

'Nicholas Fermbaud, it is good to be here. The road is dusty and my men would welcome refreshment.'

'Of course, my lord,' said Fermbaud, 'you will find my servants eager to meet all your needs.'

Edward dismounted and removed his gauntlets and helm before handing them to a page. He walked up the steps to stand beside the Castellan before turning to look back into the courtyard where the eyes of hundreds of men were upon him. The King stood head and shoulders taller than Nicholas Fermbaud, as he did most men and it was this stature that had earned him the nickname, Longshanks.

'I see you are well manned, Nicholas, a situation that is to be welcomed.'

'Your edicts were clear, my lord, and you will find our quota has been well met.'

'Good to hear it,' said Edward. He signalled to his sergeant at arms to stand down his men before turning to the Castellan.

'Lead us in, Nicholas, and show me to my quarters. I would divest myself of my armour.'

'Of course, my lord, and I will see you are well attended.'

They walked down the passage of the keep and stopped at the bottom of a stairwell built into the thick walls of the keep tower.

'Your room is near the top, my lord, and your guards will be barracked on the floor below. I trust that is in order.'

'It will be fine. Tell your staff we will eat at dusk but keep the meal modest. This is not a time for feasting, Nicholas, but more of that on the morrow.'

'Of course, my lord,' said the Castellan and bowed his head as the King disappeared up the winding stair.

–

That evening saw the Castellan entertain the King and his guard and despite Longshanks' demand for simple fare, Fermbaud couldn't help but wince when he saw the amount the men ate. He also knew that his kitchens were working overtime to keep the rest of the King's entourage fed in the outer halls and though his stores were full, he knew that if the visit was to last more than a few weeks, he would have to dig deep into his treasury to keep the supplies coming.

Finally the meal ended and while many of the knights left the castle to explore the taverns of Bristol, Longshanks suggested Fermbaud join him in walking the ramparts.

'An impressive fortress,' said Longshanks as he peered out over the castellations of the outer wall. The city spread away before him but despite the darkness, the full moon meant he could see the never-ending sea of rooftops.

'It is, my lord,' replied Fermbaud. 'I understand you were once a prisoner here?'

'I was,' said Longshanks, 'though not for long and rest assured, those responsible for my captivity did not live long enough to enjoy the notoriety of having once held a prince as a prisoner.'

'Your rule goes from strength to strength, my lord,' said Fermbaud, 'and I trust French soil will soon be added to your kingdom.'

'If God wills it,' said Longshanks.

'I am sure he does,' replied Fermbaud, 'and I will be proud to lead my men under your banner.'

'The sentiment is appreciated,' said Longshanks, 'but there is an itch I must first scratch and that is why I am here.'

'My lord?'

'Fermbaud, I have a never-ending list of tasks to administer if we are to sail with the spring tides. Yet across the river, there are stirrings of dissent from amongst the nobles of Wales. Rumours are reaching me about talks of rebellion and though this is nothing new, it is a distraction I can do without.'

'Do you intend to ride into Wales?'

'Not I, Fermbaud. You. I want you to lead your command and deal with any dissent you find with an iron fist.'

'Of course, my lord,' stuttered Fermbaud, 'but can I ask, why me?'

'The reasons are twofold,' said Longshanks. 'It is obvious from what I have seen that your garrison is at full strength and in good heart. The castle is indeed an impressive fortress but it will make no sense for two forces to grow idle within these walls while the preparations for the invasion are finalised. My guard have grown accustomed to conflict but I fear your men are yet inexperienced and would benefit from drawing steel in anger.'

Fermbaud nodded.

'And the second reason?'

The King turned to face him.

'I will be frank, Fermbaud. I am still not sure of your loyalty to me and this will be an opportunity to put that doubt to rest.'

'My lord,' interrupted Fermbaud, 'I can assure you…'

'Quiet!' interrupted Longshanks, coldly. 'What I am trying to say is this. Yes, you pay your taxes on time and prepare a fair table in my presence, but this is no more than I would expect from any knight. If you are to ride alongside me on the fields of France, I need to be sure your mettle is sound. Unfortunately, this remains a trait unproved in your case but I do not hold you responsible as you have not had the opportunity to prove otherwise.'

'My lord, I have won many tournaments and was knighted by your father's own hand.'

'Tournaments do not reflect the battlefield, and many men who succeed in these staged contests often balk at the sight of a speared man's innards. I suspect you are not such a man but I need to be sure. This is a chance to put those doubts to rest and if you deal with this Welsh irritation on my behalf, then my promise to you is that you will enjoy my favour on campaign, have a chance of glory and indeed a share in the spoils. I trust this is in order?'

The tone of the King's voice made it quite clear that negotiation was not an option.

'Of course, my lord,' said Fermbaud. 'I will need some time to put together the necessary supplies for such a campaign but can be gone in a few days.'

'You will be gone tomorrow morning,' interrupted Longshanks. 'Take enough food for two days' march and seek replenishment from my castles as you go. I will furnish you with notes to ensure the castellans look after your needs.'

'Of course,' said Fermbaud.

Both men stared at each other for a few seconds before Longshanks spoke again.

'Well?'

'My lord?'

'What are you waiting for? Don't you have a campaign to organise?'

'Of course, my lord,' said Fermbaud and after bowing to the King, turned away to return to the keep.

Longshanks watched him go and a few seconds later a figure approached from the darkness.

'What do you think?' asked Longshanks without turning.

'I think he will be dead within a month,' said the man before biting into an apple.

Longshanks turned to face the newcomer. The man before him was no knight, yet was one of Longshanks' most trusted men, Orland of Denmark. Orland was a giant of a man with long golden hair tied back from his head. His ancestors were Scandinavian and Longshanks had bought him from a slave trader in Acre while on Crusade years earlier. Orland had sworn fealty in return and since then had become not only the King's best fighter but also his most trusted confidant.

'I think you may be right,' said Longshanks, 'which is a shame.'

'Why? It would be no great loss.'

'Perhaps not, but despite the fat around his belly his men rate him highly, which bodes well in any campaign. Perhaps he will prove us wrong and deliver what I ask.'

'I will wager not.'

'I will accept your wager, Orland, for I want you to go with him.'

'To what end?' asked Orland.

'To see if he has the mettle I desire, but more importantly, to ensure he extinguishes this pathetic little rebellion.'

'And if he dies on the way?'

'So be it, but waste not his men needlessly. Their crossbows will be welcome in France.'

'Crossbows are nothing against the longbow.'

'Granted, but they become beneficial when behind fortifications and when we take French positions, as we must, then they will be useful in defence.'

'What authority will I have on this campaign into Wales?'

'Are you known to Fermbaud?'

'No.'

'Then go as scouts in my name. Take a dozen trusted men with you, each sworn to secrecy. If there comes a time to step in, then do so with all necessary force. I will furnish you with a document giving you my authority.'

'My blade is all the authority I need.'

'Perhaps so but if in doubt, my castellans may pull the drawbridges up at the sight of a Saxon barbarian riding toward them.'

Orland smiled at the banter.

'And the thrust of this campaign?'

'Find the ring leaders of any rebellion with all haste and make an example of them. I don't care what you do but make sure that all who know them are so terrified by their demise, they hide away for another five years.'

'Understood,' said Orland and threw the apple stump from the castle wall.

'You have three months, Orland, no more. If you are not back by the first snows of winter then I will sail without you.'

Orland nodded.

'Leave it to me, my lord,' he said. 'If there is nothing more, I will be away for I have business to attend.'

'Does this business have jet black hair and serve wine at the table of Fermbaud?' asked Longshanks.

'Indeed she does,' laughed Orland.

'Then be gone,' said Longshanks, 'and travel well. Report back to me within two months and together we will crush the French beneath our heels.'

'I will look forward to it,' said Orland and left the King to stare out over Bristol.

—

The following morning Longshanks stood at the window of his room, sipping warmed ale as he watched the scene below. In the courtyard, fifty mounted lancers and almost two hundred foot soldiers jostled into position as they awaited their leader. At the back, Orland and twelve men stood to one side with their horses and the King raised his tankard in salute as the Dane caught his eye.

Within moments, Nicholas Fermbaud emerged from the keep doorway and made his way across the courtyard to where a page held the Castellan's horse.

Longshanks sighed in disappointment when he saw Fermbaud was wearing full ceremonial armour for though it had its uses, it was too impractical for any campaign. He would be better served with leather leggings and chain-mail.

'You are going to have to learn quickly, Nicholas Fermbaud,' said the King quietly to himself, 'or I am afraid my Danish friend will win the wager and you will be dead within the month.' He turned away from the window and returned to his bed where a serving wench lay waiting.

—

Outside, Fermbaud climbed aboard his horse and turned to face his command.

'Men of Bristol,' he called. 'We are to engage on a campaign on behalf of our monarch. When we return, our names will be spoken alongside the greats of this country. Display the mettle I know we share and have courage at arms.' He looked up at the window of the keep. 'Hail King Edward, ruler of England, Scotland and Wales. Long may he reign.' The gathered men stared upward, waiting in vain for acknowledgement.

Behind them, Orland laughed quietly and shook his head in amusement.

'Come,' he said to his comrades, 'let's get out of here.'

Chapter Four

The island of Ynys Mon

Geraint rode into the clearing and acknowledged the guards posted to look after the horses.

'Is your master here?' he asked.

'He has continued on foot, my lord. He has wounded a stag and seeks to finish him by hand.'

Geraint nodded.

'How long has he been gone?'

'Most of the morning but his return is imminent. He has already sent a page back with instructions to prepare the horses.'

'Good,' said Geraint, 'I will wait.' He dismounted and engaged in conversation with the men at arms, sharing stories of battles fought and victories won, a common trait of all such men. Finally the sound of someone approaching made them stand up and they walked forward to greet the young prince.

'Geraint,' called Madog as he saw his friend, 'your presence is unexpected yet perfectly timed. Behold the beast I brought down with my own hand.'

Geraint acknowledged the kill was indeed impressive.

'I wounded him with an arrow and then tracked him to a small valley not two leagues hence,' continued Madog.

'He was weak with blood loss and my spear gave him a noble death. What do you think?'

'A grand kill indeed,' said Geraint. 'The meat will be welcomed in your kitchens.'

'The meat will be gifted to the poor,' said Madog, 'and the rack hung in the great hall. The need was for sport this morning, a chance to clear my mind of matters of concern.'

'You have given my tale some thought?' asked Geraint.

'I have thought of nought else since we talked,' said Madog. 'My eyes are heavy through lack of sleep; such is my worry.'

'And what conclusion have you reached?'

'Come,' said Madog. 'Walk with me a while. My words are for your ears only.'

The two men started back down the track, leaving the rest of the men to bring the kill and the horses behind them. For a while both walked in silence until finally, Madog spoke.

'Tell me, friend, what is your judgement on this matter?'

Geraint thought for a while before answering.

'Truth be told, my feelings are mixed,' he said. 'When I first came here, my aim was to see you safe to manhood for exactly a task such as this. Every spare minute we have had, I have taught you in the ways of warfare but now the time is upon us, I find my resolve weakening.'

'Why?'

'I have seen you grow from a boy to a man and though we share not the same bloodline, I have to admit I have come to think of you as a kinsman. My eagerness for you to lead our country into battle is balanced against my fear for your safety.'

'But you have taught me well.'

'Perhaps so but war is a risky business and Longshanks a dangerous adversary. If we do this, we have to succeed or you may not live to see your own children grow up. Edward's reach is long and he is renowned for taking revenge on his adversaries, even after treaties have been signed.'

'Surely the man is a knight and a king. Any foe would be treated with respect even after the last blows have been struck, no matter who the victor.'

'Not always, my lord. Don't forget he has already put down one rebellion and if he sees you as a potential recurring problem, he will have no alternative but to rid himself of you. No, if we are to do this, we need to be sure the mood of Wales is such that the whole country raises up in anger.'

'And your gut feeling?'

Geraint stopped and looked at the young man.

'There is a need for someone to take a lead, Madog, and history tells us it should be you but this is your decision alone. Few people know your heritage as I do so if you feel it is not your place, nobody will be the wiser and you can live your life in peace here on Ynys Mon.'

'But if I accept?'

'Then there are people you should meet. Your lineage needs to be unveiled before the nobles of Wales and your banner recognised as the true successor to Llewellyn and his line. Take your time, Madog, for if you take this path you must do so with all your heart even unto death. Anything less will be an insult to yourself and your country.'

Madog turned and signalled the page to bring up his horse. Geraint helped him up and waited as the young man stared into the distance. Finally Madog looked down at the man who had brought him up since childhood.

'As usual your counsel is wise and balanced. I thank you for this but your worry is unfounded. I need no time, Geraint, for my path is clear to me. Arrange the meetings with the nobles, my friend, our country waits for us and freedom is a hard-earned right.'

'Then you will lead us?' asked Geraint.

'Was it ever in doubt?' asked Madog.

'I suppose not,' said Geraint, 'but there is one more thing to be discussed.'

'Which is?'

'If we are to unveil your claim to the throne then you will have to publicly lay claim to the title of Prince of Wales.'

'Is that really necessary?'

'It is.'

'Then so be it. Make the arrangements, Geraint. If God wills it and the people of Wales see the strength to my claim then we will free this nation together.'

Fifty miles away, a lone rider made his way along narrow trails through one of the densest forests of Mid Wales. His cloak was closed against the cold and the furred hood drawn tight against the snow-laden branches clawing at his face. The forest was silent except for the heavy breathing of the horse but despite this, the man knew he was being watched every step of the way. Finally he emerged onto the brow of a path leading down into a deep ravine. For a moment he paused and removed his hood long enough for any watchers to see his face before urging his horse forward to descend the tricky slope.

Half an hour later he rounded a corner in the ravine and smiled as he saw the place he had called home for the last few winters. At first glance it looked no different to any other stretch of the river but he knew that behind the trees along the base of the jagged cliff face lay a labyrinth of hollows and caves where water had eaten away the limestone over countless years. At the front of each, the inhabitants had created wooden palisades to keep the weather at bay and form warm shelters that could house dozens of men and their horses for many weeks if need be. Garyn knew that despite his notoriety as an outlaw, he was safe from harm here as this was the winter home of the Blaidd, the mercenaries who harassed the supply lines of the English in return for money from the Welsh Lords.

'Garyn,' called a voice, 'you have returned. Stable your horse for we have a deer's haunch still dripping fat into the flames. For a coin I will carve a small slice in your name.'

Garyn peered up to the crag, seeking the owner of the familiar voice. For a few moments the man was hidden from his gaze but as he stood up, the movement gave away his position. The defender was swathed in the grey furs of a wolf, not only as protection from the cold but as an effective camouflage against unwelcome eyes. This was Derwyn, the second in command of the Blaidd in Garyn's absence and one who had become a close friend. He was a giant of a man and the owner of a magnificent beard, complementing the mass of black hair that hung down past his shoulder.

'Derwyn,' answered Garyn, 'judging by your girth I suspect there is nothing left worth eating.'

Derwyn laughed and descended the crag to meet his friend. Garyn climbed the slope and grasped his friend's arm in greeting.

'It has been a while, Garyn,' said Derwyn. 'We thought you may be dead.'

'And leave you in charge? The world is not ready for such a thing, my friend.'

'Perhaps not. Come, I was not jesting regarding that haunch. Your timing is perfect.'

The two men walked around the carefully placed bushes and ducked into the cavern that formed the main hall of their group.

'Garyn,' called out a few voices, 'welcome back.'

Garyn acknowledged his comrades and made his way to the fire at the centre of the cavern. One of the women took his wet cloak and waited until he had stripped to the waist before handing him a sheepskin.

'Here,' said another, 'sit. I shall bring you warm wine.'

Derwyn carved a slab of venison from the carcass above the flames and placed it on a trencher before handing it to Garyn. A small crowd gathered around their leader as he ate his meal, but kept the talk to minor things out of courtesy. Finally he threw the trencher to one side and drained the wooden tankard before letting out a satisfying belch and looking around at the people he had come to call family.

As he picked the meat from between his teeth, he contemplated the events that had led him here. Ten years previously he had been swindled out of his father's lands by a crooked abbot and having been wrongly outlawed, had fled to join the armies of Llewellyn in the north. En route he had encountered Goddeff, the leader of the Blaidd, a band of mercenaries who had struggled to settle after returning from crusade, so plied their trade fighting for whatever lord paid the heaviest purse.

The Blaidd had quickly become notorious for their battle skills as well as their loyalty to whatever master they served at the time, but though this meant they often fought against other Welshmen; they never took English coin against their own countrymen. When Goddeff had found out that Garyn's father had been a fellow knight, he took the young man under his wing and Garyn joined the Blaidd. Goddeff taught the young man the skills needed to survive in the harsh political landscape and Garyn had soon become a valued and skilful member of the feared band. Since then, as the original members fell to death's call either by blade, arrow, age or disease, he had risen through the mercenary ranks until finally he stood alongside Goddeff as an equal. Finally, when the leader died through an infected injury, Garyn had stepped seamlessly into the role of leader and was respected by every man and woman who called the Blaidd their brethren.

Garyn had at first continued their role of mercenaries but as time went on and resistance against the English occupation grew, the barons of Wales joined forces to pay the price of the Blaidd and commissioned the outlaws to harass the supply lines of Longshanks, a task they were notoriously successful in administering. Despite this, Garyn was growing tired of hiding away amongst the valleys of Wales and craved the opportunity to fight in the open against the English, so when he received news of a possible uprising against the occupiers, he lost no time in offering the services of the Blaidd to the cause. He had attended many secretive meetings across Wales since then, culminating in the one at the Pilgrim's Rest tavern. At these many meetings, deals were made and promises of support pledged as final plans were laid to raise the resistance against the English.

'Garyn,' called a voice, interrupting his reverie, 'what news of war?'

Garyn looked up at the blunt question and saw dozens of eyes peering at him in expectation.

'Phillip,' interrupted Derwyn, 'let the man rest; he has been on the road for many weeks and will answer in his own time.'

'Let him be, Derwyn,' said Garyn quietly. 'It is a fair question.' He looked around at the men he had fought alongside for so long.

'The news is this,' he continued. 'The will is strong amongst the villages across the country and even as we speak, blacksmiths sharpen pikes and fletchers increase production of arrows for the longbows. The Lords Cynan and Morgan have garnered the support of most of the minor barons and many Englishmen sleep nervously behind their fortifications knowing any movement after dark invites an arrow between their shoulders.'

'So is there an agreed date?' asked Derwyn.

'Alas no,' said Garyn, 'at least not yet. Despite their willingness to fight, as usual the barons' eyes are already on the greater prize before a sword has been drawn. They quarrel about whose flag we will fight under, for all crave the glory success will bring.'

'In the name of Christ,' shouted Derwyn, 'what is wrong with these people? Every minute they bicker like children, more stones are added to English fortifications. Conwy is already impregnable and the word is that work on Caernarfon's walls has doubled in intensity. It will be finished within the year and once done there will be little chance of getting a foothold in the north.'

'All this was discussed,' said Garyn, 'and they are fully aware of the situation but there has been a significant development. There is a rumour of a man in the north with a legitimate claim to the throne of Wales, a noble with direct lineage to Llewellyn himself. If this is true then we could have a leader who cuts through all the argument and a figurehead to lead us against Longshanks.'

A gasp whispered from the gathered men.

'I know of no such man,' said Derwyn. 'Surely such a claim would be common knowledge?'

'You would think so but it is said this man's heritage has been kept from him all his life to protect him from an assassin's blade. It would seem that he is now of age and willing to take up the mantle.'

'This is nonsense,' said Derwyn. 'The lineage of every line is well known and you can be sure that even the slightest rumour of such a man would have brought Longshanks' henchmen like a swarm of bees.'

'You are right, my friend, but my contact, a man called Meirion ap Rhys, has been told by someone called Tarian that such a man is currently being groomed for leadership.'

'Someone who knows someone,' sneered a voice. 'It seems like a tale for babes to me.'

'Meirion ap Rhys is a respected man. He would not give false hope for the sake of rumour.'

'He may well be a respected man but who is this Tarian you speak of?'

'I do not know him directly but Meirion speaks highly of him. If he says this would-be Prince exists then I for one believe him, as should you.'

'Why?'

'For Tarian pays into the purse that fills our bellies.'

'So who is this prince?' asked Derwyn, 'and when will he declare himself?'

Garyn paused.

'I tell you this in confidence,' said Garyn, 'and ask that until he is revealed, his name is not spoken outside of this cave. His name is Madog and he is a minor noble on the island of Ynys Mon. It seems his grandfather bore the same name and was the bastard son of Owain Gwynedd.'

'If this is true,' said Derwyn, 'then even I can see the strength of the lineage but surely the barons will not accept this without proof?'

'You are right,' said Garyn, 'as you can imagine, all the barons were taken aback by this news and at first refused to accept his right. Despite this, the evidence provided by Tarian was overwhelming and caused many to doubt their own claims. Tarian and his comrades, men of like mind, have made it their mission to champion Madog's claim. Most have now pledged allegiance but one has withheld his support until the claim is proved.'

'Who is the dissenter?'

'Cynan ap Maredudd, the most powerful warlord in Wales.'

'Did you not just say he had given support?'

'To the cause, yes, but to Madog, no, at least not until this prince carries out a holy task to prove his claim.'

'And this task is?'

Garyn looked around and paused.

'Cynan ap Maredudd has demanded Madog presents him with the Sword of Macsen.'

Again a gasp rang out around the room.

'The Sword of Macsen,' said Derwyn slowly, the incredulity evident in his voice. 'That is impossible.'

'Perhaps so but that is the price demanded.'

'Nobody knows if the sword even exists,' said Iolo, a young man with a severely scarred face. 'It is an impossible task.'

'And I have no doubt that is why Cynan demanded it,' said Garyn. 'He knows that the sword is a myth and Madog will fail in his claim thus leaving the way open for his own path to the crown.'

'So we are no further forward,' said Derwyn.

'You would think so but there is one final piece of the puzzle that adds intrigue to the story. When the task became clear, Tarian sent word around Wales offering a reward for any information that may lead to the discovery of the sword and though many tried to claim with hearsay and rumour, there was one who seemed to have information that was valid.'

'Who is this man?'

'A troubadour who has travelled the country from coast to coast, his story is that he once met a man who claimed to have seen the Macsen Sword with his own eyes.'

'And Tarian believed him?'

'He did.'

'But why, surely this man plies his trade in the telling of tales?'

'Because he made no claim to the reward, requesting only that should the sword be found then a prayer be made in his name.'

'Nevertheless, a lead without much substance.'

'Like I said, Tarian is a man of great intellect and he judged the minstrel to be telling the truth. If he thinks his tale was true, then it is good enough for me.'

'So where is the man who claims to have seen the Liberty Sword?'

'He is in Castell du Bere, an English fortress in the north.'

'If his location is known,' said Iolo, 'why doesn't Tarian send word for him to come forth and declare the location.'

'He did but unfortunately the man is unable to do that.'

'Why?'

'For he resides in the dungeons of the castle, a prisoner of the constable, Robert Fitzwalter.'

'So where does that leave us?' asked Derwyn.

'The situation is this,' said Garyn. 'The armies of Wales need unification if we are to have a chance of ridding our lands of the English yoke. To do this we need the army of Cynan ap Maredudd but without the Sword of Macsen, he will not contemplate an alliance.'

'And?' said Derwyn slowly, realising where the conversation was going.

'If it's a sword he wants, a sword he will get,' said Garyn.

'How?' asked Iolo. 'Even if the tale is true, the only man who knows where it is, is locked up.'

'And therein lies our path,' said Garyn. 'The only way to find out is to ask him face to face.'

'How do we do that?' asked Iolo.

'I have promised Tarian that the Blaidd will free this man from Castell du Bere.'

'And how do you propose we do that?'

'I haven't thought that far ahead,' said Garyn, 'and seek your counsel, but after a few days here I aim to visit the castle to get the lay of the land. When that is done, we will make our plans accordingly.'

—

In the north, Geraint strode amongst rows of men testing their pike drills against each other. In the distance, hundreds of archers fired volley after volley toward a line of straw-filled sacks suspended from ash frames. He knew that all across Wales, similar scenes were being carried out in secret preparation for the conflict to come. Despite this, he knew that though the numbers were impressive, they were still nowhere near ready to take on Edward's army. They needed unity, luck and many, many more men.

'The Prince!' came a call and every man in earshot drew back from their training to watch the approach of Madog.

Geraint also watched and noted how the boy he had tutored only months earlier was growing into the role. Already he was recognised as the true prince by many in the north, but some dissenters still needed encouragement to join his cause.

Madog rode into the training camp flanked by the trusted men of his personal guard. As he passed, the men at arms cheered and he acknowledged them with a mailed fist. Geraint stepped out and took the reins of Madog's horse as the young man dismounted.

'My lord, it has been many weeks,' said Geraint.

'Indeed it has,' said Madog, 'and I have news to share.'

'As do I,' said Geraint, 'but first I have tents set up back amongst the trees and your retainers have prepared a meal.'

'Excellent,' said Madog and walked alongside Geraint as they headed to the encampment. When they reached the tent, he threw his gauntlets onto the cot and dismissed the servant waiting to divest him of his chainmail shirt. 'It will be a sad day when I cannot don or discard my own armour,' he said.

'But you are now a prince,' said Geraint sarcastically, 'surely such things are beneath you?'

'Perhaps this is true of English princes, but I am no less a man than I was before.'

Geraint smiled. Madog was becoming a man after his own heart.

'So, what news do you have, my friend?' asked Madog.

'Mine will wait, my lord. Perhaps first you could share the result of your diplomacy.'

'Indeed,' said Madog, 'mixed results but overall, very good. I have dined with peers across the north and seven more have pledged men at arms. We are close to our aim and with a few more weeks, we should be able to field an army of ten thousand souls. Even Edward would balk when confronted with such a force, would he not?'

'Perhaps,' said Geraint, 'but we should not get carried away with such thoughts for the support from Mid Wales is not yet secured.'

'What do you mean? I thought your contacts had already extracted the required pledges.'

'From most, yes but there is one ally upon which we wait, Cynan ap Maredudd and without his support we are doomed to failure.'

'How so?'

'The south is dominated by those loyal to the English and Cynan is the only man with strength and allies enough to face them on the field of battle. Even if we are successful in the north, all that would happen is that Edward would rally those loyal to the crown in the south and simply ride northward to meet us. This is a situation we cannot contemplate.'

'Why not? Surely if we are successful with the first strike, our success will swell our numbers and we need fear no enemy.'

'We cannot fight this war on so many fronts,' said Geraint. 'Our numbers are yet small and too inexperienced. It is all or nothing, and we need to hit Edward with an overwhelming force when he least expects it. To do that we need the forces of Cynan. This brings me on to my news, my lord, there is a man whose counsel I hold in great esteem.'

'And who is this man?'

'I will unveil his name in due course but suffice to say, he is instrumental in getting the barons to combine behind our cause. Even before I unveiled your heritage to you, he was dining at the tables of nobles across Wales, sounding out their allegiance and preparing the way for a cause such as this. He carries the flame of freedom in his heart like no other man, an intense furnace of patriotism that will never die, and if we are victorious in this campaign, it will be mainly due to years of hidden work by his hand.'

'He sounds intriguing,' said Madog, 'and I would indeed like to meet him face to face. Send word and invite him to my manor.'

'There is no need, my lord, he is already here and awaits your summons.'

Madog's eyes widened in surprise.

'Here? Then by all means, bring him in.'

Geraint left the tent but within minutes returned with his friend.

'My lord,' he said, 'may I introduce Rhodri ap Gruffydd, also known as Tarian, Shield of the Poor.'

Madog stood to meet the white-haired knight but before he could say anything, Tarian dropped to one knee.

'My lord,' said Tarian, 'it is my great honour to meet you at last.'

Madog glanced at Geraint, unsure how to react. Geraint gave him a nod of encouragement and Madog cleared his throat before speaking.

'Sir Rhodri, please, regain your feet, I am no king yet.'

The man stood and gazed into the boy's eyes.

'My lord, I once travelled halfway across the world seeking the right person to bear the title Prince of Wales and when I first saw you as a young boy, I knew then what the world did not, that you were indeed of royal blood.'

'So you are the man who shared the voyage that Geraint has oft retold?'

'I am that man, my lord.'

'Then the honour is all mine, and to be paid homage by a man as great as you is humbling.'

'Then I am doubly proud to have been the first, my lord, and proclaim now before you and my God that I will forthwith serve you loyally even unto death.'

'Then I am honoured to accept your pledge, sir knight, and if even half the tales that Geraint has shared prove to be true, then I am also honoured to know one of the bravest men of our time. Please, be seated.'

'Before I do, my lord, there is one boon I humbly request, after which, no favour will ever be asked of you again in my name.'

'And what boon is this?'

'That henceforth, you and all your subordinates, whether knight or knave address me by the name by which I have become accustomed, Tarian.'

'Shield of the Poor?'

'In my day, yes, but Tarian will now suffice.'

'Then your boon is granted, of course,' said Madog. 'Tarian, please, be seated. Henceforth my houses are your houses and will offer shelter or support whenever requested in your name.'

'Thank you, my lord.'

Madog turned to the servant and requested ale be brought as well as food.

'So, Tarian,' said Madog, 'Geraint has regaled me with tales of savages and sea voyages in lands afar. Tell me, is there any reality in these stories or has he embroidered the truth better than a lady of the court does a doublet?'

'I have no doubt Geraint speaks truly, my lord, for I have found him an honest man without equal. Our journey was indeed a crusade of epic proportions and though it has been many years coming, it may well finally meet fulfilment in the coming months.'

'I take it you speak of the liberation of Wales?'

'Indeed I do, and it has taken half of my life to see this day. I see before me the one man capable of unifying my country against the invader and knowing that you have accepted the call to arms should see me a happy man.'

'Should?'

'My lord, I understand Geraint has explained the stance of Cynan in the south.'

'He has but surely this is a simple case of diplomacy?'

'Ordinarily yes, but Cynan is a stubborn man. He is also a great leader and a valuable ally but he has seen too many false dawns to commit without being certain of success.'

'Nothing can offer such certainty.'

'Perhaps not, but he has still requested a gesture to prove your claim. A holy task in God's name.'

'And what is this task?'

'He wants you to locate the Sword of Macsen.'

Madog looked across at Geraint before returning his gaze to Tarian.

'The Sword of Macsen?'

'Yes, my lord. Are you familiar with the dream of Macsen Wledig?'

'I am not.'

'Then to understand the importance of the sword you must first hear his story.'

Chapter Five

The eastern border of Wales

Nicholas Fermbaud sat astride his horse at the head of the column. Behind him, fifty lancers and two hundred foot soldiers followed the well-trodden road to Monmouth, a necessary supply point on their journey into Wales. Ahead of him, the twelve scouts supplied by Edward ensured they didn't walk blindly into any traps laid by the Welsh brigands known to infest the area. Fermbaud had been reluctant to take the scouts on the campaign, but Edward had insisted, and Fermbaud guessed correctly that part of their role was to report back on the aptitude of the untried knight. As they rode beneath the broad-leaved trees of the forest, he saw the leader of the scouts riding back toward him, a dislikeable foreigner of dubious heritage and even worse manners. Fermbaud held up his hand to halt the column and waited for the Dane to approach.

'Lord Fermbaud,' said Orland, reining in his horse.

'Orland,' greeted the knight, 'how lays the path?'

'The road is clear but divides in two not ten leagues hence.'

'The maps are clear,' said Fermbaud. 'The right fork leads to Monmouth while the left takes us into Welsh territory. Our men need supplies so our route lies with the former.'

'My lord, ordinarily I would agree but there is another option for consideration.'

'Explain?'

'My lord, there is a village half a day's ride westward with farmed livestock and well planted fields. I suggest we take a detour and replenish the wagons from this village.'

'We do not have the coin for such a trade,' said Fermbaud.

'I do not suggest we pay,' said Orland. 'We will just take what we need in the name of the King.'

'I don't think that would go down well with the locals.'

'Why not? Either they are loyal to the King, in which case they should gladly meet our needs, or they are hostile, in which case we are entitled by force of arms to take what we require.'

'Surely if the latter was the case, they would offer resistance?'

'Perhaps so but isn't that scenario exactly why we have been despatched on this campaign? To put down such dissent and send a message to the conspirators against the crown?'

'I'm not sure,' stuttered Fermbaud.

'My lord, the choice is of course yours but this is an opportunity to send an early message to the enemy and will also take several days off our journey. On top of this, the men will have an early taste of success and Edward receives word of a successful start to your campaign. Of course, this is my opinion only and I will leave the decision to you.' He turned to ride away but was called back by Fermbaud.

'Wait, what arrangements need to be made?'

'My lord, I would not deem to take the place of your sergeants but if it was me, I would make all haste while daylight remains and make camp as close as we can without risk of discovery. Then, at first light surround the village with my men at arms so nobody can send for help. When we are ready, send in an emissary with a protective guard to issue our demands but be wary of treachery, these villages are often nests of brigands and you can wager many men already plot against Edward.'

'And my lancers?'

'Make them ready to ride into the village at any sign of dissent. Tell them that if their services are required, they are to not hold back and strike with the full force of their weaponry. If there is conflict, we have to take down as many as possible. Hopefully it won't come to that but we have to prepare.'

'So be it,' said Fermbaud. 'I will ready the column; you find a place to lie low for tonight.'

'It is already done,' said Orland, 'a dense forest less than a mile away from the village yet connected to the same by no path. We will be unobserved there.'

'You deemed to second guess my decision?'

'It is always prudent to prepare for all eventualities, my lord,' said Orland and turned to ride the way he had come. This time there was no call to return.

The following morning, a delegation of tradesmen stood across the entrance to Elm's wood, a small village just inside the border between Wales and England. A hunter, up before the dawn to check his snares, had raised his concern that a column of armed men were making their way to the village and a group of respected inhabitants had quickly gathered to meet the unexpected visitors.

'Who do you think they are?' asked Robert, the village blacksmith.

'I don't recognise the coat of arms,' said the hunter, 'but they are dressed for trouble.'

'In what way?'

'They wear their helms and chainmail. Why would they do such a thing unless they expected trouble?'

'Who knows?' answered Robert. 'But they will get no trouble here. We will see what they want, offer refreshment and see them peacefully on their way.'

'Should we inform Lord Gwion?'

'I have already sent message. Hopefully he will be here soon.'

The group fell quiet and waited as the early morning mist faded away in the warmth of the sun. Finally the sound of hooves on the small wooden bridge crossing the stream alerted them to the nearness of the horsemen.

'Remember,' said Robert, 'stay calm. As far as we know they are friendly and until proven otherwise, they deserve a warm welcome.'

Within moments, ten lancers rode into the village, closely followed by twenty infantry, men at arms carrying pikes. They stopped before the welcoming party and the lead rider raised his visor to look down at Robert.

'Welcome, my lord,' said the blacksmith with a nod of the head, 'and a warm welcome to our village.'

'What place is this?' asked the rider. 'And whom do I address?'

'This is the village of Elm's Wood and I am Robert ap Evan, village blacksmith.'

'Do you speak for this village?'

'Only in the absence of our lord, Sir Gwion of Mont-gomery.'

'I do not know this knight,' said the rider.

'He is a Welsh lord, knighted by Llewellyn himself.'

The rider sneered.

'A title not recognised by me,' he said, 'but neverthe-less, I will speak to him. Send word that Godfrey of Bath, second in command to Sir Nicholas Fermbaud, Castellan of Bristol Castle seeks audience with immediate effect.'

'May I ask to what end, my lord?'

'No you may not for such matters are between men of nobility, not men of labour.'

'Of course, my lord, my apologies. Sir Gwion has been sent for but in the meantime, perhaps we could make you comfortable?'

'You may bring water for the mounts and ale for my men. Is there any bread?'

'The village oven has been fired but alas it will be a while yet before the first loaves come forth. As soon as it is ready, we will distribute it amongst your men. We also have some cold pork if that would be acceptable.'

'It will,' said Sir Godfrey, dismounting from his horse. 'While we wait for your master, show me around this village and in particular your cold stores.'

Robert's eyes narrowed slightly but he nodded slowly in agreement. Godfrey turned to address the guard.

'Dismount but stay alert. Sergeant Bister, place these people under close guard until I return.'

'Is that really necessary, my lord?' asked the blacksmith. 'I can assure you we offer only peace and friendship.'

'Friendly words, but we know you not and your true intentions may be shielded from us. It is purely a precaution.'

'Of course, my lord,' said Robert. 'Please, follow me.'

Godfrey turned again to his men and beckoned the two lancers at the front. 'You two, come with me. Sergeant, if any harm befalls us, you know what to do.'

'Yes, my lord,' said Bister.

Robert led the knight through the small village and headed to a barn. Inside they saw one wall piled high with hay. Against another, two dozen barrels stood side by side while a wooden platform was filled with hessian sacks.

'What's in these?' asked Godfrey.

'The barrels contain dried fruit while the sacks are our seed stock for the spring.'

'Is there any grain?'

'We have a granary half full,' said Robert, 'a small amount but with care it will see us through the winter.'

'What about salted meat?'

'Seven hams and three sides of beef.'

'Who owns these?'

'They are to be sold on behalf of farmers in the outlying fields. There is a market tomorrow.'

'Geese?'

'A few dozen around the village but there is a large flock under the control of the egg man.'

'The egg man?'

'Sorry, my lord, a term we use for Tom Davies. His family earns their living tending flocks and he has become known as such.'

Godfrey nodded.

'And what about livestock?'

'There are only milk cows in the village. Beef is reared on the hills along with sheep.'

'Ale?'

'You will have to speak to Sir Gwion, my lord. He controls the ale for the taverns. We have no wine.'

'Where are your cold stores?'

'At the rear of the barn.'

'Show me.'

They walked outside and down a slope at the rear. A doorway had been cut into the hill and inside, the walls had been lined with stone. A steady trickle of water ran down the rear wall and along a channel in the floor before flowing out of the room and joining a nearby stream.

'The running water keeps the temperature cool,' said Robert, 'and in the winter, we place ice from the streams along the walls. It lasts deep into summer.'

'A clever arrangement,' said Godfrey and looked at the meat hanging from the rafters.

'Whose are these?'

'They belong to many people, my lord. Oft, the families gather their coins to buy a side between them. It is the only way many can afford meat.'

'Anything else of value?' asked Godfrey.

'Only our chattels.'

'Nevertheless, you seem well stocked for such a small village.'

'All taxes are paid to Gwion, my lord, I can assure you that. We are a humble population who work hard and share the bounty. We have known hunger and look out for each other but we are also prudent in times of plenty and take measures to ensure the winter is as comfortable as we can make it. The harvest you have seen today is evidence of such prudence.'

'Are all villages in Wales as blessed?'

'I cannot answer for them, my lord.'

'Robert,' came a cry, 'our Lord Gwion approaches.'

The blacksmith and the knight ducked out of the cold room to watch a group of riders approach across the fields below.

'Is that your master?'

'It is he.'

'Then come, we will return to my men.'

Ten minutes later, four men rode their horses into the village and pulled up before Godfrey.

'Sir Gwion,' said Godfrey, 'I understand you are the lord of these parts.'

'I am, and whom do I have the honour of addressing?'

'I am Godfrey of Bath, riding under the command of Sir Nicholas Fermbaud. We are carrying out a task on behalf of the King himself.'

'Longshanks?'

'Do you pay homage to any other?'

'Of course not. I am just surprised to see his emissaries in these parts. He usually leaves us well alone.'

'He may well have done but we now seek your support in his name.'

'In what way?'

'We need supplies enough for five days' riding. I have examined this village and there is ample here. I suggest you are well placed to meet the needs of the King's men.'

Gwion looked around and counted Godfrey's men.

'I think this is acceptable,' he said. 'I will arrange a pack horse immediately.'

'A welcome sentiment,' said Godfrey, 'but alas a pack horse will be insufficient. Our numbers are ten times this and we will need at least two carts filled with supplies. If you empty the cold stores and include the salted meat it should suffice but in addition you will include twenty loaves and ten barrels of dried fruit. You can keep the grain and the seed for next year's harvest but we need twenty bales of hay for the horses.'

'My lord, this will decimate our winter stores,' said Robert.

Godfrey lashed out with his fist and knocked the black-smith to the ground.

'How dare you interrupt your betters,' he snarled, 'now stay quiet or I will have my men give you the beating you deserve.'

'Good knight,' said Gwion, 'there is no need for such a thing. The man only speaks that which is on all our minds.'

'Nonsense,' said Godfrey, 'you have already said you look after each other in times of need. Show the same mettle and you will no doubt survive. Besides, you seem like a generous soul, I am sure a good master would not see his villagers starve.'

'Assuming we meet your demands,' said Gwion, 'pray tell what payment these people will receive in return.'

'If you want to pay them, feel free to do so, we will pay nothing as we act in the name of the King.'

'That is not just,' said Gwion. 'We always pay the King's taxes in full without default. I accept that your need is great but even the Crown accepts that fees must be paid and people fed. Do not these villagers come under the protection of the King's reach?'

'An interesting question and one that is yet to be resolved,' said Godfrey. 'However, I accept your protest and invite you to take your complaint to the court of Edward for recompense. In the meantime, we will take the supplies we need, with or without your blessing.'

'And if we do not accept?'

'Then we will take them by force and that, my friend, is something you do not want to countenance.'

'You are free with your threats, my lord, yet I see no sign of strength.'

'Trust me, sir,' answered Godfrey, 'as we speak there is overwhelming force just a moment away. Indeed, there are over a dozen crossbows aimed at your heart as we speak.'

Silence fell between the men until finally Gwion turned to Robert.

'Blacksmith, I suggest you give this man what he desires.'

'But, my lord…'

'Do as I say, Robert, and I will replenish what I can from the manor's stores. Rest assured I will take this disgraceful behaviour to the court of Edward himself and seek compensation.'

'A sensible resolution,' said Godfrey. 'I will return at noon to collect the stores and make sure there is no trickery, for if there is, this village and everyone in it will pay the price.' Godfrey climbed back into the saddle and without another word, rode back out of the village.

The rest of the morning saw the villages collecting the supplies and by the time Godfrey returned, two carts lay full of goods including hams, sides of beef and barrels of dried fruit. Another two were piled up with hay. Gwion was also there and as two of Godfrey's men climbed aboard the carts, he once more faced the knight.

'You have left this village destitute, sir knight. Since when has that been in the honourable code?'

'Chivalry has its place,' said Godfrey, 'but in this case it lies second to fealty. My pledge is to my king and my god. Sometimes there are casualties along the way and if some of these people die as a result of this campaign, then so be it.'

'A harsh judgement on those less fortunate than ourselves, I suggest.'

'It is no different to losing one of my men in battle, sir. Now, let us end this verbal joust and get on with the task in hand.' He turned around to call to his men. 'Sergeant Bister, are we ready?'

'We are, my lord,' answered Bister but before he could say another word, his head jerked back as an arrow thudded into his eye, smashing open the back of his skull in an explosion of bone and brains.

For a moment nobody moved until suddenly, Godfrey stood up in his stirrups and drew his sword.

'Treachery,' he roared, 'to arms.'

'Wait,' shouted Gwion, 'I did not order this, it is not of our making.'

'Liar,' shouted Godfrey and swung his sword at the standing knight, cutting deep into the man's throat. Behind him, a horn sounded the alarm as the men at arms ran forward with their pikes. Within moments, screaming peasants tried desperately to escape the armed men and panic ensued as villagers ran everywhere to escape the killing. The sound of horses thundering across the bridge heralded the approach of the rest of the lancers and from the trees around the village, a hundred more men at arms poured forth to join the slaughter.

'Stop,' screamed Robert, grabbing the reins of the knight's horse, 'call them off I beseech thee. Take what you want but spare our lives.'

'Too late for that, peasant,' shouted Godfrey. 'You spoke of compromise but had betrayal in your heart.' He spurred his horse forward knocking the blacksmith to the ground. Robert got to his knees but before he could say anything else, a crossbow bolt thudded into his back. He fell forward into the dirt choking on his own frothy blood as the village filled with Fermbaud's men.

'Kill them all,' shouted Godfrey, 'and when you are done, burn this treacherous village to the ground.'

–

Up at the edge of the forest, Fermbaud sat astride his horse watching the events unfold. Alongside him was Orland astride his own charger.

'Well, it looks like you were correct, Orland,' said Fermbaud. 'It would seem these Welshmen cannot be called trustworthy.'

'Treachery abides in the breast of all men, my lord,' said Orland, 'but in some it is deeper seated than others.'

'So what now?'

'Now we carry out the task before us. To wipe out a community is a terrible thing but the signal it will send to those who plot against the King will be immense. The next village we encounter will drop to their knees in fear.'

'Perhaps they will fight first?'

'Then they will also die. Now, if you excuse me, my lord, I will join those below. It has been a while since my blade felt the resistance of living flesh.'

Fermbaud watched the man ride away and scowled in disgust. He had disliked this man from the very beginning but every day that passed meant his hatred deepened.

Chapter Six

Castell du Bere, Dysynni Valley

Castell du Bere stood proudly on the spur of a rocky hill overlooking Dysynni Valley. For many years it had lain in the hands of the Welsh, but since the conquest by Edward ten years earlier, it had been occupied by the English and had become a strategic post of vital importance.

Its position meant it oversaw the main route from the south and though there were other paths leading through the mountains, they were difficult to navigate and drew the attention of brigands. This route lay in the shadow of Du Bere and it enjoyed the protection of the garrison within.

The strength of the fortress lay in the location. It was protected on three sides by sheer cliffs, unassailable by any siege engines or cavalry and the high stone walls built directly onto bedrock meant that tunnelling was impossible.

The only approach was via a winding road which led to the base of the hill through lands cleared of trees. This meant that the castle would have plenty of warning of any approaching enemy and could pull up its drawbridge long before anyone came within bowshot of the castle walls, and the occupants slept safe in the knowledge that their castle was impregnable.

Deep in the valley at the base of the castle, Dysynni village was waking to another day. Barrows were wheeled to the market square, and farmers herded flocks of geese from their holdings amongst the slopes of the nearby hills.

Within an hour of the dawn, the village was alive with the sounds of livestock and the chatter of people as they prepared for the day ahead. New flames were lit in old fire pits to warm pots of ale and cook the cawl, the meaty broth that was a staple food in the area and a favourite of the many visitors to the market.

As the people went about their business, at the edge of the village the inhabitants of a large stone building were also stirring into life. The hall was a sanctuary, a place of shelter offered to travellers who simply could not afford the prices of the boarding houses and taverns. Inside, a lone figure rose quietly from one of the cots and walked into the outer hall where he was greeted by the warm smile of a well-fed monk.

'Welcome to another wonderful morning, my son. My name is Brother Simon. Pray be seated and you can break your fast shortly.'

'Thank you,' said Garyn, 'I am thankful to have found such a place. My arrival last night was late and I feared I would once more be sleeping with only my cloak and the stars as a blanket.'

'God's heavens are indeed a spectacular cover but alas offer no physical warmth to us mere sinners.'

'Your refuge is certainly well placed to help the weary traveller, that much is true.'

'Oh there are several taverns that offer lodgings,' said the monk, 'but all have a price and some do not offer suitable surroundings for men of piety. Can I assume you are such a man?'

'Alas no, Brother, but my purse is light and I have other matters to attend. The attentions of ale and whores could not be further from my mind.'

'You will find our hospitality simple yet honest,' said the monk, 'and if you are able to leave a coin or two when you leave then we will see it goes to feeding others with similar need. If not, then please, go with our blessing and we pray that God sees fit to lighten your load.'

'A coin I can manage, Brother, thank you.'

'Then I will leave you in peace,' said the monk and disappeared through a nearby door.

Garyn looked around the hall. It was empty except for one other man, staring into a half empty tankard. Within moments another monk appeared carrying a pot of maize porridge and a tankard of watered wine. This man was dressed in a coarser habit, obviously too big for his frame and his stature was frail. He placed the fare on the table before Garyn.

'Thank you, Brother,' said Garyn once more.

'Oh, please, don't refer to me as Brother,' said the man. 'I am not worthy of such an honour and only serve those better than me.'

'My apologies,' said Garyn, 'your attire suggested otherwise.'

'A kindly jest made at my expense,' said the servant. 'The brothers allow me to dress so but alas I will never reach their level of holiness.'

'Why not?'

'I committed a heinous crime in my youth and begged sanctuary at the monastery. The brothers sought leniency on my behalf and were granted custody of me for the rest of my life. My service is my penance, a gift for which I am eternally grateful.'

'Will you never be a free man?'

'I am free in the eyes of the law but not before God.'

'A strange set of affairs,' said Garyn. 'Will they never accept you into their order?'

'It is not in their hands. I am well versed in the psalms and litanies but alas have never made a pilgrimage to Rome, nor ever will.'

'Why not?'

'I am destitute, my lord, and rely on the monks for my living. I could never afford passage nor sustenance for such a journey. Alas, my sentence is just and I settle for servitude.'

'Elias, back to the kitchens with you,' said Brother Simon coming back into the room. The servant bowed his head and scurried away.

'My apologies, friend,' said Brother Simon walking over to the table. 'Elias is a kindly soul but of simple mind. How is your fare?'

'A nourishing meal indeed,' said Garyn, 'you have my gratitude.'

'Have you travelled far?' asked the monk.

'From a place called Builth,' said Garyn, 'do you know it?'

'I know of it but though I am well-travelled, I have never been there.'

'You should, it is a very friendly place.'

'Perhaps one day.'

'So this Dysynni,' said Garyn. 'I have heard it is a prosperous village and a man can make a good living here.'

'Indeed he can,' said the monk, 'for the opportunities are equal. The safe road provided by Fitzwalter means that most travellers between north and south pass this way, many of whom take the opportunity to rest before continuing their journey.'

'Fitzwalter?'

'The Castellan of Du Bere and constable of this village.'

'I only saw the castle in the failing light last night, it seemed very impressive.'

'Indeed it is,' said the monk, 'and while the necessity of such fortresses is a sad indictment of our lives, until such time as all men can live in peace, then they are a necessary evil.'

'Is the Castellan a fair master?'

'He is not the worst I have seen, but let's just say he often administers justice with a heavy hand.'

'What do you mean?' asked Garyn.

'I will give you an example,' said the monk. 'This morning there is to be a public flogging. A boy of no more than twelve years was found hidden in a wagon taking cargo from a ship in the north to Caerphilly castle in the south. His crime was only to flee a brutal ship's captain and seek freedom but he was caught and imprisoned in Du Bere. The captain's envoy arrived yesterday to reclaim the runaway and wants an example made before he takes him back to the ship, so the boy is to receive a flogging this very morn. Despite our protestations, Fitzwalter has quashed any hope of clemency and insists the punishment goes ahead.'

'That seems a bit harsh for one so young.'

'I agree, but it seems the captain is angry his reputation is besmirched and I hear five silver pennies passed between the envoy and the Castellan to ensure an example was made.'

'A steep price for a mere gesture, methinks.'

'It is a sad day when the value of a captain's reputation far outweighs the life of a boy,' agreed the monk.

'Such are the times we live in,' said Garyn.

The monk proceeded about his business and left Garyn to his meal. As he ate, the other man in the room got up and walked to sit down opposite him. Garyn looked up and stared at the man.

'Greetings, stranger,' he said quietly, 'are we known to each other?'

'Strangely enough, this was to be my question to you,' said the man. 'My name is Hywel ap Rees and I couldn't help overhearing your conversation with the monk.'

'Then I apologise for disturbing you,' said Garyn, slowly lowering his spoon to the table.

'No apologies needed,' said the man, leaning back and picking at some pork stuck between his yellowed teeth, 'though I am intrigued at your conversation.'

'And why would that be?'

'I am from Builth myself and though I admit I can't know everyone who hails from my birth town, I am surprised that your face is not familiar to me. We are of a similar age, you and I so this is an unusual state of affairs, wouldn't you agree?'

'Perhaps. Builth is a big place.'

'It is but your accent also confuses me for you see, I have a sister who wed a miller in Brycheniog. That miller has a distinct accent and is oft teased by me for the way he says his words.'

'What is your point stranger?' asked Garyn, leaning back.

'Oh, no point but if I was a gambling man, I would wager you hailed from Brycheniog, not Builth.'

'And if I do?'

'It matters not to me where any man calls home,' said Hywel.

'Then is the matter closed?' asked Garyn.

'Of course.'

Garyn picked up his spoon once more.

'Except of course it does beg another question,' continued the man unexpectedly as he leaned forward.

Garyn looked up once more.

'Which is?'

'Why would a simple traveller pretend to be from one place when he is clearly from another, especially when he is talking to a man of God? Indeed, it may lead a suspicious person to conclude that the man had something to hide, wouldn't you think?'

Garyn lowered the spoon again and pushed the bowl away from him.

'State your business, stranger, for you have already interrupted my meal uninvited.'

'Again, you have my apologies,' said the man, 'but I will be honest with you. My name is indeed Hywel ap Rees and I do hail from Builth, however I am no merchant trader, I am a liegeman of the sheriff of that town and earn my bread returning those with a price on their heads to justice.'

'I see,' said Garyn, 'and I suppose you suspect me of being a brigand?'

71

'Not necessarily though my calling does indeed make me a suspicious man. You never introduced yourself,' said Hywel, 'or indeed said why you claimed to be from Builth. Perhaps you could ease my rude but suspicious nature.'

Garyn paused and considered ramming the bench against the man's midriff but thought better of it. There was a greater prize at risk.

'Hywel,' he said with a smile, 'you are correct and I have indeed been frugal with the truth. I am of course from Brycheniog and only used Builth as a means to avoid revealing my true identity.'

'And why would this be?' asked Hywel.

'My father owns a farm deep in the heart of the South Wales hills,' lied Garyn, 'and without my knowledge or consent, promised his friend I would marry the man's daughter as soon as she was of age. Her birthday approaches and though I love my family dearly, an uglier girl you have never seen. On top of this she is a simpleton and though I know I am being dishonourable; I cannot live my life alongside such a beast so I ride north to seek my fortune on the ships that ply their trade from the north coast.'

The liegeman stared for a moment then burst out laughing.

'You ran away from an arranged marriage?' he said.

'I did, to my shame.'

'Fret not, stranger,' said the liegeman. 'I know of no law that forces marriage on any man.'

He stopped laughing suddenly.

'She's not with child, is she?' he asked coldly, his eyes narrowing with suspicion.

'Not unless she has rutted with a bear,' said Garyn, 'but I suspect even bears have standards.'

The liegeman laughed again and stood up.

'If this girl is as afflicted as you say, then I suspect I too would have chosen flight over matrimony. Thank you, my friend, it is always good to start the day off with laughter. I wish you well in your future but will now leave you in peace.' He turned to leave but stopped once more.

'One last thing,' he said, 'you never introduced yourself.'

'I didn't,' said Garyn.

'So, can I have your name, you know, just for me to verify your story the next time I am in Brycheniog?'

Garyn was growing tired of the irritating man's questioning and his hand crept to his sheathed dagger beneath the table.

'My name is Garyn ap Lloyd,' he lied, 'and my family farm lies in hills above a village called Y Bont. It lays just south of Brycheniog.' He watched the man's eyes carefully for any flicker of recognition or disbelief but there was none.

'I know of Y Bont but have never been there. Have a blessed day, Garyn ap Lloyd, it has been good talking to you.' With that he left the sanctuary and headed into the town.

Garyn breathed a deep sigh of relief and stood up before draining his tankard of warm ale. The servant returned to take away the bowl and tankard.

'Thank you, Elias,' he said and placed two coins on the table. 'These are for the monks.' Taking the servant's hand, he placed a third into the wretched man's grasp. 'This one, however, is for you.'

Elias stared at the silver penny on his palm, not sure what to say.

'My lord,' he said eventually, 'this is a generous gift and I will donate it to the monastery in your name.'

'No, I want you to keep it for yourself, Elias and there could be many more if you are interested.'

'What use would I have of such wealth?'

'How about that pilgrimage to Rome you dream of?'

Elias looked at the treasure. He had never held such an amount in his whole life.

'It is only a down payment, Elias and for certain services there can be many, many more.'

'What would you have me do, sir?'

'All will be revealed in good time,' said Garyn, 'but if you are a man able to keep things in confidence, then perhaps we can go a long way to meeting the cost toward that pilgrimage you crave.'

'If that is a possibility,' said Elias, 'then the devil himself wouldn't make me talk.'

'Good,' said Garyn. 'I will be in contact soon enough. In the meantime, are you able to provide a secure room where a man can sleep in safety for a few weeks?'

Elias thought for a moment before answering.

'There is an old apple store at the back of the barn, sir. It is small but dry and can be made comfortable with the addition of a few bales of hay.'

'Do the monks frequent the barn?'

'Only the stalls where the donkeys are kept. The rear is rarely visited for it is where we bed the diseased when they seek shelter. You could use that.'

'It will suffice,' said Garyn. 'Prepare the store with clean blankets, I will return this afternoon.' He placed another silver penny on the table. 'Keep this between you and me, Elias, understand?'

'Understood,' said the servant, pocketing the coin and looking furtively around. 'Our secret?'

'Our secret,' confirmed Garyn.

—

Outside, Hywel ap Rees lifted the saddle onto his horse. Another two riders trotted up and reined in their steeds alongside him.

'My lord, there is talk of a known thief expected in the Three Saints tavern this evening. It may be worth waiting to see who he is.'

'Forget him,' said Hywel, tightening the girth strap. 'We have other business to attend.'

'He may be worth a silver penny or two,' said the rider.

'Perhaps so, but I met a man this morning and if he is who I think he is, we can be rich men before this month is out.' He looked up. 'Ride to Builth with all haste. Talk to the constable there and tell him to send fifty men at arms immediately.'

'Fifty?' answered the rider. 'What outlaw demands such a force?'

'A man called Garyn ap Lloyd,' said the liegeman, 'but unless I am mistaken, this is not his true name and he is really known as Garyn ap Thomas, one of the most wanted men in Wales.'

'I do not know of him,' said the rider.

'Not many do,' said the liegeman, 'for he keeps such things close to his chest but those in the know suspect he leads the biggest band of brigands in this land.'

'The Blaidd?' asked the rider.

'The Blaidd,' confirmed Hywel.

'If this is so, then why do you not seek support from Fitzwalter at the castle?'

'The reward is substantial for any Blaidd member but for this one, there is a special prize on offer, one that can make us rich in our old age and I will share it with no other.'

'What prize is this?'

'One from the abbot of Brycheniog. I hear he has been personally slighted by this man and has made a lasting oath to administer his own retribution. The only condition is that he is captured alive but to do so will take overwhelming strength. The Constable of Builth has his barracks well manned and has oft expressed his desire to bring the Blaidd to account. Bring them back with you and we will rendezvous ten days hence at the entrance to the village.'

'Surely our quarry would have fled by then?'

'I don't think so, this morning he was full of questions and unless I am mistaken, is up to no good. Why else would the leader of the Blaidd sleep amongst the poor and diseased unless he has his eyes on a greater prize? Now, be gone and return with all haste.'

'Are you not coming?'

'No, I am going to Brycheniog. I need to speak to a certain abbot.'

'So be it,' said the rider and turned his horse. Within moments they were galloping in different directions leaving Dysynni far behind them.

Chapter Seven

The dream of Macsen Wledig

Madog, Tarian and Geraint dined on a fare of boar and roasted vegetables before Madog dismissed his servants and the three men sat alone around a trestle table in the tent.

'So,' said Madog, 'what is this dream you tell of, but before you start let me say this. I am a practical man and do not take easily to portents of fate by witches or omens. I feel a man makes his own way in this world, guided only by the hand of God.'

'A wise philosophy,' said Tarian, 'but when a leader deems to lead the masses, then he would be wise to at least know of such things.'

'So be it, Tarian,' said Madog. 'Tell your tale and I will let you know how much heed I pay to it.'

Tarian supped on his ale before starting.

'My lord, what do you know of the history of our land?'

'Mostly what we are taught at our mother's knee,' answered Madog. 'I learned the tales of the Welsh princes back as far as Hywel Dda the lawmaker. However, I also sat in wonder at the stories of Arthur and his knights as I suspect do all young boys even today.'

'I suspect they do, my lord, and whilst the true stories of Arthur are perhaps different from that told to excited

77

boys, that is a lesson for another day. My question relates to times beyond recent history, before Lion Heart or Harold, even back past the age of saints and the times of the Northmen. I am talking about the times of the Romans.'

'I am aware of some stories,' said Madøg, 'but very little is known of those people apart for the statues and ruins they left behind them.'

'What if I was to tell you that way back before any of us can even imagine, this land was ruled by such men, men who not only excelled in warfare but provided political systems and wealth across the whole country? They brought culture never before seen in our lands, which has never been seen since and not only ours, for they ruled all lands from here to the Holy Land and even further down into Africa. Their ships sailed the seas in their hundreds seeking new lands, either as trading partners or as conquests. They were feared by all and ruled the world for hundreds of years.'

'If this is so, where are they now?'

'Like all civilisations, they rotted from within but their legacy lives on across the known world. They brought water where there was draught, culture where there was barbarianism and religion where there was darkness. The Roman Empire was like nothing we have ever witnessed.'

'And how do you know of this?'

'My lord, in my time I have had cause to talk to many learned men including those who have religion as their calling. They have seen sights that we can only imagine and read many documents dating back to that age. In Rome, which was of course the seat of the Roman Empire, there are records documenting wondrous things and though the early Romans worshipped Pagan gods, eventually they saw Christ's holiness and converted to Christianity. Now it is the churches and monasteries of our faith that hold such records and are the source of such tales. I have been fortunate to hear some such stories and though they may be embellished in the telling, I believe enough to know they bettered us in many ways, not just warfare.'

'So what has this to do with this so-called dream of Macsen?'

'The story I am about to tell is from that age, my lord. It is said a great leader called Maximus Clemens sat in power over all of Rome's greatness. He was an emperor and all powerful. He ruled lands from Africa to England and feared no man. Yet he was unhappy for though he had everything, he lacked the one thing he craved most, love.'

'Is this not the case in many men?'

'Often it is. One night, Maximus Clemens dreamed of a beautiful woman sitting on the crest of a mountain overlooking a fishing village. In this dream, the woman had golden hair to her waist and eyes of azure. She was beautiful beyond compare and the emperor was enthralled. In the dream she beckoned him with gentle hands and bid him find her for she waited for him in lands afar. They sat next to each other in the dream and looked out over clear waters in a beautiful land but all too soon she was gone.

'When he woke,' he continued, 'he was distraught that the vision had ended and fell into a great depression. For seven times seven nights he refused to leave his bedchamber, desperate to dream again of this goddess but alas the dream never returned. Finally he sought the wisdom of the old gods and his way was made clear to him, he was to find this beauty for she waited for him still.'

'I suppose he set out on a quest,' sneered Madog.

'He did not,' said Tarian, 'for Maximus Clemens held power untold and riches only dreamed of, so he sent out ten thousand men in his name to all the corners of the earth, each seeking the woman who promised to be his love.'

'Am I to believe this tale of unrequited love or is there a serious outcome to all this?' asked Madog.

'Please, bear with me, my lord, for though the build-up has perhaps been embroidered over the years, the outcome is deadly serious.'

'Then continue, Tarian, for I am intrigued.'

'For two years his men sought the girl until finally, a weary priest reached the north shores of Wales, not far from your own manor here in Ynys Mon. He heard tell of a great beauty and when he laid eyes upon her, he knew she was the one. He sent word to Rome immediately and Maximus Clemens left his empire behind to see the subject of his dreams. When he arrived, he was astonished at her beauty and asked her if she had ever dreamed of him. She retold the very same vision he had dreamed two years earlier and he knew the quest had been fulfilled.

'Immediately he sought her hand in wedlock but though she consented, there was one condition, they would never leave Britannia. Maximus Clemens agreed without second thought for though he was Emperor of Rome, his love of the girl was greater than his love of power. He stayed in Britannia as emperor and together they ruled the country bringing great wealth and happiness.

'It was a peaceful and bountiful time but though they ruled half the world, the girl loved her homeland more than anywhere else. Maximus Clemens made sure Wales prospered under his rule and made a holy pledge before God that as long as his sword stayed in Wales then no foe would ever take her liberty. From that point on, though we could never claim to be equal partners of Rome, we prospered as a nation and traded with the world as equals, free from the yoke of all men.'

'A pretty tale,' said Madog, 'but just a story nothing more. You have not convinced me of anything apart from your love of stories, Tarian.'

'Then what if I was to tell you that the woman he wed was Helena Lledogg, also known to us as Saint Helen of the Hosts.'

Madog slowly put down his tankard and stared at Tarian.

'That's impossible, before she was canonised Helena was wed to the King of England.'

'She was, but that king was called Macsen Wledig which was the Welsh name given to him by our people in honour of his protection. His real name was Magnus Clemens Maximus and he was the Emperor of Rome.'

Madog looked between the two men, allowing the news to sink in. Finally he spoke again.

'Even if this is true, how does it help us?'

'It helps us because it gave birth to a legend. While Macsen was alive, the country prospered, however, he died relatively young leaving Helena distraught. His role as emperor quickly passed to another claimant in Rome but she was allowed to stay in Wales as his widow.

'Helena was a very clever woman and knew about Macsen's pledge to the people regarding his sword. She also knew that though Macsen was dead, as long as the sword was displayed then the people would believe in their freedom. Subsequently she arranged to have it displayed in the chapel that held his tomb and for many years, people prayed for his soul beneath the liberty sword hanging high above his final resting place. It soon became a symbol of freedom and stories spread that if Wales was ever subject to conquest, then any man wielding Macsen's blade would be granted holy power to restore the land to liberty.

'Despite his death, Wales continued to prosper and Helena devoted her time to the building of roads in Macsen's name. Her legacy lies even now between most towns but eventually she turned to the church and died in service to Mary, mother of Christ, and before long, the tales became shrouded in folklore.'

'So what happened to the sword?'

'Therein lies the problem,' said Tarian. 'The sword is said to still be hanging above the tomb of Macsen but the thing is, nobody knows where the tomb is. The death of the Emperor was almost a thousand years ago and since then, Wales and England have fought many battles and when people run screaming for their lives, tales of ancient heroes are oft forgotten in the need to seek safety.'

'Wars are terrible things, Madog,' said Geraint, 'and take their toll on flesh and bone but often buildings have their own price to pay, especially those of a religious nature. Churches are ransacked for treasure but sometimes they are just torn down as a reminder to the local population of who is in charge. Some believe the chapel that contained his tomb was ransacked by the Saxons when they first arrived but others believe it still lays somewhere in the north of Wales, waiting to be discovered.'

'And there is no record of such a place?'

'There is not.'

'So how is this of relevance to us? Are you suggesting I set out on a quest to find a tomb of a man dead a thousand years or more, in a chapel that may not exist to find a sword that may just be the outcome of a fable?'

'Ordinarily I would agree it begs an unlikely outcome,' said Tarian, 'but I have news of a man who claims to know the location of the tomb and though he cannot be reached at present, things are afoot to locate the sword and if we can find it, then your claim will be irrefutable.'

'And if this man's claim is false?'

'Then we will be no further forward than we are now.'

'But there is also another problem,' said Geraint.

'Which is?'

'Cynan ap Maredudd has sights on greatness. His army grows under his influence and it is said he seeks the title for himself.'

'Has this situation not drawn the attention of Longshanks?'

'Edward prepares for his French campaign as we speak and a minor Welsh lord flexing his muscles is of secondary importance. However, Cynan knows the feeling in the country is swelling toward war and sees an opportunity. He is a passionate Welshman and seeks the same as us but his lineage is poor and I feel he would not unite the country under one banner.'

'So is he friend or foe?'

'He is neither and can fall either side. However, if we can find this sword your claim will be unchallenged and he will acknowledge your lineage.' Geraint paused. 'The thing is, my lord, we need his army if we are to succeed.'

'So without this sword we are dead in the water.'

'Not exactly, we can continue to offer resistance but this is the one opportunity to unite our countrymen. Without the sword, we could wait generations for the mood of the nation to once more ignite but with it, our people can be free within the year.'

'Then our way is clear,' sighed Madog, 'whether truth or fable, we need to at least seek this blade.'

'We do, my lord, and already we have taken steps to locate the tomb. The task has been given to the one group with resolve enough to take on such a challenge, the Blaidd.'

'You have engaged the Wolves?'

'We have, my lord.'

'Are they not just brigands?'

'Brigands no, but they are mercenaries who work for the highest paymaster. I understand Cynan approached them with the same request and offered them their weight in silver to return the sword to him. An astonishing price but their leader turned the offer down and came to one of our comrades, Meirion ap Rees, to request a different deal.'

'Geraint, I cannot better that offer, what can you have possible promised in my name that is greater than the wealth of kings?'

'The one thing valued above all riches, my lord, and the one thing only you, as King of Wales could ever deliver, their liberty.'

'They want amnesty?'

'They do. They require no silver or gold, no coins or riches of any description. All they ask, if you are eventually announced as the true monarch of these lands is a proclamation absolving them of all crimes and allowing them back to their families.'

'Is this within my power?'

'At the moment, all you can do is promise to meet the request but if we are successful and you are indeed pronounced king, then everything is within your power.'

Madog sat back, deep in thought.

'And you believe this sword exists?'

'I do, my lord, with all my heart.'

Madog paused again, deep in thought. He got to his feet and walked around the tent before returning to stand before the two men.

'I accept your counsel, gentlemen, and will follow this path. Keep me abreast of matters concerning the sword's location. Until we find the weapon, we will continue to drill our men in preparation.'

'A wise decision, my lord,' said Tarian, 'and one I feel you will not regret.'

Chapter Eight

Dysynni Village

A large crowd was gathering as Garyn made his way to the village square. A public flogging always drew interest but to see the brutal punishment on one so young was a particular novelty. Many of the people crowded around the cart which had carried the boy from the castle. He was tied to a cross-rail as the manacles in the castle had proved too large for such wiry wrists and though he posed a forlorn figure, his demeanour was defiant.

Garyn ignored the prisoner and cast his eye around the market square, seeking a certain man he knew would be present. For half an hour he scanned the crowd and thought he would be too late but finally he spied the man he sought. The person in question was of little significance at first sight. He wore ordinary clothes and sat at a trestle table drinking ale amongst his peers. Garyn moved closer and as soon as he had a chance, sat on the bench alongside his target.

'Ale, if you please,' he said as the serving wench walked by.

'Of course, sir,' said the woman, 'that will be a copper penny.'

Garyn put three pennies on the table.

'Just the one, sir,' said the girl.

'Bring two tankards,' said Garyn, 'and a trencher of bread and pork.'

'Of course, sir,' said the girl and scooped the coins into the front pocket of her apron.

'You have a healthy appetite,' said the man alongside Garyn.

'I have not eaten since dawn,' said Garyn, 'and would have a full belly before sampling this afternoon's entertainment.'

'And a strong thirst it would seem.'

'The second tankard is for you, my friend,' said Garyn.

The man looked up at him.

'I do not recall your face, sir. Do I know you?'

'I do not believe we have met, though I suspect I know who you are, or at least, what it is you do.'

The man looked down at his backpack on the floor and saw the wooden handle of his whip sticking out of the side. He looked back up at Garyn.

'If it is trouble you want, then you have picked on the wrong man. I have been engaged by the Castellan himself and one call from me will bring his men running. That boy broke his contract and the punishment is a legal decree. He may be young, but if we let them get away with breaking the law then all boys of his age will follow his example, and then where would we be?'

'I want no trouble,' said Garyn, 'indeed, I agree that contracts should be met. However, I wonder at the severity that has been agreed.'

'He is to receive six lashes,' said the man before draining his tankard.

'A severe test,' said Garyn.

87

'It has been reduced from twelve,' said the man reaching for the full tankard placed before him by the serving girl. 'However, six is enough for most and I have seen bigger men die of the pain.'

'This is what concerns me,' said Garyn, 'it seems very harsh on a boy so young.'

'Don't fret too much, sir, for the boy is not even English. He hails from France and was sold as a rigging monkey by his family for a tidy sum.'

'Even so,' said Garyn, 'I suspect the lashes will prove too much.'

The man shrugged his shoulders.

'They may, they may not, it depends on my aim and my mood.'

'How so?'

'If my aim is true and I hit the same wound, I can cut a man to his core and have been known to break a man's backbone, however, that sort of attention is reserved for murderers.'

'And if the crime is minor?'

'Then the force of the blows is lighter and spread across the back. The pain is more severe for a short term but the wounds usually heal within weeks.'

'Tell me,' said Garyn, 'which style is to be administered today?'

The man shrugged his shoulders.

'It has not been discussed but despite my trade, I am not a cruel man.'

Garyn breathed a sigh of relief and pushed the plate of bread and pork toward the man.

'Please,' he said, 'share my meal. What is your name, stranger?'

'I do not share my name outside of my family for my trade attracts unfriendly attention but you can call me the Friar.'

Garyn frowned.

'The Friar?'

'Let's just say it hails from a past best forgotten,' said the man.

'Well, Friar,' said Garyn, 'I accept that you have an important job to do but I also suspect you take no great joy in it.'

'I have long lost any emotions,' said the Friar, 'and now only wield the whip to earn a crust.'

'Then can a man ask if you are open to conducting some business on the side?'

'Why, is there someone you want whipped?'

'On the contrary, there is someone whom I want treated gently.'

'The boy?' asked the Friar.

'The boy,' confirmed Garyn.

'I have already told you; the commission has been accepted.'

'I understand but would request it is administered with compassion.'

'Ha,' sneered the Friar, 'a compassionate flogging? That would indeed be a double-faced punishment. How do you administer such a thing?'

'All I ask is that the blows are spread and are as light as you can get away with without drawing awkward questions from your masters.'

'And why would I do this?'

Garyn reached across and took a piece of bread from the trencher, uncovering a golden coin. The Friar looked up for a moment before sliding the coin from the wooden board and into his pocket.

'Do we have a deal?' asked Garyn.

'My arm is indeed weary today,' said the Friar eventually, 'and I suspect my blows will not be as strong as usual.'

'And your aim?'

'Is still sharp, the blows will be spread evenly.'

'Good,' said Garyn. 'One more thing, if the boy is conscious at the end of his punishment, there will be a similar coin waiting for you at the conclusion of today's events.'

'Agreed,' said the man.

'Good. I will leave you now my friend but would welcome confidence in this matter for I am as generous with my blade as I am with my coin.'

'Understood,' said the Friar returning his attention to the pork.

Garyn joined the crowd and wandered toward the village centre. Midday was approaching and there was one more deal he wanted to make. Eventually he stood at the centre of the village square and watched as the previous occupant of the whipping post was dragged away, a man beaten to within an inch of his life by the family of a woman he had raped. Strangely, Garyn felt no compassion at all for this man as his punishment was well deserved.

The sound of horns filled the air and a column of twelve men at arms forced the crowd apart to make way for the Castellan. Garyn watched as the extremely fat man made his way to the elevated seats placed upon a platform at the edge of the square. Another man joined him and from the cut of his garb, Garyn guessed correctly he was the emissary of the sea captain.

Garyn watched for several minutes until he saw an opportunity. He approached the platform and passed a note to one of the guards. The guard passed the note to the seaman who looked up with interest toward Garyn. Garyn nodded his head slightly in acknowledgement and watched as the seaman whispered in the Castellan's ear.

Fitzwalter laughed and said something back before the seaman descended the steps and walked through the crowd. Garyn swallowed hard and felt for the reassuring feel of his dagger at his waist. This was to be the most dangerous deal of the day. The seaman disappeared around a corner of a house and Garyn followed closely. Finally they stood face to face.

'Are you the man who sent the note?' asked the seaman.

'I am, sir.'

'Then I am intrigued. Your note promises riches for a simple deal.'

'It does, and my purse is heavy with coin.'

'Then tell me what this deal is?' said the seaman. 'But make it quick for there is a flogging to be witnessed.'

'I know of the flogging and therein lies the subject of the deal,' said Garyn. 'I want to buy the boy from you.'

The man paused but then laughed.

'That wretch? Why is he of value to you?'

'My mistress is French, my lord, and requires a serving boy who can speak the language. I understand he is from France?'

'Indeed he is, from an island called Corsica, a place famed for its seagoing people, but why your interest in this one?'

'No reason, my lord, except that as you can imagine, French speaking boys are a rarity in these parts.'

'I would imagine so but alas, he is not for sale.'

'Why not?'

'Because my captain wants him flogged and returned.'

'But surely, as a businessman, a heavy purse would be just as welcomed. He could buy another boy and make a handsome profit.'

'That depends on the weight of the purse.'

'Name your price, sir, and I will say whether it can be met.'

Garyn could see the man thinking furiously, calculating what was in it for him. Finally he settled on an amount that he thought may be in reach of the stranger's purse.

'Five gold coins,' he said, 'and the boy stays here with you.'

'A steep price for a mere boy,' said Garyn.

'Perhaps so but you don't know the temper of my captain. I could well be flogged myself for this but five gold coins may calm his ire and leave me with a healthy profit.'

'I understand, sir,' said Garyn, 'and accept your price. However, if I add another coin, will you release him unharmed?'

'Alas, I cannot. The flogging will go ahead but as he will be damaged goods, I will sell him to you when the punishment is concluded.'

'So be it,' said Garyn. 'When the boy is cut down, deliver him unto the tavern and I will hand over the payment.'

'And if you are not there?'

'Then you still have the boy, there is nothing to lose.'

The seaman thought for a moment then held out his arm.

'We have an agreement,' he said and Garyn grasped the offered wrist to seal the deal.

'I will see you later,' said Garyn and turned away as the seaman returned to his seat.

Garyn returned to the crowd and forced his way to the front, much to the annoyance of some of the old women jostling for position. A few moments later the boy was led from the cart and placed against the whipping post. The thongs around his wrists were attached to a rope which was then fastened high on the pole so should he pass out, his body would still be upright. The boy was defiant in demeanour but despite this, Garyn could see fear in his eyes.

A man stepped forward and cut the jerkin from the boy's back and a murmur rippled around the crowd as they saw how skinny he was.

'He is but a puppy,' said one of the old women, 'the poor mite will be cut to the bone.'

'He is nought but a Frenchy anyways,' said another. 'Let him bleed, I say.'

From the side, the Friar stepped forward and unravelled his leather whip, its blood-stained surface glistening in the midday sun. A couple of hisses and insults came from the watchers but on the whole, the crowd fell silent. The Friar walked up and placed a leather wrapped stick up to the boy's mouth. The boy shook his head but the Friar insisted.

'Better to bite on this than your tongue, boy. I have seen bigger men than you bite through their own flesh. Take it for you own good.'

The boy opened his mouth and accepted the leather stick.

'Listen,' said the Friar, 'I will not lie, it is going to hurt but there are only six lashes to bear. Pant like a dog between each and bite hard as each lands. I will get it over as quickly as I can. Ready?'

The boy nodded but even from his position ten paces away, Garyn could see he was terrified.

'Friar,' called the Castellan, 'enough chit chat, let the punishment commence.'

'Aye, sir,' said the Friar and walked away, unravelling the whip as he went. When he was ready, he called out to the boy once more.

'Whoever it is you pray to lad, I suggest you call on them now.' He flicked the whip twice and drawing it back behind him, let the leather fly to land squarely across the boy's shoulders.

The crowd gasped and many eyes turned away as the first lash landed, opening a wound across the boy's flesh. A muffled scream came from the victim but he remained upright. The Friar looked across at Garyn and saw the look in the man's eyes.

'A good strike,' called the Castellan, 'continue.'

'Aye sir,' answered the Friar and sent the second lash whistling through the air. This time the weal appeared a few inches below the first and again the boy cried out. The next three lashes followed in quick succession and by the time the fifth stripe appeared, the boy was hanging from his ties, passed out through the pain.

'Revive him,' shouted the Castellan, 'he will not escape his punishment through lack of consciousness.'

'He has had enough,' shouted some of the crowd.

'Release him,' shouted others.

'Nonsense,' roared Fitzwalter, 'he is a criminal and will be treated as such. Revive him, Friar and add another lash for his impertinence.'

'No,' shouted the crowd.

'Silence,' roared the Castellan, 'or I will have him whipped to death. Friar, continue immediately or take his place.'

The Friar picked up a leather bucket and poured water over the boy's head. The boy gasped in shock as the water revived him.

'Stand up, boy,' said the Friar, 'let's get this over with.'

The victim struggled to his feet and leaned his head on the whipping pole.

Friar returned to his place and with lightning speed, sent the final two lashes through the air in quick succession. The first made the boy cry out and as he collapsed again, the second caught him as he still fell.

The crowd ran forward to the pole and caring hands cut the boy down. Wet sheets were carefully placed over his back and he was carried back to the cart.

'The punishment is done,' roared Fitzwalter, 'and let this be a lesson to all who would break the law. Justice is equal across all men, irrespective of age. Now, prepare a fire for I have ordered an ox killed and brought to the village to be roasted in this very square. Let it not be said that I do not administer pain and pleasure in equal measure.'

Approving voices were heard amongst the crowd and as many turned their attention away from the boy, the Friar approached Garyn.

'Satisfied?' he asked.

'Was that the gentlest you could have been?' asked Garyn.

'Trust me, any lighter and the Castellan would have known I was withholding my arm.'

'I see the last blow was administered quickly; I suppose that was to ensure a second coin.'

'The quickness of the last lash was for his sake not mine,' spat the Friar, 'he could not have taken resurrection a second time. Keep your stinking coin, I want nothing more to do with it.'

'No, wait,' said Garyn and pressed two coins into the man's hand. 'You did your job and I am a man of my word. You have my gratitude.'

The Friar glared at Garyn but took the money.

'You have made me conscious of my work and for the first time in many years, I felt compassion for the victim.'

'Surely this is a good thing.'

'On the contrary, I hate you for it. This job is hard enough without the weight of guilt it can bring.'

'Rest assured you have done the right thing, Friar,' said Garyn.

'That is not your decision to make,' said the man. 'Now, I am going to leave this place and hope to never see you again.' Without another word he walked away into the crowd.

'Do you know him?' asked a voice over Garyn's shoulder.

Garyn turned and saw the seaman.

'No, I was just complimenting him on his accuracy.'

'If you say so,' said the seaman. 'I trust our deal is still on?'

'It is.'

'Then be at the tavern at dusk. Make sure you have the money.'

'The money is secure,' said Garyn, 'but I will not pay for a corpse.'

'Understood,' said the seaman, 'I will see you then.'

—

Eight hours later Garyn stood at the side of the tavern alongside Elias, the servant from the sanctuary. Together they watched as a man pushed a handcart down a muddy side street. Behind him strode the seaman and two of his henchmen.

'Do you have the price?' asked the seaman.

'I have it,' said Garyn. 'Does he still live?'

'He does,' said the seaman, 'but who knows for how long?'

Elias pushed aside the sheepskin covering the boy and nodded toward Garyn.

'His breathing is shallow but regular. I need to get him back and apply ointments.'

Garyn threw a purse over to the seaman.

'Our business is concluded,' he said, 'good day to you, sir.'

'And to you,' said the seaman and returned back the way he had come.

Elias pushed the handcart out of the village and toward the sanctuary, closely followed by Garyn. When they arrived, Garyn pulled back the sheet, now red from the boy's blood. The boy groaned as the cloth pulled at his wounds.

'Do you think he will be all right?' asked Garyn.

'I think so,' said Elias. 'I have been trained in the ways of herbs and these are clean wounds.'

'Good,' said Garyn. 'Here are some more coins, buy what you need from the apothecary.'

'Sir, can I ask a question?'

'Go ahead.'

'What interest do you have in this boy? Is he known to you?'

'Not at all,' said Garyn, 'but many years ago my brother was also hurt and imprisoned in a foreign country far from home. He was older than this boy but in just as desperate a situation if not worse. I dread to think what would have happened but luckily, I found him just in time. This boy's plight reminded me of him and I thought it a suitable way to repay the good fortune I had in finding my brother.'

'I understand,' said Elias. 'And when he is well, what would you have me do with him?'

'I hadn't thought that far ahead,' said Garyn, 'but if you can look after him for the time being, I will return within the next few weeks and check on you both. Besides, it has just occurred to me, he may have some information I may be interested in.'

'What sort of information?'

'Don't worry yourself over that, Elias, just make sure you get him fit and well again.'

'Of course, my lord, he will be as sprightly as a week-old colt before this month is out.'

'Good, I will return then. Don't forget, Elias, this is our secret.'

The servant nodded and watched Garyn walk back the way he had come.

Chapter Nine

Brecon Castle

'Hold there stranger,' said one of the pikemen at the entrance to the castle, 'state your name and your business.'

The rider reined in his horse and dismounted.

'My name is Hywel ap Rees and I hail from Builth. I seek audience with Father Williams, abbot of the Monastery at Brycheniog. I understand he is here?'

'The abbot is a guest of the Castellan this past week and is not taking visitors. I suggest you go to the abbey and await his return.'

'My business will not wait,' said the liegeman, 'and I demand audience.'

'Take your demands elsewhere, stranger,' said the pikeman, 'we have our orders.'

'I respect your loyalty,' said Hywel, 'but let me say this. I have information for the abbot, information he has been seeking for many years but it will become useless within days. If he finds out he missed this opportunity, which I can assure you he will, then I suspect you will suffer a heavy price and we all know he is not a man of good temper.'

The pikeman looked at his comrade nervously.

'What do you think?' he asked.

'What is this information that you proclaim so important?' asked the second soldier, turning to face Hywel.

'It is for his ears alone but I will say this: go to the abbot and tell him there is one at the gate who knows the whereabouts of the blacksmith. That will be enough.'

The men paused but eventually one turned to stride under the raised portcullis.

'Your mount looks tired,' said the remaining guard, 'it would seem you have ridden far.'

'Two days with little rest,' said Hywel, 'and would welcome shelter and hay for my horse.'

'If your news is as important as you claim, then I suggest you will be well stabled within the hour.'

'Perhaps so,' replied Hywel. 'Tell me, it is a long time since I have had cause to visit this place and the last time I came the castellan was a man called Ellicott. Does he still hold the responsibility?'

'Alas no, for he was a kindly man. He died in suspicious circumstances and many suspect poisoning but such matters are beyond the likes of us.'

'So who is your new master?'

'Our new lord is known as Gerald of Essex, an English knight who wed the daughter of Cadwallader. Since he took over her father's lands his star has risen and he has acquired huge influence hereabouts. He is a brutal master and feared by many so when the position of castellan became available, his petition for consideration was well received by the King and Gerald was appointed Castellan of Brecon Castle as well as Sheriff and Constable of Brycheniog.'

'A position of much power,' said Hywel.

'Indeed, but a position supported by Longshanks himself for Gerald keeps the Welsh in their place with a brutal hand. Between him and the abbot, there is not a dissenting word to be heard from Builth to Caerleon.'

'Is the abbot a close friend of this Gerald?'

'Indeed he is and between them their power in these parts is second only to the King.'

'And what do you think of this?'

'Me? I have no thoughts on such matters. I am a soldier of the King and takes the penny to obey orders.'

'Nevertheless, are you not of Welsh birth?'

'There are many Welsh in the King's army,' said the pikeman. 'It doesn't mean we are any less patriotic, it's just a living and perhaps one with a view of reality rather than fantasy.'

Before Hywel could say anymore the other pikeman returned.

'Let him through,' he called. 'The abbot will see him.'

'It seems your tale is good, stranger,' said the second guard. 'Go through to the inner ward.'

Hywel grunted and led his horse under the portcullis. As he walked, he could see dozens of men along the upper castellations, each cradling a crossbow in their arms.

'Are you expecting trouble?' asked Hywel.

'Nobody would dare raise their fist against Gerald,' said the guard, 'but there are rumours of revolt and it is always good to be prepared.'

The sound of the horse's hooves echoed around the castle's courtyard as a page ran forward to take the beast away.

'Feed and water him well,' said Hywel.

The guard handed Hywel over to a waiting squire and within moments he was walking through the double doors of the great hall. He was shown to an oaken table near to a roaring fire built into the far wall.

'The abbot will be along shortly,' said the squire. 'Have you eaten?'

'I have not,' said the liegeman, 'and would welcome a crust.'

'I will have the kitchens bring you a meal,' said the squire.

Ten minutes later, a serving girl carried a tray of food for the liegeman consisting of half a chicken, a bowl of cawl and a hand of bread, along with a jug of watered wine. Hywel mumbled his thanks and tore into the chicken, taking large gulps of wine between each mouthful. When he was done, he ripped the bread into chunks and dipped it into the rich cawl gravy between spooning vegetables into his mouth. Slowly he became aware of being watched and looked up to see a man staring at him in distaste. He swallowed hard and wiped his mouth with the back of his sleeve.

'Is there a problem?' he asked.

'I think the only problem here is your lack of manners,' said the man.

'I apologise if my manner offends you,' said Hywel, 'but a hungry man often forgets such niceties when faced with a feast.'

'Granted but irrespective of your table manners, do you not show the courtesy of hospitality?'

'Indeed I do, and await the arrival of my host, the abbot of Brycheniog.'

'On the contrary,' said the man, 'the abbot is a guest here as are you. I am your host, Gerald of Essex, castellan of this castle and Edward's trusted constable.'

'My apologies, my lord,' said Hywel standing up and bowing his head. 'I was not expecting one so young.'

'A mistake often made,' said Gerald, 'but one to which I am taking a dislike. Since when is age a guarantee of loyalty, lineage or indeed prowess? I have seen many aged knights who are not worthy to carry such a title.'

'Your point is well made, sir,' said Hywel looking around him. 'Is the abbot not available?'

'He is indisposed,' said the Castellan, 'but I will arrange an audience shortly. Finish your food and then ask the squire to bring you through.'

'Thank you, my lord,' said Hywel and as soon as the young knight had left, he sat back down, returning his attention to the unfinished bowl of cawl.

—

Father Williams was being pulled into an upright position in his bed. His face was gaunt but his strength was returning after suffering another bout of dysentery, a recurring problem after his time in the Holy Land many years earlier.

'Where is he?' he wheezed.

'He is partaking of my hospitality in the main hall,' said Gerald. 'I will bring him through shortly.'

The abbot sipped on a goblet of water.

'Excellent,' he said. 'Does he seem of sound mind?'

'I have no idea,' said the Castellan, 'but he doesn't seem like a simpleton if that's what you mean.'

'You know what I mean,' said the abbot. 'I have seen too many cold trails these past few years and time is running out if I am to catch the man I seek.'

'I don't see why you still pursue him,' said Gerald. 'It has been fourteen years since your paths last crossed and since then you have become a powerful man, not to say rich.'

'We have both shared the spoils, Gerald, never forget that. I have indeed achieved most things and will go to my grave a satisfied man but this one thing escapes me. If I can deliver on my oath then I will die a happy man.'

'But I still question the reason why. You killed his family, confiscated his father's lands, broke up his marriage and made an outlaw of him. What more does he have that you could possibly want?'

'His life,' said the abbot. 'I want to see the light fade in his eyes. If I can be the wielder of the blade, then all the better but I will accept being close by.'

'Remind me again of his crime?'

'He blocked my passage to greatness,' said the abbot. 'The true cross of Christ was within my grasp but he interfered and placed it in the hands of the crown. To add insult to injury, I then had to deliver the cross to Rome on behalf of Longshanks and it is now in Papal hands. Without this blacksmith's interference, I could have used the cross to great affect and perhaps sought a path to cardinalship.'

'Is that possible for a monk?'

'With the right tools and enough wealth, all things are possible, even within the church. Imagine if I presented the holy fragment to the Pope in my name, not the King's. The Papal gratitude would have been overwhelming.'

'But what is so important about being a cardinal?'

'Only a cardinal can become pope,' said Father Williams.

Gerald paused as the information sunk in.

'You wanted to become Pope?' he asked with incredulity.

'Why is that such a shock to you?' asked Father Williams.

'I thought that the position was pre-ordained and only the privileged could hold sway in such a position.'

'Gerald, my friend. You of all people know me better than most and I believe that had I gained access to that privileged circle, then I would have been perfectly placed to take advantage of any opportunity. Stranger things have happened throughout history.'

'Indeed they have,' said Gerald, 'and actually, I believe that once you had become close enough, then nothing would have prevented you achieving your aims.'

'And therein lies my ire,' said the abbot. 'God gave me one chance, one opportunity to gain the leverage to open certain holy doors but it was denied me by Garyn ap Thomas and that, my friend, is precisely the reason I want to see him suffer before I die.'

'Understandable, I suppose,' said Gerald. 'Are you ready to receive your guest?'

'I am, bring him in.'

—

Hywel ap Rees stood at the side of the abbot's bed, breathing shallowly to avoid the underlying stench of human faeces beneath the heavy perfumes.

'They tell me you are the Sheriff of Builth,' said the abbot.

'No Father, I am only his liegeman, tasked with returning the guilty to justice.'

'A noble role,' said the abbot.

'And one I am very successful at,' said the liegeman, 'hence my claim to know the whereabouts of the man you seek. However, I am also aware this information is of value to you and we all have to pay our way in this world.'

'You get quickly to the point,' said the abbot, 'a trait I admire in men. Tell me what you know and what it is you desire.'

'Let us agree a price first,' said the liegeman, 'and then I will share my tale.'

'And what if I think your story unworthy?'

'Some things are out of my control, Father, and I am aware that by the time we return to whence I came, our quarry may have fled but I don't think so. Therefore my proposal is this. We agree a price and I take you or your forces directly to him. The price will be one hundred gold coins dead, or thrice that alive. In addition, I want ownership of all other bounty claimable upon the heads of his men. That way, I am only paid if we are successful.'

'I like the way you barter, liegeman. The price is high yet based on success. The deal is acceptable to me.'

'One more thing,' said Hywel, 'I want the details written down and signed under a seal of authority. It can be yours or the Castellan's it matters not but it must be legal and admissible in front of any court of the land.'

'Such matters are not usually committed to parchment,' said the abbot.

'We are doing nothing illegal, Father. It is a deal between honest men based on the apprehension of those outside the law. The practice is sound.'

'Agreed,' said the abbot. 'I will have the papers drawn up straight away. Now, tell me what you know.'

'Many years ago I was in the pay of an English lord as a lancer. My master took the cross and undertook a crusade to Acre where I stayed for three years. During that time, I was oft stationed within the constable's hall and was on one such tour of duty when a petition was made by many men regarding ownership of the true cross.'

'You were there?'

'I was, Father, as a guard on the hall doors. At the time, Acre was rife with the stories of Garyn ap Thomas and his recovery of the true cross. As we shared a homeland I was particularly interested in the stories and I saw him close up on several occasions.'

'I am aware of that meeting,' said the abbot, 'and hear tell that the blacksmith represented himself before the King. Is this true?'

'Alas, Father, it is not. The man who spoke for him was a follower of your own order, a Benedictine monk called Brother Martin.'

'And you are sure it is the same man you saw?'

'I am. We even had cause to talk briefly but never became comrades in arms. Since then I have oft wondered about his whereabouts and wasn't surprised that a man of his mettle eventually ended up as the leader of the Blaidd.'

'A rumour only,' said the abbot, 'for no one knows the leader of the Wolves.'

'I mix with many men of distasteful character, Father, and I can assure you the rumours are true. Anyway, our paths crossed again not three days past and I recognised him straight away though fortunately, it would seem he has no recollection of me.'

'So what was he doing?'

'He seems to be planning something for he mingles with the destitute, asking questions of the locals. I have been told he has frequented several taverns in the area and the conversation always falls to a certain castle and its defences. I believe he may be planning a raid on the supply lines of this fortress and spies upon it to judge the strength of its patrols and the urgency of the response.'

'Can you be sure of this?'

'Nothing is certain, my lord, but if we take him alive, then I am sure the Castellan's torturers can extract the truth.'

'So where is this castle?'

'Father forgive me but the location will be revealed only upon receipt of the signed agreement. I'm sure you will understand.'

'You are a suspicious man,' said the abbot. 'A trait of value in these difficult times.'

'It is why I have lived so long,' said Hywel.

The abbot lay back and closed his eyes for a few moments. Finally he opened them again and turned to one of his servants.

'Have quarters prepared for our guest and furnish them with food and ale.' He looked at the liegeman. 'Am I to assume you would like company to warm your bed?'

'That would be good,' said Hywel.

'Arrange it,' said the abbot to the servant and turned to face the liegeman again. 'I will have the document drawn up overnight. In the meantime you will stay here and, in the morning, set out with a patrol of men in the pursuit of my quarry. Bring him to me alive, Liegeman, and I will double the price you ask.'

'A generous gesture,' said Hywel.

'Coins I have aplenty and as I suspect I am not long for this world, what use is there in keeping a hoard when the one thing I most desire is within my grasp. Now, I weaken from my illness so be gone, the scroll and the men at arms will be waiting for you at dawn.'

Hywel bowed and retreated from the room. When the door closed, a tapestry moved to one side and Gerald of Essex stepped out.

'Do you think he tells the truth?'

'I do,' said the abbot, 'for I too was at that meeting in Acre and I just cast a line of questioning to the liegeman to uncover any untruths.'

'What do you mean?'

'I suggested the blacksmith represented himself but this Hywel ap Rees corrected me and said it was a Benedictine monk who spoke.'

'And was it?'

'It was indeed,' said the abbot, 'one of my own monks had a mistaken sense of loyalty and turned from his brothers to support the blacksmith's crusade.'

'Does this monk still live?'

'Of course not and I had cause to rob his grave many years ago.'

'You robbed a monk's grave?' laughed Gerald.

'There was a need,' said the abbot, 'and again that cursed Garyn came between me and glory. No, I think this liegeman speaks true and we have a good opportunity.'

He paused. 'I have a task that needs doing, Gerald and I would entrust it to no other man but you.'

'And what task is this?'

'I want you to carry a message to Garyn ap Thomas, a sealed note that should be handed to him alone. If you do this for me, I expect the blacksmith to return here of his own free will.'

'Did you not just charge the liegeman with returning the outlaw here?'

'I did but the blacksmith is a resourceful man and will not submit easily. Just in case, I have another string to my bow, a ruse that will ensnare him as a spider does a fly.'

'I am not surprised but why me? There are countless messengers of lower standing you could call on.'

'Indeed I could but the contents of the letter cannot be seen by normal men. You, Gerald, are not a normal man.'

'I will take that as a compliment,' said Gerald, 'but nevertheless, I have a castle to run. Send someone else.'

'You are quick to turn away my request but have not yet heard the terms.'

'What terms?'

'When he returns, as he will, then I will reveal to you the location of my treasury, making you a very wealthy man.'

Gerald paused.

'I know you have hoarded away some baubles, Abbot, but I am already a rich man, why would I risk my life for more?'

'Because the measly pile you call wealth is but an apple in a barrel compared to what I have amassed over the years. Bring Garyn to me alive and I will reveal exactly where it is hidden, every last coin.'

'How do I know you are telling the truth?'

'I am not long for this world, Gerald, and despite these robes, I find myself believing there is nought but darkness awaiting my soul. I have no need of wealth in the grave so would rather exchange it for one last earthly desire, to see the blood of the blacksmith running down the hilt of my dagger.'

Gerald stared for several moments before replying.

'And there is as much as you say?'

'More,' said the abbot. 'In my life I have had access to more churches than you can imagine and at every opportunity sought tribute in the Lord's name. In the beginning it was for good cause for we had an abbey to furnish. War was looming and I soon found out that in return for promised salvation, people were willing to give up their most precious possessions to the church. Gold, precious stones, silver coins, religious artefacts, you name it, I received it. The tributes poured in and within a year there was more than even I could handle. I should have stopped or sent them on to Rome but the greed was upon me and always I sought more. Many were the moonless nights when I buried my gains and they lay there still, a wealth no man could spend in a hundred lifetimes.'

'And you would bequeath this to me?'

'In a heartbeat. The second I feel the blacksmith's last breath upon my face I will give you the location.'

'If so much has been hidden, how do I know it has not already been found?'

'Because no man will dig up a grave.'

'The treasure is buried within a grave?'

'In the graves of many men,' said the abbot. 'I could not risk being seen digging open ground so I used the newly turned soil of the recently deceased to hide it away. In each grave there lies a sack of goods no more than a spade's depth from the surface, each enough for a poor man to become rich.'

'And where are these graves?'

'Ah, now that information is known only to me, but bring me Garyn and I will gladly dictate a list of the dead men sharing their soil with a king's ransom.'

'You are willing to swear this on your mortal soul?'

'I am, but you can believe me when I say I have no interest in what happens after I die. Bring him to me, Gerald, and I will make you one of the richest men in England.'

Gerald paused and stared at the abbot; their eyes locked together for several seconds.

'Write your letter, monk,' he said eventually, 'I accept your commission.'

Chapter Ten

Dysynni Valley

Garyn paused at the crest of a hill and looked across the valley below him. In the distance he could see Castell du Bere outlined against the backdrop of a moon-filled sky.

'Impressive,' said Derwyn, his second in command.

'It is well positioned,' said Garyn, 'and can be accessed only via the spur to the front. All other approaches are impossible to climb.'

'And the defences?'

'The walls are protected by a ditch and earthen ramparts. A drawbridge is pulled up at night and covers two portcullises. I know not what lies within the walls themselves but there are many arrow slits and I have seen crossbow men along the castellations.'

'It is as good as I have seen,' said Derwyn, 'yet you insist we can get inside.'

'I do.'

'Then pray tell what you intend to do for I see no weaknesses.'

'All in good time, my friend, for the plan relies on the input of another.'

'Who?'

'Come, I will introduce you.'

They turned off the crest and rode down the path toward the village. Just before the bridge leading over the stream on the outskirts, Garyn turned off and rode into the small courtyard of a building at the side of the road.

'What is this place?' asked Derwyn, looking up at the cross above the doorway. 'Some kind of church?'

'Not quite,' said Garyn, 'it is a sanctuary for weary travellers.'

'And our man rests here?'

'He does,' said Garyn, 'though it is not a man we seek but a monkey.'

Derwyn stared after Garyn as he rode around the back and dismounted outside a barn.

'A monkey?' said Derwyn catching up with him. 'I once saw such a beast on a dock in Caerleon. How could such a thing help us breach a castle wall?'

Garyn tied his horse to an iron ring in the barn wall, as did Derwyn.

'It is not the furry kind of monkey we seek, Derwyn, but a different kind, a rigging monkey.'

'And what pray is that?'

'A rigging monkey is a young boy used to scale the masts of sailing ships. They are usually sold into service by their families and hail from places where they farm goats on rocky crags. Such boys are as sure footed as the goats they herd and are valued for being light and nimble between the rigging.'

'And how does this help us?'

'Like you said, the front of the castle is unassailable due to the defences but the other three approaches are only lightly manned. When my path crossed with this boy several weeks ago my aim was just to save him from a tortured life, but I have visited him many times since and developed admiration for his character.'

'In what way?'

'He is a boy aged beyond his years, Derwyn, and during one conversation, expressed a desire to kill Fitzwalter. When I laughed at his ambition, he took offence and assured me that not only could he access the castle by climbing the cliff face to the rear but he could also scale the walls.'

'Impossible.'

'So thought I, but not ten days ago he demonstrated on the walls of this very sanctuary. He climbed barefoot, his fingers and toes seeking out the smallest of cracks.'

'And was he successful?'

'He was. All the time I feared he would fall but he soon sat astride the upper wall, laughing at my concern. It is truly a sight to behold.'

'And you think he can access the castle?'

'I do, but at first I had no intention of putting him at risk. My plan was to bribe some of the servants and gain access that way.'

'Were you successful?'

'Only partially but the man could not gain access to the mason. I was willing to be patient but events have overtaken us and I find myself limited by time.'

'Why?'

'Cynan ap Maredudd has grown impatient and has decided to take the initiative. I have received word he is mobilising his army and intends to take the fight to Longshanks.'

'In what way?'

'He is no longer willing to wait for the freedom sword to be discovered and rides to strike a major blow against the King.'

'What does he intend to do?'

'His target is a castle,' said Garyn, 'and his rallying call is that he intends to take back that which was once ours.'

Derwyn glanced up at the castle on the hill.

'This one?'

'Exactly,' said Garyn. 'Castell du Bere was built by our ancestors, and Cynan has used the pull of history to gather forces to his banner. Men flock to him and I know this village has already been swollen by many of his supporters awaiting his arrival.'

'A noble challenge,' said Derwyn. 'There is nothing a patriotic Welshman likes more than a call to arms to oust an English lord.'

'Perhaps so but I believe the castle is just a cover for his true aim. I suspect his real target is the mason for only he knows the location of the sword of liberty. If Cynan can lay hands on that as well as taking a castle from beneath the rule of Edward then his claim to the Welsh throne will be unassailable.'

'So what do you intend to do?'

'I intend to use the boy to achieve what I could not, get access to the mason. I could not share this with you sooner, for the boy's injuries meant I had to wait for his strength to recover but now he is well, he strains at the leash to gain revenge. Come, you will meet him in a few moments.'

Once inside the barn, Garyn walked past a huge pile of logs and through a dilapidated horse stall before ducking to crawl through a hole in the wall and into a room lit by a single candle, standing in a bowl of shallow water.

'Philippe, are you there?' he whispered.

'Garyn,' came a man's voice. 'Over here?'

'Elias,' said Garyn, 'I did not expect to find you here at this time.'

'I now sleep out here also,' said Elias. 'It was proving impossible to keep up the pretence with the monks so I told them about your mercy. I know it was supposed to be kept a secret but they suspected me of stealing bandages and ointments. At first they demanded I treat the boy at the monastery but I said he was diseased so they keep their distance but insisted that I too stay out here until you return to take him away.'

'An unfortunate circumstance,' said Garyn, 'but it can't be helped. Does anyone else know of this arrangement?'

'I don't think so but I am glad you have returned; the boy drives me mad.'

'Why?'

'He is a young pup, Garyn, and needs to stretch his legs. The confines of a sanctuary are not for him, he has the heart of a lion and the patience of a winter storm.'

'Fret not,' laughed Garyn, 'after tomorrow your role in his recovery will be done and I have not forgotten my promise to you. By the day after tomorrow, Rome will be a little nearer for you.'

'Garyn, is that you?' asked a voice in the darkness.

Gary smiled at the French accent.

'It is, Philippe, and I have brought a friend. This is Derwyn and I trust my life to him, as can you.'

'Welcome Derwyn,' said the boy and turned back to Garyn.

'Do we go tonight?'

'Patience, Philippe,' said Garyn, 'you have but one more day to wait. Tomorrow night, you can show us what you are really capable of, now, be a good lad and bring something to drink for our throats are as dry as dust.'

The boy grabbed an empty pitcher from a table and ducked out of the room.

'How is he?' asked Garyn.

'As strong as ever,' said Elias. 'The whip marks play a pretty pattern upon his back and he oft has bad dreams but he is like a caged animal, desperate to be free.'

'Good,' said Garyn. 'I will spend a few moments with him but then have to leave. I will return tomorrow for the last time, after that, you will never see me again.'

'I understand,' said Elias. 'Is it too much that I ask what it is you intend to do?'

'It is,' said Garyn. 'For your own sake you must remain ignorant of our task and if we succeed, nobody will ever know. However, if we fail, then our lives will be forfeit, including yours.'

'Well, whatever it is, I wish you luck,' said Elias.

'Thank you. Now, please, give us some time alone. We will be gone within the hour.'

–

Three hours later, Garyn and Derwyn rode down a dirt track several miles away from Dysynni. The night was now dark and both men reined in their horses as the sound of an owl echoed through the darkness. Derwyn nodded to Garyn and they turned off the track to head for a dense forest a few hundred paces away. Within a few moments a caped figure rose from the grass and aimed a longbow at Garyn's chest.

'State your business,' said the armed man.

'Stand down Eric,' said Derwyn. 'It is your leader returned from Dysynni.'

'And how fare the poor in the village?' asked the man without lowering his bow.

'They send their regards,' said Garyn, knowing full well that any other answer would alert the guard that they either were not alone or were being followed.

The man lowered the bow.

'Welcome back,' he said. 'Ride straight ahead and you will be met. There is food but no fires so cold meat and bread will be your fare.'

'It is sufficient,' said Garyn. 'How many men have heeded the call?'

'I believe we have over a hundred,' said the man.

'A goodly number,' said Garyn and spurred his steed onward into the forest. Within ten minutes both riders were welcomed back amongst their comrades, the most feared band of outlaws in the land, the Blaidd.

Chapter Eleven

Mid-Wales

The English column led by Fermbaud headed deeper into the mountains of Wales. They had been travelling from castle to castle and during the six weeks since leaving Bristol, had visited many towns and villages, displaying their support for those lords loyal to Longshanks and administering brutal penalties on any suspected of anything short of total subservience. Word of their actions quickly spread around the country and soon, any men involved in resistance to the King hid amongst the forests until the patrol had passed. Though this oft avoided the physical punishment of such men, Fermbaud was not a stupid man and where the number of women in a village was disproportionately high, he exacted a heavy price on what limited wealth lay within their control. Soon, even his many store wagons were full, so wherever rebellion was suspected, winter stores were destroyed and buildings burned. This was even more prevalent in Mid Wales where nationalistic pride was to the fore and Fermbaud left entire Cantrefs destitute. It was after one such destructive day that Orland once more rode back to speak to the knight.

'Orland,' said Fermbaud, 'you have been gone two days. I was beginning to suspect you had left us.'

'On the contrary,' said Orland, 'I have always been within half a day's ride. I find this place fascinating and though the terrain can be difficult, there are many easy pickings to be had.'

'Remember, this is a mission of subjugation, not devastation.'

'Is it not much easier to achieve the first aim by applying the second?'

'I suppose so but our time here is limited and I feel the King's message has been made clear. We will head south and pay our respects to the castellan of Brecon castle before re-joining the King at Bristol. To be honest, I for one will welcome the comfort of my own bed rather than the hardness of a cart floor.'

'I trust you have not seen many campaigns?'

'My expertise lies elsewhere,' said Fermbaud, 'however, even I can see this has been a success and look forward to relaying my account to the King.'

'I accept your decision, my lord, but there is one more thing before we head back. Ten miles to the east there is a village of a few hundred souls. The village has a church at its centre and yesterday I took the opportunity to look inside. It is well furnished with treasures, in fact, embarrassingly so.'

'What do you mean?'

'For such a small village to have such wealth may suggest it has been obtained by foul means.'

'Not necessarily, many such villages oft gift their wealth to their church.'

'Perhaps so and ordinarily my suspicion would not have raised but the men of this village have an arrogance about them.'

'In what way?'

'They roam freely with weapons at their side.'

'This is not a crime.'

'It is not but why would ordinary men of a quiet village need such arms at short notice unless they were men used to trouble. Also, I heard many talk freely of their hatred of Longshanks and voicing impatience that a planned revolt is long overdue.'

'Treason?' gasped Fermbaud.

'Exactly,' said Orland, 'and that is why I rode hard back here to relay this information. I submit that our path is clear and we should attack this village immediately.'

'But surely the King should hear news of this rebellion as soon as possible and we should make haste to inform him?'

'Accepted but one more day will matter not. Even if we leave for Bristol immediately our path lies less than ten miles from this village. We can make a detour, inflict the King's justice on this traitorous people and gain many treasures to help fund the Longshanks' French campaign at the same time.'

'Did you not say they were well armed?'

'Carrying weapons is one thing,' said Orland, 'being able to use them against a tested army is another. Our men are now well blooded and will not have any trouble against these peasants.'

'What do you suggest?'

'There is no need for subtleties for their allegiance is obvious and they talk openly against the King. I suggest we attack at first light without thought of negotiation. Give the men their freedom to enjoy the spoils of war so when they eventually land on French soil, their desire to fight hard will be underpinned by their previous experiences. They have campaigned hard, my lord, and deserve a chance of spoils. Cut them loose and see what they have become.'

'And the church?'

'Destroy it for it is no longer a holy place but a nest of vipers. The treasures are spoils of war and will be warmly welcomed by Longshanks. Our parting gift to the Welsh will be the bodies of their kinsmen and the ashes of their poisonous church. The message sent will be overwhelming; bend the knee to your rightful King or suffer similar consequences.'

Fermbaud's thoughts rested only briefly on the cost in human life, lingering much longer on the imagined treasures of the church. If they were as plentiful as Orland said, then Longshanks surely wouldn't miss a few golden goblets or jewel encrusted crosses.

'Agreed,' he said and turned to his second in command. 'Godfrey, rest the men at the next river. Get them fed and watered but ensure they are prepared for one final assault. We will approach the village before dawn and attack at first light.'

'So be it,' said Godfrey and turned his horse to gallop back to the column.

'I will prepare the scouts,' said Orland. 'We will lead the charge and take the edge off any immediate retaliation. The only position of strength is the church itself and it is important it's secured before anyone has a chance to rally there.'

'No,' said Fermbaud, 'you will sit this one out. If this is to be the last offensive of this campaign then I will lead it myself.'

'But what about the church?'

'I will make it my personal goal to secure it in the King's name.'

'And the treasures?'

'Are not of your concern. Now, get back to your business and mark out a route easily followed in the dark.'

Orland stared at Fermbaud with interest. There was no doubt the Castellan was only interested in any spoils to be gained from the sacking of the church, but it was also fascinating to see the soft man who had lived a life of leisure behind his castle walls developing a much harder edge. There may be hope for him after all.

'So be it,' he said.

The following morning, almost two hundred of Fermbaud's men crept along the edge of a river leading through the village, keeping their heads low so as not to be seen above the bank. At either end of the valley, twenty-five lancers waited for the signal to advance and close off any means of escape. At the head of one of the mounted groups, Fermbaud himself waited nervously on his horse. He wore his full armour and sweated heavily, even though the pre-dawn mist was chilling upon any exposed flesh.

Eventually everyone was in place and all eyes looked eastward at the lightening sky. Finally Godfrey came back up the river and approached the knight.

'My lord, the men are in place and undiscovered, all we need is your command.'

'Then we will wait no more,' said Fermbaud. 'Before this day is done, we will be well on the way home. Return to the men, Godfrey, and upon the signal, let them loose.'

'Aye, my lord,' said Godfrey and returned to the riverbank.

Ten minutes later, Fermbaud turned to a man at his side.

'Soldier, the hour is here, give the signal.'

The foot soldier lifted a horn to his mouth and sent a deep haunting tone echoing around the valley. Fermbaud drew his sword and held it high.

'To arms, men,' he shouted, 'and show the mettle I know we share but let your hearts not be weakened by pleas for mercy, for this day there will be no quarter.'

The twenty-five lancers spurred their mounts forward while a mile downstream, the rest of the mounted men approached from the opposite direction. At the sound of the horn, Godfrey stood up from his crouched position below the riverbank, as did the rest of the foot soldiers.

'Men at arms,' he called, 'take this day as a reward for your service. Leave no man breathing and no building standing. Make no mistake, you are about to face men willing to fight to the death so we will do our utmost to provide them that outcome. Look to your weapons, men, and show these peasants who really rules this country. For King and country, *advaaance!*'

The line of infantry clambered up the riverbank and ran toward the houses. The need for secrecy was long gone and the sounds of their shouting ripped through the morning mist as they charged into the village.

High on a hill above, Orland looked down with concern evident on his face.

'I don't understand,' he said, 'something is wrong.'

'My lord?' asked the man at his side.

'There is no barking,' said Orland as he watched the figures racing through the morning mist, 'where are the village dogs?'

Four men at arms ran toward the nearest building, a cottage with stone walls and a thatched roof sweeping down to meet the floor. The first man ran up and kicked hard at the door. To his surprise it swung in easily and they ran into the firelit gloom.

Immediately they headed for the sleeping figures in the beds expecting resistance at any second but nobody moved. The first man pulled back one of the sheepskin covers and stared confusedly at the rolled-up sack of hay beneath.

'There's no one here,' he said turning to his comrades.

'Same here,' said his fellow turning over an empty cot. 'What's going on?'

The men returned outside and were joined by their comrades as similar scenes were revealed across the village.

'Where are the treasures?' roared Fermbaud, storming around the church, 'that cursed Orland said there would be treasures.'

'I don't understand,' said the man at his side, 'the church is bare. How can this be?'

'I don't know,' growled Fermbaud, 'but I will hold Orland to account for this.'

Behind him the church door crashed open and Godfrey ran in.

'My lord, we are compromised, the village is empty of all souls.'

'What?' gasped Fermbaud. 'Is there nobody here?'

'None, my lord. It looks like they knew we were coming and fled the village.'

'I am being made a fool of,' snarled Fermbaud, 'and someone will pay the price.'

'We should get out of here, my lord,' said Godfrey, 'it could be a trap.'

'Agreed,' said Fermbaud, 'assemble the column but fire the village first. At the very least they will know I have been here.'

Godfrey ran back out of the church to organise the destruction.

–

Within half an hour the village was ablaze and thick black smoke poured into the morning air. The column was reassembled ready to march out, two hundred infantry flanked by twenty-five lancers on either side. Fermbaud mounted his horse and faced the ranks.

'Men, it would seem we have been outwitted on this occasion but fret not for I swear you will have the opportunities I promised. The first village we come across on our journey home will suffer our wrath.' He turned to his second in command. 'Godfrey, bring up the rear, I will lead the column.' He turned his horse and headed to the bridge, followed by his entire command.

Fermbaud had gone no more than a thousand paces before he raised his hand to stop the patrol. Silently he stared at the scene before him and waited as Godfrey galloped forward, reining in his horse beside him.

'Who is it?' asked Godfrey, staring at the two knights blocking their path.

'I don't know,' said Fermbaud, 'but there's only one way to find out.' He spurred his horse gently and rode forward to meet the two men blocking the road astride their own chargers. Within moments Fermbaud and Godfrey faced the two unknown knights face to face.

One of the strangers was clad in a black hauberk, a lightweight shirt of chainmail hanging down to his thighs. Over it he wore a tabard emblazoned with a single red lion, rampant upon a yellow shield background. The lightweight fighting armour was complemented with plated greaves upon his legs and a chainmail aventail hanging from his open-faced bascinet. A shield hung from his saddle bearing a matching emblem and a sheathed sword hung at his side.

'Sir, you block our path,' said Fermbaud.

'On the contrary, sir,' said the opposing knight, 'it is you who block our path for we would return to our village.'

'And who is it I address?' asked Fermbaud.

'My name is Cynan ap Maredudd,' said the knight, 'and I am lord of this place.'

'And I am Nicholas Fermbaud, Castellan of Bristol Castle,' came the response.

'I know who you are, my lord, for your deeds this past month have travelled the breadth of this country faster than the swiftest steed. Pray tell what brings you and your army to our lands.'

'I think you will find this land belongs to Edward and I am abroad on his business.'

'To what end?'

'Bringing a warning to those who would challenge his kingship,' snapped Fermbaud, 'and to remind them that these lands fall under the rule of the English crown.'

'The ownership of the soil beneath our feet is the subject of much discussion and has been for many generations,' said Cynan, 'but perhaps that is a conversation for another time.'

'Your words border dangerously close to treason, sir knight,' said Fermbaud, 'and I suggest you choose them carefully.'

'In my own lands my words will be delivered in whichever way I wish.'

'This is not your land,' said Fermbaud, 'it belongs to the King.'

'These Cantrefs belong to the families of Gwynedd,' answered Cynan, 'and no matter what brutality you may inflict on those unable to defend themselves, I know of no man hereabouts who has bent his knee to Longshanks.'

'I warn you for the last time,' snarled Fermbaud, 'guard your words or you will force me to defend my monarch's honour.'

Cynan paused and looked at the black smoke bellowing from the burning village behind the column.

'The King's honour,' he sneered, 'is this the deed of an honourable king?'

'And what is it to you? Do you own this village?'

'I am lord of many such villages in these parts so take an interest in such things.'

'We had cause to exact the King's retribution on the people here.'

'Retribution for what, exactly?' asked Cynan.

'For treason against the crown.'

'And do you have examples of this treason?'

'They were heard talking openly of rebellion. This village harboured traitors.'

'Is not one man's traitor another man's liberator?'

Fermbaud fell silent and the two men stared at each other for several moments.

'I sense your discourse is intended to raise my ire, sir, and will joust no further. Now, get out of the way for our path lies beyond.'

'This path is not yours,' said Cynan, 'it belongs to the Princes of Wales. If you want to use it, there will be a toll to be paid.'

'I will pay no toll,' growled Fermbaud, 'and demand for the last time, remove yourself from my path or suffer the consequences.'

'On the contrary, sir,' said Cynan. 'There will indeed be a toll but whether that is paid in gold or blood, only you can decide.'

'Your impertinence astounds me, sir,' shouted Fermbaud, 'and I will suffer it no more.' He drew his word and ten lancers galloped forward but Cynan did not move.

'You had your chance, Fermbaud,' said Cynan, 'and could have been back between the walls of your fancy castle within days.' He lifted his arm and hundreds of armed men rose from the long grass on either side of the road.

Fermbaud looked around in astonishment, but his anger outweighed his sense.

'You dare to challenge the King's messenger?' he roared. 'How dare you?'

'My lord, we are heavily outnumbered,' said Godfrey. 'I suggest we seek terms.'

'I will do what I will,' shouted Fermbaud and stared at Cynan once more. 'I offer you one last chance, Welshman, get out of my way.'

'I can't do that,' said Cynan, 'so I will make a counteroffer. Meet me on the field of combat, man to man as champions of our respective claims. Do this and only one man needs die this day.'

'I do not recognise your claim,' spat Fermbaud, 'and will not lower myself to the challenge of a lesser man.'

'Then prepare your men, Sir Fermbaud, for if you are to take this road, then it will have to be over the corpses of myself and my men.'

'So be it,' said Fermbaud and turned to Godfrey. 'To arms, Godfrey, the men will yet have their day.'

Cynan turned to ride back toward his own men and gave a signal. Each flank ran inward to form a line three deep across the valley, presenting a wall of lances and pikes. Fermbaud rode back to his own forces, the lines now also deploying to face the enemy to their front.

'They outnumber us two to one,' said Godfrey. 'It will be a hard fight.'

'They have no horsemen, Godfrey,' said Fermbaud leaning down to receive his shield from his squire, 'and each of our lancers is worth ten infantry men. Our lancers will lead the charge and shatter their lines. As soon as they do, attack their left flank only. The rest of his men will be too busy engaging the lancers leaving an equal fight on the left. Don't forget, our men are well blooded and are more than a match for these peasants.'

'I hope you are right, my lord,' said Godfrey and galloped away to join his command.

Cynan reined in his horse in front of his own lines and dismounted. A squire climbed into the saddle and galloped the knight's horse away to safety.

'William, you know what to do,' shouted Cynan as he secured his helm strap.

'We are ready, my lord,' answered a sergeant at arms, 'let them come.'

Cynan stared across the field to the deploying enemy.

'They see us as underlings,' he called, 'nothing more than servants in our own lands. Well today it stops and we will send Edward a message he cannot ignore.' He raised his voice so Fermbaud could hear him across the open ground. 'Do you hear me Englishman, I challenge your false king's right to this country and swear by all that is holy we will wrest his crown from him, alive or dead.'

'Defend yourself, Welshman,' roared Fermbaud, 'for this day will be the last you see of these cursed lands.' He turned to his own command. 'Men of England, today we earn our bread, wipe this filth from our path and return to our king in triumph.' He raised his sword high in the air. 'For Edward and England, advaaance.'

The fifty horses, already skittish in the excited atmosphere needed no more urging than the shouts of the lancers and lurched into a gallop across the open field. At fifty yards the riders lowered their lances parallel to the ground and leaned forward to anticipate the impact.

'Ready yourselves,' called Cynan as they neared the Welsh lines, 'steady... steady... Now!'

In one smooth motion the solid line of Welshmen split in the centre and ran toward either flank leaving a gaping hole in their ranks. The unexpected manoeuvre caused confusion in the charging lancers and many swerved to either side, effectively splitting their strength.

'Deploy the archers,' roared Cynan and as if from nowhere, two hundred crossbow men emerged from a fold in the ground behind Cynan's lines.

'*Target the horses,*' roared William, the sergeant at arms commanding the archers, '*release.*'

Two hundred metal tipped bolts flew through toward the lancers and within seconds, thirty of the horses fell to the ground, many screaming in agony as the bolts drove deep into their innards. Men were thrown to the ground at full gallop with many incurring serious injuries. Those who were still able, staggered to their feet, confused at what had just happened, but before they could gather their thoughts or retreat to the perceived safety of their own lines, the second volley cut them down along with the rest of the horses who had escaped the first barrage. The whole thing was over in less than a minute, and Fermbaud's infantry watched in horror as their most potent strike force was wiped out with not a single casualty sustained by the enemy.

'Reform,' shouted Cynan and his lines closed once again. Apart from the snorts of dying horses and the groans of wounded men, the battlefield fell silent.

'I am insulted you saw us as mere striplings, Fermbaud,' he shouted. 'I am a Knight of Llewellyn and these men defend what is rightfully theirs.' He drew his sword and held it high. 'Men of Wales, the time has come to rid the lands of our fathers of the English invader. There will be many days like this but it begins with this one. Account yourselves worthy of freemen for that is the prize before us.' He lowered his sword toward the enemy. 'For Wales and Freedom, *advaaance*.'

The Welsh lines marched line abreast across the field, picking up pace as they went.

'My lord, we are undone,' shouted Godfrey, 'we must take to the hills.'

'I will not flee this man,' roared Fermbaud, 'and if I die this day it will be serving my king.' He turned to his own lines. 'Men of England,' he called, '*advance*.'

The English lines walked forward to meet the oncoming enemy, their own pace increasing as they went. Weapons were banged on shields by both sides raising the blood in their veins and within seconds, the insults and shouts of self-encouragement soared to screams of aggression as the armies broke into a run, racing toward the conflict.

Up above in the treeline, Orland stared down in horror.

'My lord, should we not go to his aid?' asked one of his men.

'I do not fear death, Gresham, but will not throw my life down for a useless cause. That man has written his own death warrant and should have sought terms as soon as he saw the size of the enemy. There are always other days for retribution and all he has done is give these Welshmen a petty battle to celebrate.'

'Perhaps he will surprise us and give a good account of himself,' said Gresham.

'It matters not,' said Orland, 'for this Welsh knight is playing games with the Castellan.' He nodded toward a hill on the opposite side of the valley and his comrade could see a huge column of riders passing over the brow.

'There are more infantry massed at the end of the valley,' said another voice quietly and both men looked downstream to see over five hundred men at arms, standing silently in ranks in case they were needed.

'This is not a petty lord with ideas of grandeur, Gresham, but a well-equipped army preparing for campaign.'

'Then the day is already lost,' said Gresham.

'It is,' said Orland, 'and we need to leave this place.'

'Shouldn't we lay low in case there are survivors who need our help?'

'Fermbaud chose his own fate and nothing we do will change it; besides, Edward needs to know of this as soon as possible or his very kingship may be at risk.'

'So be it,' said Gresham and the scouts turned their horses back into the treeline to join their comrades. Within moments they were through the forest and galloping as fast as they could away from Mynydd Fach, leaving the ill-fated castellan and his doomed command behind them.

Back in the valley the two walls of armed men closed in on each other beneath a wave of spears thrown by both sides. Dozens fell as a result but the charge maintained its impetus. Seconds later the lines crashed together in a melee of steel and hewn flesh. Men screamed as wielded pikes reached over the shield wall to pierce the exposed flesh of their enemy and heavy maces smashed against the helms of any man within reach. Those lucky enough to have shields crouched behind them, pushing against the enemy with all their might, the adrenaline of combat matched by the fear of death. Swords were thrust between the shields whenever gaps appeared though were often deflected by chainmail armour.

Cynan stood alongside his own men, fighting with a fanaticism born of nationalistic fervour and hardened battlefield experience. Fermbaud on the other hand stood behind his men urging them on and often hitting the backs of their heads with the hilt of his sword whenever he perceived a weakening of the line.

'*Heave*,' roared Fermbaud, 'break their lines or we will be overrun.'

The English fought like demons and acquitted themselves well but eventually the overwhelming numbers of the enemy told and the line broke. Almost immediately, individuals turned to flee and within moments the call to retreat could be heard along the line.

'Revoke that command,' screamed Fermbaud, 'hold the line,' but it was too late, the damage was done and his men broke to flee back the way they had come. They had not gone a hundred paces when they saw another equally strong force coming from the direction of the burning village.

'It is a trap,' shouted Godfrey, 'we are surrounded!'

Fermbaud finally realised the risk and looked frantically around for safety.

'Across the river,' he shouted, 'head for the trees.'

By now the battlefield was covered in individual battles to the death. Chainmail shirts were no protection against heavy pikes and many men were speared through or had their bodies cleaved open by the heavy blades. Men screamed for mercy as they were overrun but in the heat of battle, most were ignored and many died on their knees, their cries for clemency still ringing in their killer's ears as they dealt the killing blow.

Dozens reached the river but had underestimated the steepness of the far bank, and Cynan's men stopped at the water's edge as they realised they had their enemy cornered. Fermbaud was frantic, demanding his men lift him up to the perceived safety of the tangled undergrowth upon the other side of the river and as he stumbled away from the battlefield, Godfrey turned to face the enemy massing along the bank behind him.

Cynan walked through the ranks of his victorious men and stared at the scene before him. Fermbaud was getting away but what was left of his command was either dead on the battlefield or standing in the river.

'My lord, do you want one of the archers to bring him down?' asked William, indicating the running man.

'No,' said Cynan, 'send some of the cavalry to bring him to me alive.' He returned his attention to the men in the river. 'You men,' he said, 'are no less victims than we. You have been led by a false king into lands that don't belong to you, but such is the life of a soldier. Ordinarily I would have you ransomed but I can't ignore what I saw this morning through the dawn mist. There was a hunger in your eyes and if we hadn't warned the people, I suspect there would not be one living soul left in the village, aged or child. Poor people who face a battle every day just to stay alive would have met the steel of trained soldiers without thought of mercy. As a boy, I once attended a church where the priest preached an eye for an eye. I have never forgotten that and feel that in this case, the justice preached by that man fits the crime.' He turned and said something to William. Within moments, a hundred archers pushed forward and loaded their crossbows.

'Wait,' shouted Godfrey, 'this is murder, you can't do this.'

Cynan turned to face him.

'Ah, I remember you. You are second in command of this campaign, are you not?'

'I am,' said Godfrey, 'and demand compassion. Kill me but let these men go, they were only carrying out orders.'

'Carrying out orders does not an innocent man make,' said Cynan, 'and there was a hunger amongst them when they thought their prey defenceless.'

'Call yourself a knight?' shouted Godfrey. 'You were quick enough to challenge Fermbaud in one to one combat not an hour since, well I now challenge you, Welshman, give me a sword and fight me as an equal. Let the prize be our deaths or our freedom.'

Silence fell and all eyes turned to Cynan. After a moment's silence he nodded to a nearby soldier who threw Godfrey a sword. Godfrey started to wade out of the water but was stopped by Cynan.

'Hold there, sir knight, for I will not suffer one more English footprint upon Welsh soil.' Saying that he threw away his shield and waded into the river to face his enemy. 'Be guarded, sir,' he said, 'for today there will be no quarter.'

'I expect none, nor offer any,' said Godfrey and without warning swung his sword at Cynan's head. Cynan lifted his sword to deflect the blow and as the weapon glanced away, punched Godfrey to the side of the head with his fisted gauntlet. Godfrey fell back but maintained his stance. Cynan took up the offensive and steel clashed on steel as the advantage swayed back and forth. Cynan tired quickly for he had fought hard during the battle but Godfrey was also exhausted and both men's swords dropped momentarily as they gasped for breath in the knee-deep water.

'Your skills are better than expected, Welshman,' said Godfrey. 'You fight like an Englishman.'

'I was taught by a man who fought alongside Llewellyn himself,' said Cynan, 'and resent the comparison.'

'I care not what you resent,' snarled Godfrey and swung a low blow against Cynan's side.

Cynan deflected the worst, but the blade still cut into his chainmail shirt, digging into the flesh beneath. He gasped in pain and stumbled to his knees, dropping his sword in the process. As quick as a flash, Godfrey lunged forward and pulled his dagger to rest it against Cynan's throat. The Welshman was kneeling on the riverbed and waist deep in water. On the bank, many men raised their crossbows but Cynan ordered them lowered.

'Hold your weapons,' he shouted, 'it was a fair fight.'

'This is where you belong, Welshman,' snarled Godfrey, 'beneath an Englishman's blade. Now, do we ride from here free men?'

'No Godfrey, you don't,' said Cynan.

'So you go back on your word?'

'On the contrary, my word is my bond and is as strong as iron. Your men will die here, as agreed.'

'But I have won the fight,' said Godfrey, 'the deal is sound.'

'The fight is not over,' said Cynan, 'we said no quarter, remember?' As he spoke, Cynan's hand thrust upward from the water and drove a dagger into Godfrey's groin, the only part of him unprotected by chainmail.

Godfrey gasped in pain but before he could retaliate with his own blade, Cynan grabbed his wrist with his other hand and forced it away from his own throat. Godfrey staggered backward toward the riverbank before turning and falling to his knees.

Cynan got to his feet and followed the wounded knight. As he reached him, Godfrey's head hung low and his hands grasped his groin in agony.

Cynan looked up at William and nodded silently. Without warning, crossbow bolts thudded into the chests of all the remaining English soldiers standing in the river and within a minute, their bodies started to float gracefully downstream, turning the water red with blood. Godfrey looked up, surprised he was still alive.

'What are you waiting for?' he shouted. 'Which of you will send a bolt through my heart?'

Without warning Cynan kicked Godfrey in the back sending the man sprawling in the mud. The wounded knight tried to push himself up but Cynan stepped forward and placed his foot on the back of his head.

'Like I said, Godfrey, today is a day of equality, an eye for an eye. For too many years we have lived under the heel of an Englishman, how ironic it is that you now die beneath the heel of a Welshman.'

As his men looked on in silence, Cynan exerted all his pressure to force Godfrey's face further into the riverbank, choking him on mud soaked with the blood of his dead comrades. Finally the man moved no more and Cynan staggered from the river.

'My lord, the day is done,' said William, 'let me see that wound.'

'It is a mere scratch,' said Cynan, 'and I will seek poultices from the physician later. In the meantime, get our dead buried and the wounded tended. I want to be out of this place by dawn.'

'Are we to disperse?' asked William.

'On the contrary,' said Cynan, 'our men have tasted English blood and you can be sure Edward will not let this lie. Send word to every man across our lands that the time has come to step up and be counted amongst their countrymen. Today we took the first step to freedom but there are many more needed before we can even dream to rule ourselves. So no, William, we will not disperse. Today we unfurl our banners to proclaim our independence, and should Edward refute that claim, let him come and deny it in person.'

'What do you intend to do?'

'I intend to take one of his most important strongholds,' said Cynan. 'Tell the men that before this week is out, we march on Castell du Bere.'

Chapter Twelve

Dysynni Village

Garyn stood alongside Philippe amongst the trees at the base of the cliff beneath Castell du Bere. The night was dark and there was a storm brewing. Ten other members of the Blaidd were with them and many more sat in taverns throughout the village, drinking watered ale and generally keeping a low profile.

'Are you sure you want to do this, Philippe?' asked Garyn.

'Yes, my lord, it is my way to repay you.'

'There is no debt, Philippe, now you are well we can seek a way to get you home.'

'No, I want to do this first. The man in charge of the castle inflicted great pain upon me and I would seek revenge.'

'Revenge is a terrible burden for one so young,' said Derwyn.

'My people are a proud one,' said Philippe, 'and we let no man beat us down without retribution.'

'Your task is to get access to the mason, nothing more,' said Garyn. 'If you try to get anywhere near the Castellan you will be caught and hung. Just get access to the mason, understand?'

'Yes, my lord,' said Philippe.

'And you are sure the window above belongs to the room that holds him?'

'Yes, my lord. I shared the room for three days and spent an age gazing out at the mountains behind us.'

'There are many such windows holding the same view.'

'There are but I recognise this approach for I considered escaping down the walls.'

'Why didn't you?'

'My lord, the bars were too solid within the opening and I could not squeeze through.'

Derwyn looked up at the sky.

'There is rain in the air,' he said, 'we should get this done.'

'Do you need extra clothing?' asked Garyn, looking at the boy's attire. He wore knee-length leggings and a thin shirt. His hands and feet were bare.

'No, they would weigh me down,' answered Philippe.

'Then if you are sure, let's get started.' Garyn and Derwyn walked with the boy to the edge of the treeline and crouched low as he continued alone to the base of the rocky cliff. Without a backward glance, he quickly clambered over the easier lower reaches before reaching the steeper cliff face. After a final adjustment of the small pack upon his back, he reached up to find his first hold and within moments, was climbing the cliff as sure-footedly as a mountain goat.

'The boy has impressive skills,' said Derwyn.

'This is the easy part,' said Garyn, 'the skill comes with the castle walls. I have never seen such a thing.'

'I will have to take your word,' said Derwyn, 'for the walls are deep in darkness and will be beyond my sight.'

'As they will mine,' said Garyn, 'all we can do now is wait.'

—

Up above, Philippe climbed steadily, his keen eyes in partnership with his searching fingers, seeking out handholds on the slippery rock. Finally he reached the base of the castle wall and after pausing to catch his breath, slid his hand upward to find the smallest of cracks between the masonry. Slowly but surely his strong wiry arms pulled his scrawny frame upward, aided by feet that sought out the tiniest of footholds. Upward he climbed, pausing only to catch his breath when a solid grip was assured. In the distance a flash of lightning was closely followed by a crash of thunder and the first drops of rain pattered down on the castle.

Philippe renewed his efforts and within ten minutes, reached the window of the cell. He extended a length of rope from around his waist and tied it to one of the bars, securing his position on the narrow sill.

'Mason,' he called quite loudly to be heard above the rain, 'Mason, can you hear me?'

Inside an old man turned in his sleep.

'Mason,' called the boy louder, 'wake up, it is Philippe, your fellow prisoner of a few weeks ago.'

Inside the mason sat up and squinted toward the window.

'Boy, is that you?' he asked.

'It is, come closer or the guards will hear my calls.'

The old man shuffled toward the window and stared out at the wet boy in amazement.

'What witchcraft is this?' gasped the mason. 'Are you dead and fly back as a spirit?'

'I am not dead but have climbed the wall,' said the boy. 'I have questions for you from a man who seeks knowledge.'

'What man?'

'He says his name is Garyn, beyond that, I cannot say.'

'And what knowledge is so important that he sends a boy to risk his life in order to obtain it?'

'He seeks the Sword of Macsen,' said the boy, 'and I chose to come of my own free will.'

'The Sword of Macsen,' repeated the mason. 'Why does he want that?'

'I know not,' said Philippe, 'except to say it is needed for a great quest.'

The mason fell silent for a few moments.

'Boy,' he said eventually, 'are you sure this man does not just seek to fill his purse with the coins such a find would bring.'

'He seems an honourable man,' said Philippe, 'and saved my life. I believe his intentions are true. He also said that in return he would do everything in his power to release you from this cell as soon as the circumstances are right.'

'Tell him not to bother,' said the mason. 'I am comfortable with my lot.'

'No man should accept imprisonment,' said Philippe.

'This is not so bad,' said the old man. 'I grow older by the day and would struggle to find such easy work in the towns. I am locked up only at night and am fed well. During the day I carry out the finer repairs on the Castellan's keep. If I hadn't called him a fat pig after too much ale one night, I suspect my quarters would be substantially finer.'

'Are you saying you will not help him find this sword?' The mason fell silent again.

'I will help him,' he said eventually, 'for if he seeks it for the right reasons, then somebody somewhere must be planning to resurrect a cause long overdue.' He looked up at Philippe. 'Listen carefully boy, I will keep it simple but I have a story to tell. Many years ago I was employed to build the walls of a castle. Stone for the walls was taken from many quarries but there was a finer stone already available in a nearby church that had been long abandoned. The walls had long since fallen and we sent many carts to retrieve the dressed stone for the chapel in the new castle.

'While we were retrieving the stone, I saw a slab within the floor. The slab was etched with an eagle grasping a lightning bolt. I had never seen such a thing and believing it may be a pit containing hidden jewels, I am ashamed to say I quickly covered up the slab with earth so no other person would cast eyes upon it. A few days later, along with my son, I returned to lift the slab and found steps leading into a tomb. The tomb contained a stone sarcophagus and the eagle emblem was also engraved upon the lid as well as words in a language I did not recognise. My son said they were Latin and I am ashamed to say that we robbed that tomb of its riches and did not work on the castle again.'

'Did you become rich?'

'For a while but alas, the money earned from the booty must have been cursed for my son drowned a few weeks later after getting drunk and falling in the river. I too suffered only heartache from the coins and spent them on ale and whores. Soon it was gone and I had to resurrect my skills as a mason. This is what led me here and I accept my fate for to steal from the dead is an unforgiveable sin.'

'So did you sell the sword?'

'I did not, for the sword is the one thing we left within the tomb and fearing we would be discovered, we fled without trying to undo the ties that bound it.'

'So where is this place?' asked Philippe.

'It is exactly where you would expect to find the tomb of an emperor,' said the mason, 'within the walls of a Roman fortress.'

'In Rome itself?'

'No. The castle walls I helped build were those of Caernarfon, one of Edward's greatest fortresses. High on a nearby hill there lies the remains of a fortress far older than you or I can imagine and I have since learned that it was built by the Romans, though its origins lie far further back in the depths of time. In its day, the Roman fortress would have been something to behold, but alas it is now no more than a ruin. When the Romans left, a church was also built upon the site but this also has gone and provided much of the material for the castle walls. Tell your friend to seek the slab I spoke of in the northernmost corner of the ruins. I expect it is now overgrown but the tomb should still be there. Beneath the eagle, I believe he will find the Freedom Sword hanging above the body of Macsen.'

'Is there any more?' asked Philippe.

'That is all I know,' said the mason. 'Now, you should be gone for I hear the guard approaching with my evening meal. Tell your master that I wish him well on his crusade and should the sword deliver what is believed, then I will go to my grave a happy man.'

Philippe paused before removing a long length of thin rope from his pack. He secured one end to one of the bars before releasing the rope already around his waist.

'Is there anything we can do for you?' asked Philippe.

'Yes there is,' said the mason, 'when you get a chance, light a candle in a church somewhere and pray for the soul of an old man.'

'I will do that,' said Philippe, 'fare ye well, mason.' Without another word he lowered himself back over the edge and walked backwards down the castle wall, using the rope to support his weight. The mason peered out and when the rope went slack, he undid the knot and let it fall.

'Fare well yourself, boy,' he said quietly, 'and whoever this Garyn may be, let God strengthen his arm.'

—

'There he is,' said Garyn, getting to his feet as the boy ran through the rain toward him.

'What did he say?' asked Derwyn as the boy reached them. 'Do you have the location?'

Philippe nodded but Garyn could see he was shivering violently.

'Where is it?' demanded Derwyn.

'Enough,' said Garyn, throwing his oiled cloak around the boy's shoulders. 'All will be revealed but first we will get to a place of warmth and safety. Come, we will go back to the sanctuary.'

—

An hour later, the two men and Philippe sat near a roaring fire. The monks had retired for the night but Elias let them in and now stood guard against any interruption. Philippe was wrapped in a warm sheepskin and supped on a tankard of hot ale.

Finally he had warmed up enough to talk and the men sat silently as they listened to the mason's tale. When he had finished, Garyn looked at his friend in silence.

'What do you think?' he asked eventually.

'A Roman fortress that no longer exists,' said Derwyn, 'right next to an English castle. This quest gets harder and harder. What's more we don't even know if his tale is true.'

'He seemed an honest man,' said Philippe, 'and I for one believe him.'

'He is a grave robber,' said Derwyn. 'That doesn't seem like an honest man to me.'

'He seeks forgiveness and asks that we pray for him.'

'Did he say the name of this fortress?' asked Garyn.

'The name escaped him but he was adamant it exists.'

'Then we should make ready to go,' said Garyn.

'Where to?' asked Derwyn.

'Caernarfon,' said Garyn.

'Caernarfon is a walled town built and populated by the English,' said Derwyn. 'On top of that it is protected by a castle second only to Conwy in its strategic location and strength of its fortifications. It is said it holds a garrison of hundreds.'

'I have no interest in the castle nor the town,' said Garyn, 'only the location of this Roman tomb.'

'If it even exists,' said Derwyn.

'Well, there is only one way to find out,' said Garyn, 'and that is to go there. Tell our men to return to the hide and await instructions. Tomorrow we travel alone.'

—

Fermbaud curled up in a foetal position, hidden in the depths of the bracken. For days he had managed to avoid the riders sent after him by Cynan and though he knew he was near the border between Wales and England, he was exhausted, weakened by fatigue, hunger and fear. His clothes were saturated from the constant rain and he shivered uncontrollably, not only from the cold but the fear of the fate awaiting him at the hands of Cynan's soldiers.

Despite his state, his eyelids dropped and he subconsciously welcomed the brief respite sleep would bring, even if only for a few seconds but he was jolted wide awake at the sound of horses passing nearby. He pushed himself further beneath the bracken and listened as the latest patrol passed his position. Fermbaud was desperate to remain undiscovered for though his situation was miserable, he knew the following day would see him across the border and in the safety of an English village. A voice carried through the gloom.

'My lord, the trail leads there.'

'Are you sure?' came the reply.

'The trail is as clear as a wayside sign, our quarry lies less than an arrow's shot from your horse.'

'Then flush him out,' said the first voice. 'I tire of this game.'

In the bracken, Fermbaud was distraught. His position was compromised and he faced discovery within moments. His heart demanded he stand and fight but his exhausted body could not deliver so Nicholas Fermbaud, Knight of Edward and Castellan of Bristol Castle, curled up in a tighter ball, hoping against hope they passed him by.

Minutes passed and though the sounds of booted footsteps came near, none seemed to get close to the terrified man. Eventually they died away but just as Fermbaud began to hope he had escaped discovery yet again, he felt the gentle press of cold steel upon his neck.

'Well, well,' said a muffled voice, 'what do we have here?'

Fermbaud froze, his face pressed into the ground as he waited the thrust that would end his life.

'Mercy,' he whispered, 'grant me life and I will make you and your men rich beyond your dreams.'

'We have no use for money,' said the voice, 'what else can you offer?'

'Anything,' gasped Fermbaud, sensing interest in the man's tone, 'land, women, you name it and it can be yours within days, all I ask is that you spare my life and return me to England.'

'Do you give your word as a knight?' asked the voice.

'I swear on my honour.'

For a few seconds there was silence before the blade was withdrawn and Fermbaud heard the weapon being sheathed.

'Then stand up, Fermbaud,' said the voice, 'and get yourself mounted. We are on the way to Bristol as we speak and look forward to claiming this bounty you speak of.'

Fermbaud scrambled to his feet and turned to face his captor. For a few seconds his mind struggled to comprehend the situation but suddenly his woes fell away and he gasped in relief as he recognised the man before him.

'Orland,' he cried, 'I thought you were one of Cynan's men.'

'A mere jest at your expense,' said Orland, 'though I will not let you forget your pledge.'

'Women and ale, I will gladly give,' said Fermbaud, 'whether gleaned by fair means or foul. I thought you were surely dead?'

'We came close to conflict several times,' said Orland, 'but in such circumstances, discretion won the day and we laid low until the Welsh army moved on. We followed your trail for days but always it was too dangerous to move in because of the enemy searchers. Still, we are here now and you are alive, that is what matters.'

'You have my gratitude,' said Fermbaud.

'Right, let's get you a dry cloak and some food. The area is clear of Welshmen but we can't be sure so daren't risk the road tonight. We will rest nearby and at dawn we will ride as fast as we are able to the border. With a bit of luck we can be in Bristol within two days.'

'I hope so,' said Fermbaud. 'I can't wait to get away from this cursed place. The luxury of the castle will be a welcome sight after these past few weeks.'

'I seek no luxury, Fermbaud,' said Orland, 'only to brief Longshanks about the rekindled threat from the Welsh.'

'Of course,' said Fermbaud, 'that as well.'

'Then come,' said Orland, 'our camp is nearby.'

Chapter Thirteen

The island of Ynys Mon

Madog was staring through an upper window of his manor when Geraint and Tarian arrived. Together they were shown in by a servant and stood at the door awaiting the prince's attention.

'My lord, we were summoned,' said Geraint eventually.

'You were,' said Madog, turning around. 'I have heard news that Cynan ap Maredudd has embarked upon a campaign in the south.'

Geraint glanced at Tarian.

'It is true, my lord, Cynan took it upon himself to exact retribution on the column that rode from Bristol.'

'On whose orders?' asked Madog. 'Did we not agree that the offensive would start once we rode under a common banner?'

'It was discussed, my lord, though Cynan is a law unto himself and oft acts on the spur of the moment.'

'He threatens this whole thing with his impatience,' said Madog, 'and will fragment the alliance of the Welsh Lords.'

'Perhaps, not,' said Tarian, 'perhaps there is another goal within his aim.'

'What do you mean?' asked Madog.

'My lord, we well know he has aspirations to the crown himself and whilst he has not declared against you, his continual preying upon the forces of Edward could rally the southern lords behind him and strengthen his claim.'

'So he garners support while I sit here and wait for an artefact that may not even exist.'

'It is the best way to unite Wales, my lord, and if the sword is found it will instantly unite everyone behind you.'

'Perhaps so, but if it turns out to be a fool's errand then this man will have a far stronger support base than I.'

'You have the lineage, my lord,' said Geraint.

'What is lineage without the support of the common people?' answered Madog. 'Geraint, I was ignorant of all this until you saw fit to enlighten me. In hindsight, it may have been better if I had remained so but that time has long passed. We are where we are and every day the fire within me grows, as does the injustice inflicted on our people. I will not just sit back and wait while history books are written in my absence. Are the men ready?'

'For what, my lord?'

'For war,' said Madog. 'I am no longer willing to wait and will take the offensive to Edward.'

'My lord, in a few more weeks, the King will have sailed for France and victory will be assured. Even without the sword, at the very least you will be in a far stronger position to bargain with him when he returns.'

'There will be no waiting,' said Madog, 'and there will be no bargaining. There will be retribution, there will be conflict and ultimately there will be freedom. This Cynan ap Maredudd may have set himself up as champion of the people but Wales will not be denied unity and I will not be denied my birthright. In two days we will send a message across the country that will proclaim the real leader of this campaign and at the same time, send shivers of fear down the backbone of Longshanks himself.'

'What do you intend to do?' asked Tarian.

'What I intend to do, Tarian, is that which has long been thought impossible. I intend to break the ring of steel.'

Tarian and Geraint fell silent as the implications sunk in. Geraint was the first to speak.

'My lord, that can't be done,' he said quietly. 'Edward's castles are impregnable and we do not have the strength to besiege them.'

'We may not have many siege engines,' said Madog, 'or the greatest armies to immediate hand but what we do have is heart and a belief born of frustration garnered by generations of servitude to a false king. Fret not, Geraint, I have not sat back and spent my days in idle chatter these past few months but have explored all options for when this day comes. I have made my plans and I swear by Almighty God that this ring of steel will be broken.'

'But, my lord, even the greatest of hearts will be shattered upon the masonry of Edward's walls. How can we possibly hope to succeed, even against the smaller fortresses?'

'We will succeed with guile and cunning,' said Madog, 'combined with a conviction of right and God's will but dismiss this talk of smaller fortresses – the message sent needs to be clear. We own these lands, they are ours by right of birth, ours by right of justice and ours by God's will. This king may build his false walls,' he continued, 'but to a man who seeks freedom they are little more than a hindrance. Two days from now my banner will fly above a castle of Edward and by doing so, we will shatter this so-called ring of steel wide apart.'

'Which castle, my lord?' asked Tarian.

'The greatest of them all, Tarian,' said Madog. 'Tomorrow we take Caernarfon.'

—

'He has gone mad,' said Geraint after Madog had left the room to collect his briefing documents. 'There is no way these men can take a fortified manor house, let alone a castle. The man has lost his mind.'

'On the contrary,' said Tarian, 'I think he may just have found it.'

Geraint stared at his friend.

'How can you say this?'

Tarian stared back.

'Geraint, you have become too close to the Prince over the years and still see the boy within him. I have not shared this closeness and see a young, intelligent man hungry for adventure and justice. Combine these with a keen mind and experience and you have the makings of a great leader.'

'Therein lies the problem, experience he has none.'

'Then this is something we shall bring to the table. Give the boy his head and stay close to the decision making. If he gives sound advice, as I suspect he will then we will just flank him as a deerhound does a stag, influencing his direction.'

'And if his choices are foolhardy?'

'Then alas we will do what the deerhound is also good at, we will bring him down.'

Geraint stared but eventually nodded in agreement.

'And what about the men?'

'The detail will take care of itself. There are enough sergeants at arms to ensure the men are well drilled. The boy's inexperience may indeed be a boon for he is not weighed down by tradition learned from old soldiers.'

Geraint sighed.

'I hope you are right, Tarian, for this has the makings of a huge disaster.'

'It also has the makings of a huge victory,' said Tarian. 'Anyway, the Prince returns, let us see what these plans hold.'

Madog unfolded a map on the table and placed a glazed figurine on each corner to hold it down.

'These are floor plans,' said Tarian. 'Never have I seen such detail.'

'They are,' said Madog, 'and show the layout of Caern-arfon castle itself. They have been drawn up over many months.'

'By whom?'

'The man's name matters not and he would have me keep it in confidence. It is enough that you know that many Welshmen work at the castle in positions of servitude. Cooks, grooms, maids and servants earn their bread within its walls and between them know it better than any man.'

'But surely such information would be kept in the strictest confidence?'

'It is, but each person was convinced to share the little they knew and over the months, a picture emerged.' He looked down at the drawing. 'Look closely he said and not only is every corridor and staircase shown but those arrow slits constantly manned are clearly identified in red.'

'What's this?' asked Geraint pointing at a list of numbers.

'That is the garrison roll call,' said Madog. 'As we speak, the castle is manned by no more than eighty men commanded by a single knight.'

Tarian stared at Geraint, the excitement evident in his face before turning to gaze at Madog.

'And you are sure of this?'

'Nobody knows a castle's numbers better than the man who feeds them.'

'A cook?'

'My own cook's brother has served in Caernarfon for many years and could probably name every remaining soldier in the garrison. The majority of the men were withdrawn to join Edward's army of campaign to France.'

'Wait,' said Geraint, 'that may be a fact but a garrison half that number could hold out for months behind those walls. The castle is defended on three sides by the sea and the fourth is protected by a loyal town behind its own strong fortifications. Even if we fought our way through, without siege engines we would never get over the walls.'

'I have no intention of getting over the walls, Geraint,' said Madog, 'nor indeed under them. I intend to go through them.' As both of the older men stared in silence, Madog pointed again at the map. 'Look at the outer wall adjacent to the town,' he said, 'tell me what you see.'

'The same thick walls,' said Geraint.

'Wait,' said Tarian, 'looking closer, there is a difference. This small part has not been inked in; the walls are represented with a charcoal line only.'

'You have a good eye for one so old,' laughed Madog. 'Of course you are correct and the reason they are not inked in is that they are yet to be built.'

Geraint's head snapped upward.

'What do you mean?' he asked. 'Caernarfon's walls are complete.'

'Apparently not,' said Madog, 'there is yet a piece of wall less than fifty paces wide, defended by no more than a palisade and a few crossbow men. Building on the main walls paused a few years ago when the threat was deemed to have diminished. That perceived safety combined with the security that a loyal walled town affords, meant that much needed money could be diverted to maintain Edward's campaigns against the Scots in the north.'

'Edward is not a man to forget such things,' said Tarian, 'and ensures his defences are sound.'

'Perhaps so, but wars are costly. Why waste money on a castle in a conquered land when his bowmen are idle for lack of arrows in the north. He always intended for it to be completed but as yet has not seen it as a priority. I suggest that shortness of sight will soon change but by the time he opens the coffers, there will be a new castellan in place. Me.'

Their attention turned again to the map.

'So, gentlemen,' continued Madog, 'this palisade is no taller than a man upon another's shoulders. Am I to expect that you are able to take such a weak defence?'

'The palisade will pose no problem,' said Geraint, 'but even though the garrison is only eighty souls, we will need thrice that to ensure victory over trained men. How will we get several hundred men close enough to reach it without drawing the attention of the guards?'

'That part is easy,' said Madog, 'and it has already been arranged.' He stared at the two men again and saw the fire in their eyes. For the next half an hour he outlined the plans which had been months in the making. Finally he looked up and asked them the question they knew would be coming.

'So, gentlemen, such is the road I have chosen. I am committed to my fate and there will be no turning back. Do I have your support, or am I on my own?'

Geraint looked at the Prince, no longer seeing a boy but a leader worthy of following.

'My lord,' he said, 'I have waited half a lifetime for this day, you have my heart and my sword.' He slammed the palm of his sword arm on the map.

'As you do mine,' said Tarian and slammed his open palm on top of Geraint's. After a pause of a few seconds, Madog's hand landed last of all.

'Then so be it,' said Madog, 'in two days we will break the biggest link in Edward's ring of steel and take it for ourselves. Gentlemen, let the liberation commence.'

Chapter Fourteen

Castell du Bere

Fitzwalter sat behind a table, clutching a roast leg of goose in one hand and a tankard of wine in the other. Globules of fat shone upon his chin and a linen cloth was draped around his chest to catch any that fell to his ceremonial robes. He chewed on the meat while staring at John, the head steward who had interrupted his meal. Finally he let out a belch and pushed the meat filled trencher away from him.

'Enough,' he said, 'remove this and let the kitchens know the bird was tough, I will not countenance such a mistake again.' He stood up and threw the cloth to one side as the servants scrabbled to clear the remains of the meal. 'So John,' he continued, wiping his mouth with the back of his hand, 'who is this man who seeks audience?'

'He is but a commoner,' said John, 'but insists he has a message for your ears alone, a message that will not wait.'

Fitzwalter yawned.

'I will humour him,' he said, 'but it had better have the importance he claims. Bring him in.'

The steward bowed and left the room. Fitzwalter turned to another nearby servant. 'Have my bed prepared,' he said, 'the food has brought a tiredness upon me.' The servant scurried away leaving Fitzwalter alone in the room. Two minutes later the door banged open and the steward led in a bedraggled man, his garb still dusty from the road.

'Declare yourself,' said Fitzwalter, walking across the room to peer out of the window into the valley below.

'My lord, my name is Justin Brewer, and I am here on behalf of Cynan ap Maredudd.'

Fitzwalter paused momentarily before turning to walk back across the room, regaining his seat at the table. His eyes fixed on the visitor for what seemed an age and his fingers played out a random beat as they tapped nervously on the table surface. Finally the Castellan spoke again.

'This man called Cynan,' he said, 'is he the same one who claims lordship of the central Cantrefs.'

'He is that man, my lord, and his claim is just. The titles are a birth right acknowledged by Longshanks himself.'

'Perhaps so,' said Fitzwalter, 'but such acknowledgement is only valid while the incumbent pays fealty to the Crown.'

'We would beg to differ, my lord, birth right is absolute, irrespective of counterclaim or conquest.'

'Your words taste of treason, stranger,' said Fitzwalter, 'and I suggest you choose them well. Now, pass me this message before I have you beaten for your insolence.'

Despite the strong words the man did not break his stare.

'My lord, the message is simple. Castell du Bere was built by the hands of men born within the shadows of these hills. It sits upon a sacred place where many generations of our people were buried and was a place of pilgrimage before the forebears of Longshanks stole it for their own use. These walls belonged to our ancestors and we would have them back where they belong, amongst the people of Wales.'

Fitzwalter's eyes opened wide and his mouth dropped in astonishment.

'What?' he gasped.

'My lord, my lord, Cynan claims ownership of this castle,' continued Justin, 'and indeed the lands upon which it sits. He thanks you for your tenancy but regrets to inform you that your presence is no longer required and he expects you gone by dawn.'

For a few seconds, Fitzwalter was dumbstruck but eventually he found his voice once more.

'Let me tell you something, little man,' gasped the Castellan, 'I don't know what game you or your master play but my temper is frayed to the point of being lost. I will give you one more chance to explain for it is surely a misguided jest.'

'It is no jest, my lord,' said Justin. 'My lord Cynan demands you leave this place by dawn, complete with your garrison and whatever chattels each man can carry without the aid of carts. Do this and you will be granted safe passage to the Welsh border.'

Fitzwalter shook his head slowly in disbelief.

'And if I don't?'

'Then this castle will be taken by force and all who resist will perish by the sword,' said the man.

Fitzwalter stifled a laugh.

'I don't know what astonishes me more,' he said, 'your arrogance, your impertinence or the stupidity that makes you think that any man alive is able to take this castle. I have guards on every road for ten leagues in all directions and if there was any hint of an army anywhere near, then I would have known about it within hours.'

'Your preparations are to be commended, my lord, but alas were of no use. Our army is already within arrowshot of these walls.'

Fitzwalter fought the temptation to run to the window.

'I was in the village just this very morn,' he growled, 'and saw no such army. Do you take me for a fool?'

'No, my lord, but perhaps you were so taken by the merrymaking you did not see how busy the market was, or the fact that every tavern was full, or that every bed space in the sanctuary has been occupied these five days past.'

'What are you saying?' asked Fitzwalter, his eyes narrowing. 'This village is on a well-travelled path and the numbers coming in are no greater than normal.'

'Perhaps so, but I think it would have been better for you to count those leaving, or rather, those who didn't leave. As we speak, my lord, Cynan has an army a thousand strong being fed and watered by those who live within your shadow. If you do not accept his terms, then these same men will lay siege to your castle with the aim of returning it to Welsh hands.'

Fitzwalter managed to restrain himself a few moments later before calling over his shoulder.

'John, call the duty sergeant and pass word to secure the main gates.'

The steward ran out of the room leaving the two men staring at each other.

'You intrigue me, Justin Brewer,' said Fitzwalter, 'your arrogance is of one who knows no fear. Surely you know that your death is a very probable outcome here.'

'I do not fear death, my lord, for death is preferable to the continued servitude of an entire nation.'

'You certainly have the courage to match your convictions,' said Fitzwalter, 'but let me assure you, that is not enough. I do not know if your words ring true or if they are falsehoods born of madness, nevertheless I am a careful man and will take precautions until your true nature is uncovered. If you are indeed a messenger of Cynan then you will be imprisoned until such time as this is resolved and then hung for treason. If you turn out to be a madman, then you will be a plaything for my torturers. Either way, your impertinence today will not go unpunished.'

A door opened and a soldier carrying a spear entered the room. His tabard bore the emblem of Longshanks, worn over a chainmail shirt that hung down to mid-thigh level. On his legs he wore linen stockings and calf-length leather boots. A sword lay within a scabbard attached to his belt and on his head was an open-faced helm.

'My lord, you summoned me,' said the soldier.

'I did,' said the Castellan. 'Stand-to the garrison. I want every man on alert and the gates secured. Lower the portcullis.'

'Are we at threat, my lord?'

'I'm not sure yet but will take no chances.'

'Yes, my lord,' said the soldier and left the room.

'Come with me,' said Fitzwalter and led Justin and the steward up a winding stairway and out onto the castellated outer wall. They walked along the fortifications and into a tower overlooking the valley. Within minutes they were at the highest point and could see clearly into the village below the hill. All around them the castle was bursting into life as soldiers ran to their posts and the rattling of chains echoed around the courtyard as the portcullis dropped into position. Eventually the sergeant joined them on top of the tower.

'My lord,' he said, 'the castle is secure but we see no threat.'

'Neither do I,' said Fitzwalter, 'but perchance we are blind and this man can make us see.' He turned to Justin. 'You have enjoyed a minor victory for you have managed to get an entire fortress to jump to your tune but now that is done, why don't you show me where this army is you speak of.'

Justin held the Castellan's gaze for a few moments before answering. 'My lord, the army is amongst the people and of the people. Every person you see in the village below is a soldier of Cynan. Even those who have wielded neither sword nor lance are the bringers of your downfall. We will no longer countenance your unjust hand and once again I offer terms on Cynan's behalf.'

'You listen to me, stranger,' snarled Fitzwalter, 'you have come into my castle with nothing but threats and tales for children. At no time have you offered me anything of substance and I tire of your game. I will give you one more chance before I have you hurled from these walls. Show me something that adds credence to your claims or suffer the consequences.'

Again Justin paused before nodding gently and turning to face the slopes approaching the castle entrance. He raised one hand into the air and waved it back and fore before turning to face the Castellan. For a few seconds there was silence before John the steward started to speak.

'My lord, there is movement amongst the bushes at the side of the approach path…'

Before he could say anything else, a steel tipped bolt thudded into his chest, throwing him backward off the parapet and hurtling into the courtyard below. The Castellan instantly ducked behind the wall as did the sergeant while Justin stayed upright, staring down at the hiding men.

'To arms,' screamed Fitzwalter, 'man the battlements.'

The sergeant crouched and ran along the parapet, calling out his commands as he went.

Fitzwalter looked up at Justin.

'I will see you hung for this,' he shouted.

'Perhaps so,' said Justin, 'and I am willing to suffer that fate. But know this. If I do not return to Cynan with your answer, he has sworn that when the castle falls, as it will, then he will roast your family alive over a slow fire, ensuring it takes days for them to die.'

Fitzwalter glared up at Justin. His wife and ten-year-old son had recently joined him in Du Bere and though he paid them little attention, the thought of them meeting such a disagreeable end turned his stomach.

'You dare to threaten my family?' he growled.

'The terms are these,' said Justin, 'cede the castle and walk away unharmed. Resist and all men above the age of ten will be hung when the castle falls. Kill me and every soul will be lost, man, woman or child. There will be no negotiation.'

'These walls will not fall as easily as you think, stranger,' said Fitzwalter. 'I have a hundred cavalry stationed within half a day's ride of here and when they find out the castle is besieged; they will ride you and your peasant revolt into the mud.'

'My lord, you had a hundred men, a hundred and seven to be exact. But by nightfall last night, there were a hundred and seven horses being led back to Cynan's army,' he paused for effect, 'past one hundred and seven corpses. Now, I must be gone with your answer or, my lord, Cynan will assume you have taken my life.'

Fitzwalter turned away and descended the steps built into the castle's outer wall before stopping before the gates. Justin followed him down.

'You go back to your master,' said Fitzwalter when they reached the gate, 'but tell him this. Before this matter is ended, I will have him hung, drawn and quartered as a rebel. So gather your so-called army but expect no ceding from this man. Castell du Bere is English and if you want it, you will have to wrest it from my cold dead hands.'

Justin's head tilted slightly in acknowledgement.

'So be it,' he said and walked toward the gate tower.

'Open the gate,' called Fitzwalter, 'let him out.'

'But, my lord…?' started the sergeant at arms.

'You heard me,' said the Castellan, 'let the peasant go. He is not worth dirtying a blade.'

The guards opened the gates just enough for the man to go before slamming them shut again and sliding the huge timber bars into the holes in the gate walls, locking them securely in place. Fitzwalter turned to the sergeant.

'Open the armouries,' he said, 'and distribute what is needed. I want a full report of our situation before the sun sets, supplies, arrows, water and cattle, everything you can think of. In the meantime, make sure the castle walls are manned day and night.'

'What about him?' asked the sergeant, nodding toward the dead manservant. 'Shall we bury him?'

'Don't bother,' said Fitzwalter. 'Throw him from the castle walls.'

Justin Brewer walked down the path from the castle, hardly daring to breathe. Though the threats would have been made good, it was still a relief to yet have his life and he still expected the searing pain of an arrow in his back at every step. Within a minute he reached the archer who had fired the lethal bolt into the steward just minutes earlier.

'Richard Ash,' he said, 'you are, for once, a welcoming sight.'

'I have to admit,' answered the archer, 'I thought we would now be picking your broken body from the base of the battlements.'

'I would suggest your part was fundamental in getting me out alive.'

'In what way?'

'The death of his manservant shocked the Castellan to the core and gave a message I could not convey. I think he has never seen such an accurate shot from so far a distance.'

'Is that what you think?'

'Take credit where it is deserved, Richard, the three of us were as close as arrows in a fist yet your bolt picked your target out with unnerving accuracy.'

'Your compliments are welcome, Justin,' answered the archer, 'yet unwarranted. I was aiming for Fitzwalter.'

Without another word he turned and walked away toward the village, leaving Justin wide mouthed behind him, the messenger realising how close he had come to death at the hands of a friend.

'Richard, wait,' he called running to catch the archer. 'What do you mean?'

As the two men walked away, the undergrowth around them came alive as Cynan's forces revealed themselves from their hiding places and took up positions across the approach road to the castle. Within the hour, an army over a thousand strong lay between the castle gates and the village of Dysynni, each staring upward at the seemingly impregnable walls. Eventually an armoured knight rode through the lines and stopped in front of the besiegers.

'Where is Justin Brewer?' he asked, looking around.

'I am here, lord,' said Justin, running over to Cynan's side.

'Did you give him my ultimatum?'

'I did, my lord, and he poured scorn upon it. He said the castle was impregnable.'

'Against frontal attack it is indeed a formidable fortress,' said Cynan, 'but the walls are only as good as those who defend them and all men need to eat.'

–

Up in the castle, Fitzwalter was shouting at the keeper of his kitchens.

'What do you mean, no food?' he screamed. 'This is a castle with a fully armed garrison. The stores are always kept full in case of situations such as this.'

'My lord,' said the man wringing his hands, 'the cold stores were full this very morn, I checked them myself when getting the meat for the afternoon meal, but when I went back a few moments ago the hooks are empty. I fear there has been a traitor amongst us and he took the opportunity to sabotage our supplies.'

'How can that be?' demanded Fitzwalter. 'Nobody could carry that much meat through the gate, it would take many carts.'

The cook glanced miserably at the man next to him before answering quietly.

'My lord, it did not go through the gate, it went out of the window.'

Fitzwalter stared at the cook in disbelief as the situation became clear. Whoever was responsible had entered the cold stores and pushed every side of beef, ham or leg of mutton they could find through the shuttered window to fall to the valley below.

'How much is left?' he asked menacingly.

'None, my lord,' said the cook, staring at his feet.

'Who is responsible?' asked Fitzwalter.

'I suspect it is a man called Lloyd,' said the cook, 'he was engaged as a kitchen help this past month.'

'A Welshman,' said Fitzwalter in disgust, 'working in my kitchen?'

'He was a good worker, my lord,' said the cook, 'and came well recommended.' His voice fell away as he realised the futility of his justification.

'Where is he now?'

'He left the castle not four hours since,' said the cook.

'So he escaped?'

'It would seem so.'

'So how much food is there?' asked Fitzwalter.

'My lord, it gets worse,' mumbled the cook, 'the grain stores are almost empty and we have been relying on getting our bread from the village ovens.'

'Why is there no grain?' shouted the Castellan.

'With respect, my lord,' said the sergeant at arms, 'our supply lines have been under assault for weeks and very little grain has been forthcoming.'

'Why wasn't I told this?'

'We did not want to worry you, my lord, and expected a column of supply wagons any day.'

'But you knew our supply lines were under pressure?'

'We thought it was nought but the actions of brigands and we had the situation under control.'

Fitzwalter stared at the men around him.

'I am surrounded by imbeciles,' he gasped. 'This is a fighting castle of Edward, based in a hostile country. For many years we have been prepared to defend ourselves yet on the very day those preparations are needed, we are found wanting.' He stood up and walked over to the cook. 'It was your responsibility to secure the food for the garrison and you have fallen short. How am I supposed to tell my men they are to go hungry because of your incompetence?'

'My lord, I will have my daily rations halved with immediate effect,' said the cook, 'as will my staff.'

'There is no need,' said the Castellan, 'if there is no food to cook, there is no need for kitchen staff.' Without warning, Fitzwalter produced a knife from his belt and plunged it upward into the cook's stomach. The cook gasped and grasped both hands around the Castellan's wrist, trying to pull the knife out but Fitzwalter pressed him back against the wall. 'One less mouth to feed,' said the Castellan as the cook slid down the wall. He turned around and stared at the men still in the room. 'You,' he said pointing at a nearby guard, 'select two men from the kitchens. Task them with stretching out whatever food remains as long as possible. Sergeant, gather the rest and place them in the dungeon along with any other servants but allocate them no food for only men at arms will eat.'

'My lord, they will surely starve within days.'

'It is of no consequence; this path has been chosen by their countrymen and I will not lose a single moment's sleep in remorse. In addition, every man is to be put on quarter rations with immediate effect. In the meantime, get me a man capable of descending one of the castle walls on a rope.'

'To what end, my lord?' asked the sergeant.

'Task him with getting to Conwy, they are well garrisoned. Tell them to bring reinforcements with all haste or we are at risk of losing these walls. We can last for a few weeks but after that, our fate is in the hands of God.'

'Yes, my lord,' said the sergeant.

Fitzwalter turned to the rest of the men in the room.

'Well,' he shouted, 'you all have positions to man, what are you waiting for?'

Within moments the room emptied as everyone ran to their stations. Fitzwalter sat back and stared around the empty room, his heart racing as the implications sunk in. Castell du Bere, for the first time in generations was under siege.

Outside the castle walls the forces of Cynan were hard at work. Staying just out of range of the castle's archers, men set up barriers against any unexpected charge from the castle gates. Branches were cut from trees and sharpened into spikes before being sunk into the ground to form lethal barriers facing the fortress. Temporary shelters were erected fifty paces apart as cover from the Welsh weather and fire pits dug to provide heat and a method of cooking food for the besieging soldiers. Due to the narrow approach, the Welsh lines did not have to be very wide and it soon became clear that Castell du Bere's strengths were also its weakness. There was no need to defend three of its walls due to the surrounding escarpment but similarly it left little option for a counterattack and allowed the attackers to concentrate their numbers on the main approaches.

Behind the attacker's lines, Cynan's men went from house to house in the village, demanding supplies and support for the army. Those faithful to Fitzwalter were also exposed and placed in hastily constructed stocks in the village square to be abused by those who had suffered at the hands of the English. Taverns were closed and the ale confiscated and every baker tasked with increasing the production of the village ovens. Riders galloped in every direction to demand support from farms near and far and within days, supplies poured into the village along with those men who had struggled long enough and now sought a share in the fight back.

Before the week was over, a timber palisade had been erected along the entire frontage of the castle and Cynan's army had doubled in number. Campfires dotted the approach slopes and though the army had increased, the constant stream of supplies ensured there was food enough for all. Behind the palisade, a workforce had dug into the slope and formed a level base with strong planks, ready to take the enormous trebuchet that had been constructed by Cynan's engineers in the village.

Finally, Cynan himself walked along the palisade accompanied by his second in command, Robert Byrd.

'You have done well, Robert,' said Cynan. 'The defences are sound and the men look ready.'

'It has indeed gone well, my lord,' said Robert.

'Has there been any communication from the castle?'

'None, my lord. It has been strangely silent.'

'Is the trebuchet ready?'

'It is, my lord, and it will be hauled up from the village this very night.'

'What about load?'

'There are over a dozen carts waiting in the valley,' said Robert.

'What have you collected?'

'The usual filth from the farms, the corpses of rotting animals and even sacks of waste from the army's latrines, all collected and bound into sacks.'

Cynan grimaced in disgust.

'Keep it away from the men until needed,' he said, 'we don't want our own forces catching disease. Have you got the fire pots I sent?'

'We have, my lord. Over a hundred have been made ready and await your command.'

'Boulders?'

'A constant supply from the rivers. We have pressed the villagers into labour to keep us supplied.'

'Excellent,' said Cynan, 'I see no reason to wait. Once the trebuchet is in place, send over the boulders to break whatever we can within the walls and keep the bombardment up as long as the supply is maintained. At the very least they will be denied sleep and will seek shelter in the deeper rooms. At dawn tomorrow, replace the rocks with the fire pots for some of them will surely find broken wood to feed their flames but as soon as night falls, call up your carts of disease and send the contents over to lie amongst the rubble. I want the pressure maintained for though they have no chance of escape, there is always the possibility of a relief force from Longshanks. The quicker we can do this the better.'

'Agreed, my lord.'

'Good,' said Cynan, 'I'll leave you to it, Robert. As soon as we are able, let the bombardment commence. I have to ride south for a few days, our assault on Builth nears a fortuitous conclusion and I would be there to take possession of the castle. It will send a message to the English like no other.'

'Understood, my lord,' said Robert, 'and perchance, when you return our men will be encamped within Du Bere's walls.'

'We will see,' said Cynan.

The following morning, the impressive trebuchet was in place and a line of carts queued on the track behind, each loaded with the enormous rocks capable of smashing a castle's walls. Most of the army had gathered to see the first strikes from the siege engine. Robert climbed up on a rock so he could be seen all along the attacker's lines.

'Magister Tormentorum,' he called formally, addressing the master engineer in charge of the trebuchet, 'stand to your task and load the sling. A cask of ale to your team if the first shot lands within the walls at your first attempt.'

'A prize easily ours,' answered Master Reynolds, and turned to his team. 'Load the sling,' he shouted and four men rolled a giant rock off the back of a cart using long poles as levers. Reynolds ensured it was securely in place and then judged how high the counterweight needed to be to propel the stone over the walls. Using chalk as a marker he indicated the height on the vertical supporting beam. 'Raise the weight,' he shouted and behind him, two teams of oxen were driven away from the siege engine, each straining on the ropes that would hoist the enormous counterweight up the supporting frame.

'Hold,' shouted Reynolds and an iron peg was inserted into the ratchet mechanism to hold the counterweight in place. 'Release the oxen.'

The ropes were released from the counterweight and the oxen taken to one side.

'Ready?' shouted Reynolds.

'Ready,' answered a muscular man stripped to the waist and wielding a large two-handed hammer.

The magister turned to Robert.

'Upon your command, my lord, and I wager this first rock will fall on the head of the Castellan himself.'

'A confident boast,' laughed Robert Byrd, 'but perhaps an outcome not even I could hope for.' He paused. 'Then if you are ready, Magister, let the bombardment commence.'

Master Reynolds turned to the trebuchet and his waiting team.

'This is what we came to do, men,' he shouted. 'Let's show these peasants what real weapons can do. Release the widow maker.'

The half-naked man swung his hammer and knocked out the retaining spike from the ratchets releasing the counterweight. Immediately the box containing over ten tons of ballast fell downward, rotating the giant arm around the central pivot and launching the sling through the air. To a great roar of approval, the first rock sailed majestically through the air and over the castle walls to smash violently into one of the inner towers.

The magister turned to Robert Byrd.

'Can I ask the ale be served cold, my lord?' he said.

'Indeed it will, Magister,' answered Robert in amazement, 'indeed it will.'

Chapter Fifteen

The road to north Wales

Gerald of Essex rode alongside Hywel ap Rhys, Liegeman of the Sheriff of Builth. Behind them they had a joint force of a hundred mounted men at arms. They had been in the saddle for just over a week and had neared the village of Dysynni before coming across a barricade manned by fifty archers and a sergeant at arms in charge of a hundred pikemen.

'Hold, stranger,' shouted the sergeant. 'State your name and your business or find your mounts felled from beneath you by a hail of arrows.'

'Let me speak,' said the liegeman to Gerald quietly, 'your accent could make this situation worse.' He turned to face the soldier at the barricade. 'I am Hywel ap Rhys,' he shouted, 'and am engaged on the business of the Sheriff of Builth.'

'What business may this be?'

'We are en route to Dysynni to apprehend an outlaw named as Garyn ap Thomas. It is believed he frequents the taverns there.'

'There is nothing for you within the village,' said the sergeant, 'and I suggest you return from whence you came.'

'I hear rumour of a siege,' said Hywel, 'and would ask is there truth in such tales?'

'It is no secret the walls are besieged by my lord, Cynan,' said the sergeant, 'and I would demand you declare your stance in such matters.'

'We are freshly travelled from the south,' said Hywel, 'and know not the politics but I will say this. An attack on any fortress of Edward will not be taken lightly and Cynan will surely suffer the consequences.'

'That is his worry, not yours,' answered the sergeant, 'but you avoid my question, sir, so I say again, declare your allegiance or I will have no option but to assume you hostile, especially bearing in mind the manner of your garb.'

Hywel thought furiously. The column was made up of both English and Welsh but despite their strength, they were surrounded by archers and had little chance of victory in any fight.

'Such clothing is easily obtained in Builth,' he answered, 'for as we know, the cursed English lords in the south favour the merchants who sell such goods. I assure you that should our swords be needed, then our allegiance lies with Cynan.'

The sergeant stared at the liegeman before giving the signal for the archers to lower their bows.

'I cannot judge the honesty of your statement,' said the soldier, 'but seek no confrontation this day so will take your word as true. I will, however, deny you the road in case my judgement falls short and you are indeed here to offer succour to the castle.'

'I can assure you we offer no such thing,' said Hywel, 'only to seek the whereabouts of the villain known as Garyn.'

'I cannot help you in such matters but suggest you leave this place with all haste. Return to your manors and brace for war for it is surely a storm upon the horizon.'

'I appreciate your understanding,' said Hywel, 'and will indeed retrace our steps. A good day to you, sir.' The column turned and rode away, leaving the defenders staring after them.

'That was close,' hissed Hywel to Gerald. 'If he had found out you were an English castellan our days would have ended there and then.'

'It doesn't bode well,' said Gerald, 'and this place reeks of treachery. I suggest we take his advice and return home in case the war flows southward.'

'Agreed,' said Hywel and spurred his horse to a canter.

—

As darkness fell the column sought shelter for the night and soon found a suitable wood offering respite from the heavy showers.

'It seems there is already an occupant,' said Gerald, spying the light from a fire. 'Let's see if we can share the flames to warm some meat.' Within minutes they entered a clearing and saw a small cart near a campfire. Nearby stood a donkey, a monk and a young boy.

'Greetings,' called Hywel, 'we are friends and seek shelter for the night. This wood is big enough for us all but my comrade and I would request a few minutes at your fire to warm our bones and perhaps cook a morsel or two.'

'You are welcome, my lord,' said the monk. 'Please, feel free to share whatever you need.'

Gerald and Hywel dismounted and tied their horses to a tree before approaching the fire. All around them, their men set up camp amongst the trees, setting up oiled leather tents against the weather.

'I am Hywel ap Rhys and this is Gerald,' said the liegeman. 'With whom do we have the pleasure of sharing this clearing?'

'I am Elias,' said the man in a habit. 'A freeman of Dysynni on pilgrimage to Rome.'

Hywel stifled a laugh, the man was obviously a simpleton.

'To Rome, you say,' said Gerald, 'and you hail from Dysynni. Surely that is only a day's ride away, is this a freshly undertaken quest?'

'Indeed it is, my lord,' said Elias. 'It is not two days since we left the village but there need be no undue haste.'

'But surely you are aware there is war afoot?'

'Indeed, but the mule is slow. We travel as fast as we dare.'

'And who is this?' asked Hywel turning to the boy.

'A Frenchy given his liberty from the ships,' answered Elias. 'He travels alongside me as comrade with the aim of returning to his homeland.'

'Given his liberty?' said Hywel in surprise. 'I hear that rigging monkeys are highly valued and it is unusual for such a boy to be given up so freely. Perhaps he is a runaway?'

'Oh no, my lord, he is as free as you or me, I swear it.'

'Can you prove it?' asked Hywel.

'I have no document to prove such a thing but swear by God that his freedom was bought just three weeks ago in a trade with the ship master. I can also assure you the price was very fair and all parties were satisfied.'

'Can I ask, what price was considered fair to release such a prize?'

'Five gold coins,' interrupted the boy, 'the trade was fair and I am a free man.'

Silence fell and both Gerald and Hywel stared at Elias.

'And how would you have five cold coins?' asked Hywel coldly. 'The way of a monk is a poor one.'

'Alas I am no monk, my lord, but just a freed servant. It was not I who paid the price, but a kind man who saw the injustice of a beaten boy and sought only justice.'

'And who was this man?'

'A stranger who was passing through,' said Elias. 'He never gave his name.'

'Why would a stranger pay a fortune for a runaway boy and then hand him over to a servant?' asked Gerald. 'It doesn't make sense.'

'It does to me,' said Hywel stepping forward and facing Elias. 'I recognise you now for I saw you within the sanctuary at Dysynni. You served our quarry with his meal as I recall and he asked you many questions about the castle. I suspect it was this man who paid such a high price.'

'I don't know who you speak of,' stuttered Elias. 'I serve many such men.'

'This one was different,' said Hywel, 'and he took a particular interest in you. Fret not, Monk for I already know his name but would hear it from your own mouth.'

'I already said,' stuttered Elias, 'I am no monk and I know not his name.'

'What was he called?' asked Hywel stepping closer. 'The man with the gold coins, I want to know his name.'

'I don't know,' said Elias stepping backward.

'Oh I think you do,' said Hywel drawing a knife. 'I also think that you will tell me in the next few heartbeats or feel my blade between your ribs.'

'I don't know,' shouted Elias as he backed up against a tree. 'I swear I don't know his name.'

'Wrong answer,' said Hywel and placed his knife against Elias's midriff. 'Last chance, false monk.'

'Garyn,' shouted Philippe in fear, 'his name was Garyn and he had me climb the wall of the castle to get information, now let him go.'

Hywel stared at Gerald before returning his attention to the boy.

'Tell me, boy, was this Garyn also known as an outlaw?'

'I think so,' said Philippe miserably, 'but he was very kind to me. He saved my life.'

'And what information did you find out on his behalf? Quickly now or both you and your friend here will be hung as traitors.'

Philippe glanced at Elias who nodded silently. Philippe spurted out what he knew as the two men listened in astonishment. When he was done, Gerald and Hywel walked away into the undergrowth to talk quietly together.

'It seems fortune smiles upon us,' said Gerald, 'not only do we know his whereabouts but also that he seeks a great treasure. I would suspect that all parties concerned would pay a grand price to have possession of such an item.'

'I agree,' said Hywel, 'and suggest our path is clear. We should head north with all haste yet stay in his shadow. Let him find this artefact at his own expense and when it is in his possession, we will fall upon him and take him into custody.'

'And the sword?'

'I fear it is but a legend for fools,' said Hywel. 'Many have sought it but if it ever existed, it is long gone. Focus on the reward for Garyn for it now lays within easy reach.'

For a moment Gerald's face remained unmoved until finally he smiled broadly and held out his arm.

'Then we are in agreement,' he said. 'Let us rest well and be gone by dawn. This quest gets better with each passing day.'

The following morning the column turned northward once more, heading for Caernarfon. Behind them in the forest glade, a donkey lay dead amongst the fallen leaves while above it, two hanged corpses swung in the morning breeze, one man and one boy.

Chapter Sixteen

Caernarfon town

A guard yawned as the first of the farmers led their wagons through the gated wall toward the market in the town centre. Behind him the huge castle walls stretched skyward, a dominating presence looming over the walled town. The sun had just cleared the horizon but the morning mist from the sea still hugged the ground like a heavy blanket. More carts could be seen further down the road as well as the expected heavy foot traffic, bearing whatever they could to sell at the monthly market.

The event was always well attended in Caernarfon town for though there was a permanent market available on a daily basis, the last day of the month was when farmers and landowners in general came from far and wide to sell their goods. Merchants also used the opportunity to bring their goods and many ships had arrived in the harbour the previous day, taking advantage of the high tide to unload their wares. Fishermen pushed handcarts of salted fish and flocks of geese were herded by young boys, all destined for Caernarfon's market and ultimately the table of anyone fortunate to afford the price.

'It looks like we may be blessed with the sun today,' said the soldier.

'Hmm,' nodded his comrade, squinting his eyes toward the horizon.

'Could get busy.'

'I suppose so.'

'I hate this watch.'

'Me too.'

'Are you all right, Edmond? You seem very quiet.'

'I'm fine, let's just get it done so we can get back to the castle.'

'Too much ale last night?'

'Listen, Eurig, I did not touch a drop of ale and haven't this week past. I just have things on my mind and would rather stay quiet so if you don't mind, keep your stinking mouth shut.'

The first guard stared in surprise at the ferocity of his comrade's response.

'I don't know what you fret over,' he said, 'but I suffer such abuse from no man. You and I will sort this out later in the barracks and I warn you now, my manner will not be so accommodating.'

'Think what you will,' said Edmond, 'my mind has no time for your drivel.' He turned his attention back to the approaching traders and stepped forward to challenge the first of many he would see that day.

'Hold there, traveller,' he said, 'I would see your wares.'

The farmer stopped his cart and watched as the soldier opened the top of one of the barrels to reveal a pile of red and gold apples. He took one and bit into it, the juices running down his chin.

'Good apples,' he said. 'I trust you will make good coin this day.'

'Good coin?' said the farmer replacing the lid. 'The price has been lowered so much I will hardly be able to purchase half a dozen geese with the proceeds. The taxes of Edward cripple me and my kind.'

'We all have our burdens to bear, farmer, move on.'

The farmer led his cart through the gate and toward the town square. For the next hour the traders increased and eventually there was a long queue waiting to gain entrance to the walled town. Most were allowed straight through but some were randomly stopped as a check against brigands or poor wares. Behind them, a large covered cart made its way slowly toward the gate and Eurig stared at it suspiciously.

'That cart is not one I have seen before,' he said.

'It may be from the port,' said Edmond, 'many boats docked last night.'

'Hmm,' said Eurig, 'it will be interesting to see what is so big it weighs the cart down so.'

Edmond looked nervous.

'Let it through, Eurig, the day is hard enough without unpacking wagons.'

'I will have my curiosity appeased, Edmond,' said Eurig, 'you watch the gate while I check it out.'

Eurig watched his comrade make his way through the foot traffic toward the lumbering wagon. Up above the gate, on the ramparts of the tower a third guard stared at the lone hill beyond the eastern gate. His eyes narrowed for though the sun often brought large numbers on market day, the amount of people approaching in the distance was unprecedented. He squinted his eyes and placed his hand on his brow to shield them from the early morning glare. Slowly his hand lowered and his eyes widened in astonishment. On the brow of the hill a line of riders had appeared and halted to stare down at the castle walls. Each bore a banner and the guard suddenly realised they bore the emblems of local lords, a display forbidden by Longshanks.

'Oh saints preserve us,' he gasped and turned to call down from the tower.

'Eurig, you'd better get up here?'

'He's not here,' shouted Edmond, 'what's the problem?'

'Come and see for yourself,' answered the sentry and ran back to the wall as Edmond climbed the ladder to the parapet.

'What's the matter?' he asked as he reached his comrade.

'Look,' said the sentry pointing at the throng now approaching, 'unless my eyes deceive me, they are in defiance of our king.'

'It would seem so,' said Edmond.

'I think you should close the gates,' said the sentry and turned to descend the ladder.

'Where are you going?' asked Edmond.

'I'm going to sound the alarm, idiot,' snapped the sentry. 'The castle needs to know we could be under attack.'

'I can't let you do that,' said Edmond quietly.

'What?' asked the sentry.

'I can't let you raise the alarm.'

'Why not?'

'Sorry, friend,' said Edmond, 'but they have my family.'

'What are you on about?' demanded the sentry.

'The Welsh lords kidnapped my wife and threatened to send her back to me piece by piece unless I gave access to this gate.'

'And you agreed?' gasped the sentry. 'You have endangered us all for the sake of a peasant?'

'What else could I do?' shouted Edmond. 'They have my wife.'

'She is probably already dead,' screamed the sentry, 'and you are about to get us all killed for the sake of a false promise.'

'I don't care,' responded Edmond. 'I cannot take that risk, now lay down your arms and I will ensure we are treated well but I cannot let you raise the alarm.'

'Not in a thousand lifetimes,' snarled the sentry and reached for his pike but even as his hand folded around the haft, Edmond drove his own spear through the man's back.

'I'm sorry, friend,' he said, 'but my wife's life is more important than yours.'

Down below, Eurig had halted the large cart, oblivious of the drama unfolding above his head.

'Your face is new to me,' he said to one of the two men on the seat at the front of the cart, 'are you new to this Cantref?'

'We are, sir, and hear Caernarfon is a good place to sell our wares.'

'It might be but that would depend on what it is you have to sell.'

'Sides of fresh beef,' said the man, 'freshly slaughtered, our cart is loaded with them.'

'I can see the cart lies heavy on the road but why are they covered in such a way?'

'The day is expected to be warm,' said the driver, 'and we would keep the flesh from spoiling.'

'Show me,' said Eurig.

The driver glanced at his comrade before getting down and walking to the back of the wagon.

'Is there any need for this?' he asked. 'We risk losing the best place if we linger too long.'

'I thought you said you hadn't been here before.'

'I haven't but my comrade has and he said there is a square with limited shade. We would like to get the best location and any delay could cost us dear.'

'Open it,' ordered Eurig, 'and be hopeful that I let you in at all.'

The man hesitated again but Eurig lowered his spear to casually point toward him.

'Is there a problem?'

'No, of course not,' answered the driver and reached up to unfasten the ties.

As he waited Eurig became aware the crowd of market traders heading for the town had stopped and were gazing back along the shores of the strait dividing the mainland from the isle of Ynys Mon.

'Who are they?' asked a voice.

'Riders,' came the answer, 'but there must be hundreds of them.'

Eurig turned to stare and his mouth fell open when he saw a wall of horses galloping toward him along the flat ground between the hill and the sea. For a few seconds he was transfixed at the sight of so many galloping cavalry and the many coloured banners streaming from raised lances but his training quickly kicked in and he spun around to race back to the castle.

'Stop there, soldier,' said a voice and Eurig glared in disbelief at the sight before him. The cart was now fully open and he faced a man with a crossbow held tightly to his shoulder, the bolt aiming directly at Eurig's chest.

'Steady, Englishman,' said the archer, 'just one choice to make, live or die.'

Eurig swallowed hard and stared at his would-be executioner. Behind the man in the cart, he could see many more, peering out of the gloom.

'Well?'

'Live,' murmured Eurig.

'Then drop that pig sticker and your sword belt and walk toward me.'

Eurig threw his spear to one side and untied the belt around his waist, bending forward to place it gently on the ground. He feigned a stumble and though he was watched closely, the archer didn't see him gather a fist full of gravel from the floor.

'Now, very slowly come toward me,' said the archer, 'and don't get any ideas.'

Eurig walked slowly forward but as he reached the cart, he hurled the gravel into the archer's face while throwing himself to one side. The archer flinched though still managed to pull the trigger but Eurig had done enough to affect his aim and the bolt flew across the road to embed itself in the body of a mule. A woman screamed and as the beast reared in terror and pain, the cart it was pulling fell over, tipping its contents over the road. Panic ensued and Eurig ran desperately toward the gate, shouting as he went.

'Alarm,' he screamed, 'send warning to the castle, we are under attack.'

Within moments people were screaming and abandoning their wares to run as fast as they could toward the town walls. The crossbow man wiped the dirt from his face and turned to his comrades.

'Get out,' he shouted, 'we are discovered. Get to the gate and pray to God our man has managed to secure it open.'

Twenty more archers jumped down from the cart while in the crowd, many more discarded their disguises and joined them as they ran toward the town walls.

'Edmond, sound the alarm,' screamed Eurig, seeing his comrade on the ramparts, 'summon the garrison.'

Edmond stared down at his long-time friend with a heavy heart but stayed still, watching the events unfold.

'Edmond,' screamed Eurig again, 'don't just stand there...'

Before he could finish, a crossbow bolt smashed into the back of his head and out through his face. Eurig fell into the dirt, dead before he hit the ground.

Up on the battlements, Edmond stepped back, shocked at the horror of his friend's death and for a few seconds, stared at the corpse before looking up to see dozens of armed men running toward the bridge.

'Dear God,' he muttered, 'what have I done?'

He stayed a few seconds more but then made a decision and clambered down the ladder as fast as he could.

'You there,' screamed Edmond, indicating some men running over the bridge, 'help me secure the gate.'

Several people stopped and joined him, pushing the gate closed.

'My family are still out there,' shouted a woman, 'please, wait for them.'

'We can't,' shouted Edmond, 'or we will surely be overrun.'

'But my family…'

'There is nothing we can do,' screamed Edmond, 'now you men help me push or we will be dead within minutes.' Slowly the gates closed and the men slid the heavy oak bar into the adjacent walls. Those people who had been lucky enough to get through the gate hugged each other in relief before making their way toward the safety of the castle. More soldiers ran from the gatehouse, pulling on their helms and fastening their gambesons before climbing the ladders to the battlements.

'Where is the horn,' one asked, 'why haven't you sounded the alarm?'

'It is around Eurig's neck,' answered Edmond.

'Where is he?'

'His corpse lies in the dirt the other side of the bridge.'

'What are we going to do?' asked the soldier. 'Twelve men cannot repel an army.'

'I will get reinforcements from the flanking towers,' said Edmond, 'you get a message to the garrison.'

The man turned and sprinted through the town as Eurig ran along the base of the wall toward the next tower.

'Stand-to the guard,' he screamed, 'we are under attack.'

The sentry atop the wall had his back to him and did not move. Edmond increased his pace, forcing his body to the limit.

'Stand to,' he screamed again and this time the guard turned to stare down.

'What's the danger?' shouted the sentry.

'The eastern gate is under attack,' shouted Edmond. 'In the name of God sound the alarm and get men over there or we are truly doomed.'

The man hesitated only a moment before turning and calling through a nearby doorway.

'Alarm,' he shouted, 'all men to arms.'

Within seconds, the sound of horns echoed across the town and soldiers emerged from the sentry towers all around the town walls. Edmond leaned on a wall to regain his breath. For a few seconds he allowed himself to think about his young wife and his face contorted in pain as he imagined the fate that now awaited her.

'My sweet Elisabeth,' he whispered through his tears, 'please, forgive me but I could not betray my fellows.' After a few more breaths, he wiped his face, tightened his belt and ran back to the eastern gate.

–

Madog looked down from the nearby hill, watching as his cavalry reined in the charge beneath the town walls.

'Damnation,' he muttered, 'the gate has been denied us.'

'It matters not,' said Tarian, 'it was always a possibility and we have prepared for such an instance. What is important is that we get our mangonels in position as quickly as we can.'

Both men turned to look at the line of carts being pulled by teams of farm horses at the rear of the army.

'They won't be ready until the morning,' said Geraint, 'but the hard work has been done. All the engineers have to do is assemble the parts.'

'Still, the element of surprise is lost,' said Madog.

'My lord, it can be regained.'

'How?'

'Place the first two mangonels before the eastern gate and commence bombardment as soon as possible. Keep it up through the night to give the impression that our route lies there but in the hours of darkness, gather the remainder midway between the eastern gate and the next sentry tower. The walls seem thinner there and they are vulnerable to a focused assault.'

'Do it,' said Madog, and a messenger was despatched with instructions.

'Don't bother with ladders,' said Geraint, 'we will go through the walls, not over them. They are but a minor hindrance and the main challenge will be the castle itself.'

'Then come,' said Madog, 'let's join our men in the assault for our blood is no more precious than theirs.' He spurred his horse and with a hundred cavalry at his back, rode down to the levels before the city walls, a place now teeming with men at arms and terrified civilians.

Chapter Seventeen

Bristol Castle

Longshanks strode into the great hall, flanked by his personal guard and made his way to the top table. Three men stood waiting and bowed as the King took his seat.

'You were expected yesterday,' snapped Longshanks, 'and it is an irritation that you have made your king wait.'

'My lord,' answered one of the nobles, 'the news is not good and we had to take time to ensure it was not mere supposition. It was felt that the need for accuracy outweighed the need for haste.'

'Granted,' said Longshanks, 'but waste no more time in colourful words. What news is so daunting that it demands the patience of a waiting king?'

'My lord,' answered the noble, 'it would seem the rumours are true. There is a tidal wave of revolt sweeping across Wales as we speak. Cardigan castle has fallen on the west coast and a string of churches throughout the north have been burned and ransacked, including Llanfaes on Ynys Mon. We are receiving messages almost daily, requesting support from the royal forces to repel the Welsh rebels. Our castles at Howarden, Ruthin and Denbigh are all under siege and Morlais in the south is rumoured to have already fallen.'

'What?' gasped Longshanks. 'How can mere rebels cause the fall of even the smallest of our castles, they do not have the manpower nor the siege engines for such a task?'

'My lord, many of the garrisons have been weakened by your call to arms for the French campaign. The fortresses were left poorly manned and led by inexperienced men. It would seem that this fact was known to the rebels and they took advantage of this weakness to coordinate their attacks.'

'How strong is the revolt?'

'At the moment it is widespread yet uncoordinated. It would seem that many of the minor Welsh lords have taken it upon themselves to take advantage of the fervour such minor victories bring.'

Longshanks stared at the messenger.

'In my experience,' he said eventually, 'such things have a habit of burning themselves out, and oft I have just waited for the fervour to die down before sending in a force to arrest the ringleaders. The castles you have mentioned, albeit important, are minor in my ring of steel and we will suffer little disadvantage from their capture.'

'My lord,' said the second noble, 'if I may?'

'Speak up man,' said Longshanks, 'there is no place for formalities in such a situation.'

'My lord,' continued the noble, 'your comments are acknowledged and it is true the temporary loss of these castles is of little consequence but I feel there is a greater danger looming on the horizon.'

'Which is?'

'There is rumour of a man claiming ownership of the title Prince of Wales, and as we speak, he gathers a massive army to his banner.'

'Who is this man?' asked Longshanks.

'A minor noble by the name of Madog ap Llewellyn. He hails from Ynys Mon and his claim provides direct lineage from the Welsh princes.'

'And is he involved in this revolt?'

'Not yet but it is only a matter of time. Our worry is that he may unite the warring lords of Wales under a common banner and if that happens, he will seek independence from your royal charter.'

'So where is this Madog now?'

'We are not sure, the last we heard was somewhere on Ynys Mon though we are pretty sure he was responsible for the burning of the church at Llanfaes.'

'So who is responsible for the attacks in Mid Wales?'

'We believe there are many responsible but the main force is led by a man called Cynan, a ruthless knight with experience of many battles. He is a formidable foe and perhaps provides us with the more serious risk unless Madog gets unification.'

'Everything you have said so far is a concern yet worries me not unduly,' said Longshanks. 'For ten years there have been many minor uprisings but always we have put them back in place. I have already sent a column of armed men under the command of Nicholas Fermbaud into Wales and have heard good things about their activities. Perhaps this uprising will yet come to nought.'

As he spoke the far door crashed open and two men walked in, pausing only to briefly bow in deference.

'Fermbaud,' called Longshanks, 'Orland, a timely entry indeed. We were talking about you this very minute and look forward to your account. I pray you have good news to share?' As he spoke, the King's voice trailed away as he saw the state the Castellan was in. His face was drawn and his clothing was filthy from the week he had spent in the forests hiding from Cynan's men.

'Alas, my lord,' said Fermbaud, 'my news is dire and I am ashamed to say my command is lost in its entirety, slaughtered by an overwhelming enemy force. I was lucky to escape and if it was not for Orland, I would now lie rotting in a stinking Welsh ditch.'

Longshanks stared in astonishment.

'The whole column are dead?' he gasped.

'They are, my lord. We fought bravely but the enemy numbered in the thousands.'

Orland glanced at Fermbaud, his brow furrowing but before he could contradict the Castellan's exaggeration, Fermbaud spoke again.

'My lord,' he said, 'there is one more thing, yesterday we stopped at a village to rest the horses and while we were there, a messenger rode in with desperate news.'

Longshanks let out a long sigh.

'Spit it out, Fermbaud, for this day cannot get any worse.'

Fermbaud glanced at Orland before returning his gaze to Longshanks.

'My lord,' he said, 'Castell du Bere is under siege.'

While Fermbaud disappeared to get food and rest, Long-shanks strode around the hall, deciding his reaction to the worrying news.

'This couldn't have come at a worse time,' he said. 'The first half of the fleet has already sailed to Gascony, there is unrest in Ireland, and Scotland continues to be a thorn in my side. There are few men left of any mettle in the southern counties and the men of York need to watch the Scottish borders.'

'My lord,' said Orland, 'I hear there is a muster in Chester you can call on. Over a hundred blooded men, mostly cavalry.'

'There are,' said Longshanks, 'and they are destined to be the van of my forces in France.'

'Surely you can divert them into Wales?'

'I can but I still need infantry, foot soldiers who can face down these barbarians in Wales and crush them as the peasants they are.'

'Then can I suggest the men of Carlisle,' said Orland. 'They are well blooded against the Scots and will have no fear against the Welsh.'

'I agree,' said Longshanks and turned to one of the scribes. 'Write a letter immediately and have it sent to my lords in the north. Tell them their king needs their support and failure to lend strength to my arm will be seen in a negative manner. I suggest a hundred men at arms from each county, fully armed and able to feed themselves for two weeks. The cost will be met from my treasuries at the conclusion of the French campaign. Tell them to assemble the men and await further instruction.'

'Yes, my lord,' said the scribe and walked over to a table with his pouch of writing tools.

'You,' said Longshanks turning to another noble. 'Send word to my ship's masters, tell them to make arrangements to load supplies if required. If this uprising gets any worse and they target our other coastal castles at least they can be resupplied by sea. We have to prepare for the worst.'

'Yes, my lord,' said the noble and left the hall.

Longshanks turned to face Orland.

'My friend,' he said, 'you have just returned from what sounds like a horrendous campaign in a hostile country. Yet I have not heard your report. Did you fare well?'

'My men and I have suffered worse,' said Orland, 'but it has to be said that Fermbaud's inexperience contributed to the death of his men.'

'Did cowardice play a role?'

'It was hard to see but at the very least it was due to rashness of decision.'

'What do you feel should be his fate?'

'Give him another chance,' said Orland, 'but keep him under your control.'

'I will bear that in mind,' said Longshanks, 'but for now, I have other matters to attend.'

'What are you going to do?'

'I have no other option than to quash this revolt myself,' said Longshanks. 'I will gather what men I can and ride into this nest of vipers with all haste. I want you to go to York and muster the northern forces. Upon your return journey, pick up the cavalry from Chester and join me in Conwy as soon as possible.'

'The winter is almost upon us,' said Orland, 'would it not be better to wait for spring?'

'It would but time is not a luxury I have. I need to get this dealt with as soon as possible for my focus is upon Gascony.'

'I understand, my lord,' said Orland, 'and will force the march to join you.'

'Good,' said Longshanks, 'now get some rest for I feel sleep will be in short supply over the next few months.'

Chapter Eighteen

Castell du Bere

For two weeks, Cynan's forces continued the relentless barrage against the walls of Castell du Bere. On occasion he sent patrols toward the fortified gate to judge the strengths of the defences, but each time they were forced back by the crossbow bolts from the battlements. Boulders from the valley were now in short supply and many of the village houses were destroyed to obtain ammunition for the trebuchet. A constant cloud of black smoke hung over the besieged castle, testament to the devastation within and though the outer walls were severely damaged, the strength of their construction meant they were still defendable.

Cynan had returned from Builth and stood alongside the trebuchet, staring at the castle walls above him. Every minute or so, the earth seemed to shudder at the release of energy from the siege engine and another boulder was sent flying over the castle walls.

'There can't be much left standing inside,' said Cynan.

'Possibly not,' said Robert Byrd, 'and that is why we target the walls but their thickness poses a problem.'

'Can we not target the gates?'

'We have tried but the accuracy needed is not there.'

Cynan turned to the master of the trebuchet.

'Magister,' he said, 'they tell me that when it comes to these beasts, there is none better than you.'

'They speak true,' said Reynolds, 'and I have taken down more walls than I can remember with such machines.'

'And yet you cannot hit the gates?'

'My brief was to build a trebuchet, my lord, and that is what I supplied. Such machines are for the purpose of hurling things over walls or at walls. If you want the accuracy needed to hit a small target such as a gate then perhaps a mangonel would better suit your purpose. I can have one made but it will be several days.'

'Have it done,' said Cynan, 'but I fear we do not have the time. Fortunately, a situation has arisen that may cut those preparations short. Rest your men but prepare to send a very special missile over.'

'What missile, my lord.'

'You will see.'

An hour later, two riders made their way up the hill. One dismounted while the other stayed in place. Cynan called out to the magister.

'Master Reynolds,' called Cynan, 'attend me.'

The engineer walked over and stood beside the knight.

'My lord?'

'Master Reynolds, this is what I want you to send over the walls.'

The engineer looked around but saw no ammunition.

'I don't understand,' he said, 'do you mean the horse?'

'No,' said Cynan. 'The second man is a messenger from within the castle before us and was sent to get reinforcements from Conwy. Luckily our men caught him before he got there but the messages within his pouch condemned him. I want you to send them back to the place whence they came so the Castellan can see there is no hope of relief. Perhaps then he will see the futility of maintaining this pointless defence.'

'A pack of letters is too light to send over, my lord, I will need to attach them to a rock but surely you can send a messenger with them under a flag of cease fire?'

'I could but I believe it will be ignored so they will indeed be sent over the walls but not tied to a rock, they will be attached to Fitzwalter's man.'

Reynolds stared at Cynan. He had often sent corpses over the walls of a besieged castle but never had he sent a live man.

'Is he to be killed first?' he asked.

'I think not,' said Cynan. 'Perhaps his screams of fear will add impetus to the Castellan's decision making.'

'My lord,' started Reynolds, but he was cut short.

'Just do it, Magister,' said Cynan, 'and do it now.'

The condemned man had heard the conversation and as the implications sunk in, he started to panic.

'No, please,' he begged, 'not that, anything but that.'

'Grab him,' demanded Reynolds, 'and bind his arms and legs together. Secure his wrists to his ankles behind his back for we need to make the profile smaller.'

'*Nooo*,' screamed the man but despite his struggles, he was soon trussed as requested and placed on the sling.

Cynan stepped forward and placed the satchel of messages around the sobbing man's neck.

'I doubt you will survive this, Englishman,' he said, 'but die in the knowledge that you did so in a good cause.'

'Let me go,' begged the man, 'in the name of God I beseech thee.'

'Can't do that,' said Cynan and stepped away from the sling. 'Magister, do your work.'

Reynolds marked the trebuchet and the oxen raised the counterweight; this time measurably lower than the height needed for the large boulders.

'Ready?' called Reynolds after the oxen were released.

'Ready,' answered the hammer man.

'Release,' roared Reynolds and every eye turned skyward as the screaming man was launched high above the castle walls, his cries coming to a sudden end as he smashed amongst the rubble within.

All around the trebuchet, the men fell silent.

'What now?' asked Reynolds.

'Now, we wait,' said Cynan.

Two hours later, Cynan felt a hand on his shoulder, waking him from a much-needed sleep.

'My lord, there is a flag of surrender,' said a soldier. 'The castle are seeking terms.'

Cynan sat up and adjusted his cloak before walking back toward the palisade.

'Where is the messenger?' he asked and was led toward two men seated on the grass surrounded by a dozen armed soldiers. Cynan stared at the condition of the prisoners. Their flesh was drawn and they stank of filth. Open scabs lay upon their faces and the pus from infection stained their skin.

'Who are you?' asked Cynan and one of the men struggled to his feet.

'My name is of no consequence,' said the man, 'but I am a soldier of Edward, serving in the garrison of Du Bere under the stewardship of Fitzwalter.'

'And you have come from the castle?'

The soldier laughed sarcastically.

'And where else do you suppose I have been in this state?'

'Curb your tongue, Englishman,' growled Robert Byrd, 'or have it ripped out.'

'Do what you will,' said the soldier, 'it cannot get worse than the hell you have already released upon us.'

'What message have you brought?' asked Cynan, cutting short Robert Byrd's angry response. 'Does your master seek terms?'

'He does not,' said the soldier, 'for he is dead as are many of the garrison. Those who still live, do not have the strength to fight the disease that ravages the castle. You are to be congratulated, Welshman, the siege was well administered and we can no longer hold you out.'

'Who is now in command?' asked Cynan.

The soldier shrugged his shoulders.

'Me I suppose. I have been sent by those who still live to beg mercy and ask that they are allowed to leave in peace in return for gifting you the castle.'

'A trade?' said Cynan. 'You seem in no position to trade. Why should I bother to grant your wish when I will have what I seek within days anyway?'

The soldier stepped toward Cynan and the Welshman's hand went to the hilt of his sword.

'I'll tell you why,' said the soldier, 'because it is common knowledge that Fitzwalter had the sense of an ass and a stubbornness to match. There was never any way we were going to sustain a prolonged siege, yet he held out against the advice of his liegemen and everyone suffered as a result.'

'This could be seen as an admirable status,' said Cynan, 'for a leader to hold out till the last is something to be admired.'

'You would think so, but he did not suffer as did the rest of the garrison. He made sure his family had food and clean water while the rest of us starved. He thought we would be relieved and though many of his kinsmen died as we waited, it was of little consequence for he and his family were fine. That is why you should grant our request, Cynan, for though you are my enemy, I believe you to be a man of honour. You are victorious, do not besmirch your victory with the actions of a murderer.'

'I thought you said Fitzwalter was dead?' said Robert Byrd.

'I did,' said the soldier, 'but not from disease or the hand of a Welshmen, he died at the end of an English blade.'

'You killed him?' asked Cynan.

'I did and wish I had done so sooner.' He looked around before facing Cynan once more. 'So, the castle is yours Welshman, do your worst. The gates are open and your men can ride in unopposed. Set us free or hang us high, you will find no resistance from us.'

Cynan didn't answer but looked up at the open gates. Finally he sighed and turned back to the soldier.

'Then the day is done,' said Cynan, 'and my judgement is this. Your comrade will ride back to Du Bere and give notice for every living person to leave within the hour. When they emerge, they will be given food and clean clothing as well as carts for the sick. This is done on condition that they return across the border with all haste and swear on the cross of Jesus they will never return to Wales.'

'A magnanimous gesture,' said the soldier, 'and what of me?'

'I understand what you did,' said Cynan, 'but I cannot ignore the fact that you murdered your master. Even though his actions were suspect and his heart false, your king granted such status for a reason and it is not the place of mere soldiers to end the life of a lord. You, sir will hang before this day is done as a message to all men to obey their betters.'

The soldier stared and his shoulders slumped.

'So be it,' he said quietly.

Cynan turned to Robert Byrd.

'Pass word amongst the men, Robert, and send messengers far and wide. The siege is done, Du Bere has fallen.'

An hour later a small group of people limped slowly through the gates and down toward the village. Soldiers mixed with civilians, and exhausted children were carried by their emaciated parents. It was a scene of misery and either side of the road, Cynan's army watched in silence, astonished at the state the enemy were in.

As soon as the castle was empty, Cynan sent in a group of soldiers with strict instructions. Within the hour they returned with the news he sought.

'Well?' said Cynan quietly to one of the men. 'Did you find him?'

'My lord, there was indeed an old man in a cell along with the tools of a mason but he was dead and has been for a long time.'

'I feared as much,' said Cynan, 'return to your unit.'

As the men walked away, Robert Byrd approached.

'My lord, it is over, the castle awaits.'

'Let it wait, Robert,' said Cynan, 'our road lies elsewhere.'

'Are you not going in?'

'No,' said Cynan, 'leave it to the crows and the rats. There is nothing there for us except disease and destruction.'

'But, my lord, you have besieged this place for weeks. Surely you want to survey your prize?'

Cynan turned to Robert.

'You still don't understand, Robert, this was never about stone and mortar, it was the fact that it was never theirs in the first place. Let it fall into ruin for I have no use for such monoliths. My aim is toward a Wales where such things have no place. What use is a castle in a land where all men are free?'

'So what next?' asked Robert.

'Next we march northward,' said Cynan, 'and test the resolve of Longshanks. The country is awakening, Robert, and we can no longer control the beast within. This is but the first step and the flame of freedom is kindled, soon it will rage as does a forest fire.'

Chapter Nineteen

Caernarfon

Garyn and Derwyn neared the outskirts of Caernarfon on the northern road and were surprised to see so many people heading in the opposite direction. Finally Garyn reined in his horse and addressed an old man on a mule being led by a young woman.

'Hold, stranger,' said Garyn, 'why pray do so many people fill the road?'

'Have you not heard?' asked the old man. 'Caernarfon is under siege from the usurper, Madog. His troops run riot in all the surrounding area and if you have an ounce of English blood in your veins then I suggest you do the same.'

'Madog has attacked Caernarfon?' asked Derwyn in astonishment. 'Surely the castle is impregnable.'

'The castle still stands,' said the old man, 'but the town walls seem destined to fall at any hour. Already there is more rubble than standing stones and the houses within are ablaze from the fire pots of the siege machines. Do yourself a favour, friend, turn and ride back whence you came. I fear this area holds nought but pain and death for any traveller not allied to Madog.'

'Thank you, old man,' said Derwyn, 'but we have one more question. We hear tell of an old fort in these parts, a ruin that was once a stronghold of a race of people called the Romans in centuries past. Do you know of this place?'

'There is such a fortress,' said the old man, 'and it is named as Segontium. The stone walls have long disappeared but it is still held in reverence by many locals. It is said the ghosts of the legions are often heard marching on stormy nights.'

'That may be the case,' said Derwyn, 'but we will see for ourselves. Where can we find this fort?'

'You would do well to stay away for it is sits upon a hill within sight of the castle itself. Like I said, the place is now a maelstrom of fighting and both sides offer no quarter. I fear travellers such as yourselves will be given short shrift by either side should you be captured.'

'Thank you for your concern,' said Garyn, 'and I hope you reach the safety you seek.'

The two men spurred their horses and rode against the tide of refugees toward Caernarfon. Within the hour they broke free of the mountains and could see the coast in the distance. Looming high above the landscape were the angled towers of Caernarfon castle and above them, clouds of black smoke pouring from the burning town.

'It would seem the young prince is a man of little patience,' said Garyn.

'Should we join him?'

'No, our goal is still the Roman fort.'

'Garyn, you heard the man, there are men at arms everywhere and in my experience, when the blood is raised such men take little time to listen to the explanation of strangers. Should we run into them, we cannot explain our presence and we will probably be robbed of our possessions or hung as English spies.'

'We haven't come this far to stop now,' said Garyn. 'We will ride as far as we are able today and lay up in whatever cover we can. Once we know the exact location of the fort, we will wait until dark before getting in close. At least that way, if we are discovered we can use the night as a cloak.'

'So be it,' said Derwyn and they spurred their mounts toward the smoke-filled horizon.

'Geraint,' roared Tarian, 'ready your men. I expect the wall to be breached within the hour.'

'They already chomp at the bit, Tarian,' shouted Geraint, 'and just await the command.' He looked across the field to the city walls. The twin round towers of the eastern gate were still standing though the battlements were damaged beyond all recognition. Behind the walls, fires raged throughout the town as thatched roofs and timber buildings fell victim to the constant hail of fire pots from the trebuchets. Before him, lines of Welsh infantry waited patiently just out of range of the archers upon the town walls but everyone knew it was only a matter of time before the final assault was launched.

Geraint looked toward the wall to the left of the eastern gate, the main focus of the assault. Six mangonels had pummelled the structure since dawn and despite the defenders' desperate attempts to reinforce any damage with timbers, their task proved fruitless and slowly the breach widened. The mangonel operators lowered their aim and the constant barrage of boulders started to pound the base of the already weakened walls. The attackers held their breath, waiting for the inevitable collapse for when it came, they knew they would be sent through the breach and into the town itself.

'There it goes,' screamed a man and thousands of voices cheered as the whole section collapsed before them, leaving a breach almost thirty paces wide.

'Mangonels,' shouted Geraint, 'change the shot.'

The mangonel operators quickly changed their choice of missiles from boulders to fire pots and aimed them through the breach, for although there was little there to burn, the constant rain of liquid fire meant that any defenders were denied the opportunity to form up in a disciplined defensive line.

'Sergeants at arms,' shouted Tarian, 'gather your men and look to your weapons. Upon my command we will take the wall and the town beyond. Do not pause at the breach but forge forward while the enemy is still in disarray. Secure a line before the fort walls but beware the civilians for there are nought but English dwelling within the town. Each one is treacherous and will stick you like a pig given half a chance.'

He looked around and drew his sword.

'Are you ready?' he roared.

The throats of a thousand men answered his call.

'Then for God, for Madog and for Wales, advaaance.'

The first thousand men ran down the shallow slope toward the breach, screaming their aggression toward the few defenders still on the town walls. For a few moments the English remained but the futility of their position soon became obvious and as one, they left their positions and raced back to the safety of the castle.

Within minutes the Welsh horde poured through the breach and as most spread out to take the town, some turned their attention to the towered gate house, killing the defenders and swinging the giant wooden gates inward to allow the remaining forces into the fortified town.

Caernarfon was quickly overrun and though Madog voiced his disquiet about the actions of some of the army, he held his counsel, knowing full well that to interfere with the raised blood of a soldier during battle courted nothing but trouble.

'My lord, leave them be,' said Tarian. 'They have suffered enough at the hands of the English over the years, it is only fair that the invader now feels some of that pain in return.'

'Agreed,' said Madog. 'Arrange for the mangonels to be brought forward and positioned before the palisade wall at the castle. I also want the trebuchets to create havoc within the fortress before we breach the walls, especially the towers guarding the palisade.'

'Of course, my lord,' said Geraint and sent a messenger back to the master of trebuchets.

The three men walked through the burning town, seeing the devastation their siege had brought. All around them, armed men wreaked their pent-up frustration against the English population and many civilians died needlessly at the hands of rabid Welshmen. Women were dragged into any buildings still standing and many brutally raped before being put to the sword. Men, women and children were all equal targets and before the day was done, hundreds lay dead in pools of blood. During it all, the faces of Edward's soldiers could be seen high on the castle walls, each peering down in horror yet unable to do anything to stop the slaughter.

'Look at them,' snarled Madog, 'they hide behind their stone walls as their people feed the dogs of war. You would think they would ride out and face us as men.'

'They are outnumbered twenty to one, my lord,' said Tarian, 'and they know their only hope is to defend the castle walls.'

'A futile hope,' said Madog. 'How long before our siege engines are in place?'

'A few hours,' said Tarian.

'Good. Once we are ready, rein in our men. The town is all but destroyed but the bigger prize awaits. Our focus must now fall on the castle and tomorrow we must be within its walls or this day will have been in vain.'

Before Tarian could answer, two soldiers dragged a struggling man across the blood-stained square and threw him at the feet of Madog.

'And who is this?' asked the Prince.

'Do you not recognise him, my lord?' asked one of the soldiers.

Madog placed the point of his blade under the chin of the man on the floor and forced him to look upward.

'Well,' said Madog eventually, 'if it isn't our old friend Roger du Puleston.'

'And who might he be?' asked Tarian.

'He is no other than the Sheriff of Ynys Mon,' said Madog, 'a king's man through and through and hated by every soul who ever lived under his jurisdiction.'

'I have only ever carried out my orders,' gasped the Sheriff. 'Is this not a trait you demand of those who pay homage to you? Has the way of things become so distorted that allegiance is seen as a weakness amongst men of power?'

'Allegiance is indeed an honourable thing, Puleston, but your actions have inflicted more pain than the sum of all the men now ravaging the town around you. Children have seen their fathers hang and many starved to death as a result. Women have prostituted themselves when faced with their cries of hunger and yet been sent to the stocks for their troubles. Land has been confiscated in the name of the King and you have pursued every penny of unfair tax as if your life depended on it. Allegiance is one thing but brutality against your own people is another thing entirely.'

'They are not my people and my role was to govern them in the name of the King. That is what I have done.'

'Indeed you did, and I have no doubt the King was grateful for the full carts sent to his treasury but one of your roles is to also administer justice in the name of the people. They looked to you for the fair application of the law yet received persecution in return.'

'I governed with a fair hand,' shouted Puleston. 'Yes, I had to discipline those who trod outside the law but those who obeyed the decrees of Longshanks had nothing to fear. I was harsh, yet fair, a trait of all good leaders.'

Madog pressed his sword harder against the Sheriff's throat, drawing a slight trickle of blood.

'If you kill me,' gasped Puleston, 'Edward will have your head on a spike.'

'I have no intention of killing you,' said Madog. 'I am going to hand you over to the very people you governed for it is they who had to deal with your edicts on a daily basis, not I. If you are seen as the fair man you claim to be then the people will have no problem releasing you. But that, Puleston, is down to them.' He looked at the two soldiers standing either side of the Sheriff. 'Give him to the people,' he said, 'his fate lies in their hands.'

'You will hang for this,' shouted the Sheriff as he was dragged away, 'do you hear me, Madog? Longshanks will see you rot in hell before the spring arrives.'

—

In the last few hours before nightfall, Madog's army set up their besieging lines before the imposing walls of the castle. Foot soldiers took shelter where they could amongst the rubble while lines of fully armed pikemen took turns to watch the drawbridge, alert against any potential counterattack. Madog, Geraint and Tarian took refuge against the rain in one of the few remaining buildings to withstand the attack.

Inside the candlelit room, a group of men lay sleeping on a floor littered with scrolls and parchments. Most of the men were fast asleep, exhausted from the day's events but some sat quietly, seeing to their own personal needs. One was washing a wound on his arm while another picked away at a half loaf of bread. As the Prince entered, the man with the wound made to get up but Madog bid him stay.

'Ease yourself, soldier,' said Madog quietly, 'there is room enough for all.'

'My lord, we only sought shelter from the rain and a place to escape the cold. I can take my men elsewhere.'

'There is no need,' said Madog, 'your need is greater than mine.' He looked around the room.

'What is this place?'

'It is the exchequer,' answered Geraint quietly, 'the building where all the town's records are kept.'

Tarian opened one of the scrolls.

'This is a detailed list of people who owe debt to the King's office,' he said.

'Same here,' said Geraint opening another.

'This one details the taxes due from each man,' said Madog studying a parchment on a table, 'it even lists the recommended punishment for failure to pay.' He threw it to one side. 'So much for judgement by your fellow man.'

The men walked slowly around the room, picking their way carefully between the sleeping soldiers.

'What's that?' asked Madog and all three men walked over to a framed document fixed to a wall. For a few seconds all read in silence before Madog answered his own question, 'It's the town charter,' he said eventually, 'setting out the legality of Caernarfon as a legal entity under the direct protection of the King. Under this document the occupants of Caernarfon are appointed burghers of the town and suffer fiefdom to no man other than Longshanks.' He turned to face his comrades. 'You know what that means?' he asked. 'It means that every serf who lives outside these city walls are beholden to those who dwell within and as the town's population are made up entirely of English, that means Edward Longshanks, with a single signature has created an entire subclass of citizen based on nationality. The Welsh people who have farmed these lands for generations became lower in class than the camp followers who populated the town when Edward first invaded.'

'It makes me sick to my stomach,' said Tarian. 'Shall I have it removed?'

Madog turned to face the soldier sat tending his wounds.

'Soldier,' he said, 'the night is indeed cold and I feel you would benefit from a fire.'

'Indeed, my lord.,' said the soldier, 'but anything worth burning has either already been fired or is wet from the rain.'

'On the contrary,' said Madog, 'look around you for there is fuel enough for the longest night.'

'You would have me burn the parchments, my lord?'

'They are now of a different time and are no use to me.' He reached up and tore the framed charter from the wall. 'Start with this,' he said throwing the document across the room, 'and then use whatever you need to secure the comfort of your men. Burn the scrolls, soldier, burn them all.'

Chapter Twenty

The Roman fort of Segontium

Less than a mile away, on a hill above the castle, two men crept through a deserted settlement of wooden houses. Most of the thatched roofs were missing, and fires still smouldered amongst the charred timber ruins. The rain had abated and the clouds broken enough to see the occasional light of a full moon.

'It would seem Madog's men were diligent in their task,' whispered Derwyn, 'the settlement is all but destroyed.'

'No doubt one of many,' said Garyn, 'and though sad to see, such devastation is the tragic side effect of war. Walls must fall before they can be rebuilt.'

'The fort must be somewhere near,' said Derwyn, climbing over a fence, 'I'm sure I just heard a marching legion.'

'Keep such nonsense to yourself, Derwyn, I hold no faith in such things. Just keep walking for I see ruins in the distance.'

Within minutes they passed the first of a series of small walls, each covered with the undergrowth of years but following a distinct pattern of straight lines.

'This must be it,' said Derwyn, 'which way lies north?'

Garyn stared at the sky for a few moments, waiting for the clouds to pass.

'There,' he said eventually, pointing to a far corner. The two men walked over to the taller walls and could see the remains of a more recent building standing higher than their shoulders.

'This must be the old church,' said Derwyn, 'so we are in the right place.'

'The mason said the tomb was before the altar,' said Garyn, 'so if the entrance is here, that means the altar would be at the far end.' They walked across the weed strewn slabs until they reached the end of the paved walkway that once formed the aisle. 'This is it,' said Garyn, 'it should be here somewhere. Look for a slab engraved with an eagle.'

Both men dropped to their knees and drew their daggers to scrape away the grass and weeds. For an age they worked diligently, being soaked by the occasional shower of rain and soon Derwyn heard Garyn's voice across the roofless ruin.

'Derwyn, come here.'

The man crouched and ran the several paces between them. Garyn was kneeling upright and before him was a cleared piece of grass revealing a stone slab.

'Is this it?' asked Derwyn. As he spoke, a cloud passed from before the moon and in the light, he could see the engraved image of an eagle with outspread wings grasping a thunderbolt. Garyn smiled up at his friend.

'I think it is,' he said, 'help me remove the spoil from around the edges.'

The two men scraped away the dirt in the joints. The attention it had received from the mason a few years earlier meant it came away easily and soon there was a clear gap around edge. Garyn inserted his dagger and slowly prized up one side.

'Derwyn,' he said, 'use your knife to aid me, I fear mine may break.'

The two men worked together and moments later the edge of the small slab raised just enough for Derwyn to get his fingers underneath. He tilted the slab upward and let it drop to the grass beyond, revealing a dark foreboding hole leading down into the bowels of the earth. Derwyn made the sign of the cross upon his chest.

'I suppose we are going down there,' he said, 'into a dead man's tomb.'

'You stay here if you like,' said Garyn, undoing his sword belt, 'I will descend alone. Just be ready to pull me out when I call.'

Derwyn nodded and retrieved some tinder he had kept dry beneath his gambeson.

'Here,' he said, 'when you are within, strike a flame to light your way.'

Garyn took the tinder and dangled his feet over the edge.

'I hope this is indeed a tomb and not a well,' said Derwyn.

Garyn grimaced at the thought.

'Only one way to find out,' he said and lowered himself over the edge. For a few seconds he hung there but after a deep breath, he let go and dropped into the space below.

'Garyn,' whispered Derwyn, 'are you alright?'

'I'm fine,' came the hollow reply, 'the floor was just below my feet.'

'Hurry up and find the sword,' said Derwyn, 'I'm sure I can hear the spirits of Romans all around me.'

Down in the tomb Garyn smiled at the superstition of his friend but took out his flint and set about striking a light. Moments later he had a flame and quickly retrieved a candle from his tunic. When it was fully alight, he stood up and held it high to see around the tomb.

The tomb was small and, in the centre, lay a stone sarcophagus. The casket was open and the lid lay discarded on the floor alongside it. Garyn took a deep breath and walked over to peer inside. The remains of a body lay within, the corpse secure within a richly decorated shroud bearing the emblem of a Roman eagle. For a moment Garyn stared at the body, his heart racing and though he was tempted to open the shroud, he could not bring himself to desecrate the man's last veil of rest. He stepped back from the casket and held the candle high to find the sword but the walls were bare, the artefact was nowhere to be seen.

Garyn sat back against the wall and recalled the story Philippe had retold.

'The sword was hanging above Macsen's head,' he had said but Garyn had examined the ceiling and there was no sign of any weapon or indeed fastenings from where it once hung. His heart sunk as he realised the tale must have been false and his journey had been in vain.

'Garyn,' hissed Derwyn from above, 'do you have the sword?'

'I do not,' said Garyn, 'and I fear it has been taken.'

'By whom?' asked Derwyn.

'Either the mason or someone else has been here since,' answered Garyn.

Silence fell until Derwyn's voice whispered menacingly from above again.

'Is the corpse still there?'

'It is.'

'Then I suggest you get out as quickly as you can.'

'Why?' asked Garyn. 'The dead can't hurt me.'

'I'm not so sure,' said Derwyn, 'his ghost could be standing in a darkened corner as we speak, wielding his sword in vengeance.'

Garyn smiled at his friend's vivid imagination.

'I think not,' said Garyn.

'You don't know that,' said Derwyn, 'this world is full of strange things. He may have heard you coming and reached for his sword to defend his resting place.'

Garyn laughed again.

'Even if he did,' he answered, looking up at the darkened ceiling, 'he would never have reached it from his coffin...' the sentence lay unfinished as Garyn's eyes widened and his mouth opened in realisation.

'Of course,' he gasped, 'the old man never said the sword was on the ceiling only that it lay above Macsen.' He jumped up and walked over to the discarded sarcophagus lid.

'Come on,' he grunted to himself, 'be there, I pray.'

With a groan of effort he overturned the lid exposing the underside. Garyn reached for the candle and breathed a sigh of relief as he saw a linen wrapped bundle secured to metal rings in the stone surface. The sword had been fastened to the inside of the sarcophagus lid and had been overlooked by whoever had robbed the tomb.

'Derwyn, you beauty,' he shouted.

'What have I done?' came the reply from above.

'You told me where lay the sword.'

'I did?' asked Derwyn in confusion.

'You did, and our quest has not been in vain. Pass down my blade.'

Garyn's sword belt thudded to the tomb floor and Garyn removed his weapon from the sheath before striking at the chains holding the package to the stone lid. Within seconds they fell apart and Garyn picked up the bundle.

'Help me up,' he said and reached up to grasp Derwyn's outstretched arm. Minutes later both men walked quickly back to the place they had left the horses.

'Will you not open it?' asked Derwyn. 'It may not be that which we seek.'

'It has to be,' said Garyn, 'and besides, there was nothing else there. If this is not the sword then our quest is over.'

'At least put my mind out of its misery,' said Derwyn, 'I would see this famed sword that holds a country's liberty to ransom.'

'Not here, Derwyn, as we know the land is alive with men eager to use their sword arm. We have come too far to have it snatched away this late in the game so when we are assured of safety, then and only then will we gaze upon what we have obtained.'

An hour later, both men were secreted deep in a nearby forest and had erected a tent against the changeable weather. Derwyn lit a candle and at last, they both gazed at the linen package between them.

'Here goes,' said Garyn and gently cut away the bind-ings with his knife. Within seconds, the rotting fabric fell away and Garyn gently pulled it back to reveal the prize within. Both men stared in silence until finally, Derwyn spoke.

'Is that it?' he asked in disgust.

Garyn stared at the weapon before him. It was indeed a sword but the condition left a lot to be desired. The handle had come away from the tang and the blade was thick with rust.

'What did you expect?' asked Garyn, barely hiding his own disappointment.

'I expected a sword of an emperor,' spat Derwyn, 'perhaps a golden blade and a jewel encrusted handle. Surely an emperor would demand such things for his funeral?'

'I expect there were jewels and gold aplenty in the tomb,' said Garyn, 'but don't forget, the mason got there first. Macsen was reputed to be a fearful fighter as well as an emperor and no doubt this sword was his favoured weapon. It has lain in the tomb for almost a thousand years and time has taken its toll.'

'Still,' said Derwyn, 'how are we supposed to unite a nation behind a lump of rust?'

'It is the idea behind the sword, not the blade itself,' said Garyn, 'but I understand your worry. Many men wait to see the sword revealed before committing to the cause so perhaps this may not be the right path.'

'What do you mean?'

'The people may lose heart if they saw the sword like this, but only we know the poor condition and I'm sure a good sword smith can get it back to its former glory.

Whatever we present to Madog will be welcomed as the true Macsen Sword and the people can embrace the tale as true.'

Derwyn looked at his comrade in the gloom.

'You would present a false sword?'

'No, not a false sword but a renewed one. We could have the blade melted down and re-forged but add in anything extra to reform it to its former glory. The original will still be there but in a form that the people expect.'

'What about the handle?'

Garyn picked away at the splintered wood.

'There seems to be some left of a hard nature. A new handle can be easily carved and what is left of this could be cut away and sunk in as an inlay. At least that way the spirit of Macsen is retained and the uprising gets its focal point.'

'We could add some jewels,' said Derwyn.

'I think you are now pushing the idea too far,' said Garyn. 'I am happy to refresh the memory of Macsen but draw back from making it a tale of frivolity.'

'A point well made,' said Derwyn, 'and I agree. If we can find a sword smith, the blade can be renewed in a matter of days. By then, Madog will either have taken Caernarfon and the presentation will be in a timely manner or he will have failed and the sword will be of little consequence.'

'Then it is agreed,' said Garyn. 'On the morrow we will ride south and find a village with a sword smith. When the task is done, we will return and find a way to reach Madog without having our necks stretched. Now we should get some sleep, this forest is dense enough to keep us safe and I expect no trouble to come this way.'

'I will check the horses,' said Derwyn, 'and then we can rest.' He got to his feet and crouched as he walked to the tent flaps but as he stepped outside, he gave a cry of pain as a spear head burst through his spine and he fell back into the tent, shaking uncontrollably as his dying body lost control of his functions.

'Derwyn,' shouted Garyn and reached over to his friend but it was too late, Derwyn was dead. Garyn reached for his sword and crouched low in the tent, not sure what to do. Before he could decide a voice called out.

'Don't be stupid, Welshman,' said the voice, 'you are surrounded by armed men. Throw out your sword and surrender yourself.'

'Never,' snarled Garyn looking around for an escape route, 'I would die first.'

'That may well be necessary,' said the voice, 'but I sincerely hope not. I have a proposition for you.'

'What trickery is this?' asked Garyn. 'You just want me out there without contest.'

'We can kill you where you stand,' said the voice, 'or indeed, fire the tent and listen to you burn but that is not what I want. Come out of your own free will and you have my word, no harm will befall you. Indeed, once you have heard my proposition, if you do not agree then you are free to leave unharmed, complete with that fascinating trinket you found in the tomb of Macsen.'

'You know about that?' asked Garyn.

'We heard every word,' said the voice, 'but I digress, the offer is an honourable one and if you decline, you are free to leave.'

Garyn paused but knew he was trapped. There was nothing he could do. He glanced down at the corpse of Derwyn and whispered something to him.

'I'm sorry, friend but I swear you will be avenged.'

He walked toward the tent flap and called outside.

'So be it, stranger,' he said, 'hold your spears, I am coming out.' He threw his sword before him and ducked under the opening flap. No sooner had he stood up than a man grabbed him from behind and he felt a blade against his throat. Garyn realised there were only two men there but he was already disadvantaged and waited for the slice that would end his life.

'Well, well,' said the same voice from the darkness, 'we meet again, Garyn ap Thomas, it has been a long time.' A man stepped out of the shadows and Garyn squinted in the moonlight, his memory struggling to recall the face.

'I know you,' he said at last, 'you are the English knight who sent me to the stocks all those years ago, a deed ultimately responsible for leading me into the life of an outlaw.'

'Indeed I am,' said the man, 'and in case your memory fails you, let me re-introduce myself. My name is Gerald of Essex and I am now the Sheriff of Brycheniog, amongst other things.' His smile faded and he stepped closer to Garyn, his voice lowering menacingly. 'Our mutual friend sends his regards.'

Garyn stared with hatred at the man who had played a large part in ruining his family.

'If you speak of the abbot, I had hoped he was rotting in hell by now.'

'Indeed it is he of whom I speak,' said Gerald, 'and truth be told, his health is indeed a worry, however, his heart still beats, his wealth is greater than ever and men still suffer from his, shall we say, unique way of doing business.'

'You waste your words on me,' said Garyn, 'for I think no more of him. I hope he dies screaming in pain as soon as possible.'

'I think you may retract that hope,' said Gerald, 'for I have a message from him, especially for you.'

'Why would I want to hear anything he has to say unless it is a confession returning my lands to me?'

'Alas, it is not that,' said Gerald with a sickly smile, 'it is however something you hold just as dear to your heart.'

'Where is the message?' asked Garyn.

'I burned it,' said Gerald, 'for I couldn't risk being caught with such a document. However, I took the liberty of reading the contents. So, do you want to hear it?'

'Spit it out, Gerald,' said Garyn, 'though I imagine nothing that snake has to say interests me.'

'Perhaps not, but what if I was to say a second person also sent their regards, someone called Elspeth Fletcher?'

Garyn stopped struggling and stared at the English knight in astonishment.

'Release him,' said Gerald and the pressure around Garyn's throat eased. Garyn shook himself free and stood before the knight.

'I knew a girl once with that name,' said Garyn, 'what of her?'

'Don't play games with me, Garyn,' said Gerald, 'I know you were both wed and if you hadn't run from the stocks would probably be still with her.'

'I ran to protect her,' snarled Garyn. 'Your henchmen had targeted me for murder and if I had resisted, she and her family would have joined me on the gallows.'

'An interesting perspective,' said Gerald, 'but let's move on. The fact is that Father Williams has incarcerated Elspeth Williams and her son in a cell of Brecon castle. Fret not, she is well cared for but her fate is in your hands.'

'Why has he imprisoned her?' asked Garyn. 'What has she done?'

'Absolutely nothing,' said Gerald, 'in fact after you left, she became a perfect citizen. Oh she re-married and had a son but as far as discretions are concerned, she has lived a quiet life.'

'You are making no sense,' said Garyn, 'get to the point.'

'It is really very simple, Garyn. Father Williams yearns to see your ugly face once more. I'm sure you won't mind me being blunt for it is obvious he wants to kill you but that is not my concern, my role is to return you to him before he dies.'

'And why would I do that?'

'Because if you don't, Elspeth Fletcher will be strangled on the day of the abbot's death.'

Garyn stared at the knight, his mind racing. He had once loved Elspeth with all his heart but that had been a lifetime ago.

'And if I return?'

'She and her son will be released immediately.'

Garyn thought furiously. His conscience demanded he return at once and free the woman he once loved but he also knew that with the Liberty Sword, the very freedom of Wales could lay in his hands.

'Your hesitation is interesting,' said Gerald, 'but unfortunately time is of the essence and I have to rush you.'

'My life has not been there for many years,' said Garyn, 'and I have not set eyes on my birth town since the day I left. My path lies elsewhere and if you kill me here, then so be it but I will not give the abbot the satisfaction of seeing me die.'

'You would abandon the woman?'

'I don't believe she has been imprisoned,' said Garyn, 'you could be lying.'

'Indeed I could,' said Gerald, 'but let me make this easier for you. After you left, Elspeth Fletcher re-married a barrel maker from the village. He was not much of a catch and indeed, a bit of a drunkard but your ex-wife accepted his proposal with almost indecent urgency and they have been married ever since.'

'Elspeth was a vision of beauty,' said Garyn, 'and of strong character. She could have had any man and would only accept the best.'

'Under normal circumstances, perhaps,' said Gerald, 'and indeed there were better men available,' he paused before delivering the line he knew would entrap Garyn as sure as a fish on a hook, 'but the thing is, Garyn ap Thomas, not many men would wed a woman already pregnant with another man's son.'

Garyn stared at the English knight for an age as the realisation sunk in. The man in front of him had sent him to the stocks for publicly challenging his authority. That in itself would not have been too bad, but when Garyn found out he was to have been murdered in the stocks at the behest of the abbot, he had no choice but to escape and face life as an outlaw. Elspeth's father had begged him to never return for if the girl had been labelled as an accomplice, she could have lost her life in his place. Garyn had agreed to run and never return even though his heart would surely break but if he had even suspected Elspeth was with child, he would have stayed and taken his chances.

'You are lying,' he said, 'Elspeth was not carrying a baby.'

'I can assure you she was,' said Gerald, 'and subsequently gave birth to a strong boy child she called Thomas.'

'That was my father's name,' said Garyn quietly.

'I didn't know that,' said Gerald. 'Of course, the boy has since grown up and is now a young man of fourteen years, however, it is unlikely he will see his fifteenth as he is also imprisoned along with the woman and the same fate hangs over him. If you refuse to return and the abbot dies, you will have the death of your son on your hands. So, are you coming with me or not?'

'You know, I will,' said Garyn eventually, 'but first I will bury my comrade.'

'An hour or so I can spare,' said Gerald, 'but we will be gone by the morning sun. Make sure you are ready.'

—

Two hours later, Garyn placed the last of the river stones over the body of his friend and drove Derwyn's sword into the ground at one end, forming a makeshift cross.

'Sleep well, my friend,' he said, 'and I swear on your grave this day will be avenged.'

'Are you ready?' called Gerald from the horses.

'I'm ready,' said Garyn turning away from the grave. He mounted his horse and rode alongside Gerald who seemed to be waiting for something.

'What?' asked Garyn.

'The Sword of Macsen,' said Gerald, 'I will take it from here.'

Garyn paused but realised he had no option. He passed over the package and watched as Gerald strapped it to his rolled blanket before him.

'Right,' said Gerald, 'let's get going,' and all three men spurred their horses southward, Garyn ap Thomas, Gerald of Essex and Hywel ap Rhys, Liegeman of the Sheriff of Builth.

Chapter Twenty-one

Caernarfon Town

The Welsh siege army stood in silence before the walls of Caernarfon castle. Behind them, the town lay in ruins as did the docks and hardly any buildings were left standing within the town perimeter. Prisoners were hard at work, piling their dead into funerary pyres, just as keen as their captors to avoid the disease that such devastation brought.

The Welsh lines lay hundreds deep and though they were narrow in width, there was no need for a wider front as the target was narrow before them. The imposing north wall loomed high but right in the middle, the unfinished section was protected by no more than a wooden palisade where the building work had come to a halt years earlier.

All along the walls, defenders watched the army below, nervously awaiting the assault. The English were heavily outnumbered and whilst this would not normally have been a problem when defending a castle such as this, the unfinished walls meant the outcome was uncertain. Privately many had shared the possibility that surrender was the better option but the Castellan was away and his second in command was a stubborn man who still felt they could withstand the Welsh attack.

'Did you send them terms of surrender?' asked Madog.

'I did,' answered Geraint, 'and they were returned with scorn heaped upon us.'

Madog shook his head.

'Why are such decisions put in the hands of ignorant men,' he asked. 'The Castellan has seen what our engines did to the city walls, how can he expect a mere wooden barricade to withstand a similar barrage?'

'Apparently the Castellan is not present and the decision lays with a young knight desperate for honour.'

'Then it is a worse situation than I envisaged. Men will die needlessly on both sides over the next few hours, a situation that could easily have been avoided.'

'Such are the ways of war,' said Geraint.

Madog grunted and walked over to the engineer in charge of his mangonels.

'Magister, are you ready?'

'We are, my lord,' he answered, 'the palisade will be removed from your path before midday.'

'Then do what you have to do,' said Madog and walked away to join Geraint.

'Mangonels ready,' shouted the magister.

'Ready,' answered the teams of operators.

'You know what you have to do,' shouted the magister. 'I want that wall blasted into kindling within hours. Check your aim and target the timber. Upon my command, steady… Release.'

The machines bucked from the sudden released energy and six boulders flew the short distance to the timber palisade. Five of the rocks hit true and wood flew everywhere as the planks shattered under the impact. Defenders unlucky enough to be in the line of fire fell to the courtyard below while their comrades ran for cover, there was little they could do to defend the wooden walls.

'This will take no time at all,' said Madog as the second volley flew through the air, 'ready the men, Geraint, I feel their skills will be needed sooner than we thought.' Within the hour, the palisade was levelled to the ground and through the breach, Madog could see enemy lines waiting for them.

'More than I expected,' said Geraint, 'it would seem your spy's information was incorrect.'

'A patrol arrived two days ago,' said Madog, 'and boosted the garrison by a hundred but it matters not, our numbers are overwhelming.'

'And you decided not to share this with us?'

'There was little need, for our numbers are still superior. Anyway, the news could have sent pangs of fear through our ranks, a situation I could not countenance on the eve of battle.'

Geraint nodded silently. The news was frustrating but he had to acknowledge the decision was one of a leader. The boy was coming of age.

'Then let's get this done,' said Geraint.

Madog turned to the engineer.

'Magister, change the load, I want fire pots rained upon the buildings inside. Raise your aim and provide smoke to cover our approach. I want any archers stationed behind the arrow loops to be denied clear fields of fire.'

'Yes, my lord,' shouted the engineer and within minutes, clay pots of burning oil smashed against the castle walls, spreading black acrid smoke around the courtyard.

'Geraint,' called Madog, 'bring the archers forward.'

A hundred archers armed with longbows stepped up to pre-marked positions and loaded their strings with weighted arrows.

'I want fifty arrows from each man,' shouted Madog to Geraint above the sound of the straining mangonels, 'target the waiting English lines. As we advance, change your aim to the defenders on the walls. The chance of a kill may be slight but at least we can keep their heads down while we advance.'

Geraint shouted the commands to the archers and within seconds, the air was full of arrows as volley after volley flew through the breach toward the defending lines.

'Tarian,' shouted Madog, 'you will lead the cavalry. As soon as the gate is taken, lead them in and mop up any continuing skirmishes.'

'My lord, if I am to lead the cavalry, who is to head the assault through the palisade?'

'I will take that role,' said Madog drawing his sword. 'I have led from the back for long enough, today is the day I earn my claim.'

'But, my lord…'

'Hold your words, Tarian, my mind is set.' He turned to Geraint. 'Ready to take a castle, friend?' he shouted.

'That I am, my lord,' shouted Geraint.

'Then let's show the English what we are made of.' Madog turned to face his army and raised his sword in the air.

'Men of Wales,' he roared, 'for country and freedom, *advaaance.*'

Hundreds of men armed with pikes, swords and lances marched forward beneath the umbrella of arrows. At their head, Madog strode with sword drawn and shield wielded in the defensive position. As they came within range of the defenders on the walls, crossbow bolts flew toward them, embedding themselves deep into the soil or the shields of the advancing army. Some got through and though men fell screaming to the floor, their comrades stepped over them knowing full well that success relied on maintaining the impetus of any assault.

Madog flinched as a crossbow bolt pierced his shield and turned to shout toward Geraint.

'The pace is too slow,' he shouted, 'they will pick us off like fish in a barrel. Increase the pace.'

'*Trumpeter, sound the charge,*' roared Geraint and as the sounds of a horn bounced off the castle walls, the Welsh attackers broke into a run, their guttural screams of aggression striking fear into the defenders.

Missiles of all sorts rained down upon the men as they reached the breach, ranging from boulders to boiling water. Lines of crossbow men fired as quickly as they could into the throng and for a while, every bolt found a target. Spears hurled from the towers above added to the carnage but despite the heavy losses, the attackers' numbers were too great and the first lines of Welshmen cleared the breach.

Those in front immediately knelt and took shelter beneath their shields as their comrades arrived, knowing it would be useless attacking a formed defensive line individually. Madog was amongst them and as they waited, he turned to see Geraint taking cover behind some fallen masonry.

'Geraint,' he screamed, 'take your men up onto the battlements and deal with the crossbows, they are costing us heavy casualties. You men,' continued Madog, shouting toward a unit of infantry freshly through the gap, 'make the gates your target, I want them open as soon as possible.'

Both detachments went their separate ways and Madog looked around to see his numbers vastly increased.

'My lord, the English advance,' shouted a voice.

'We cannot wait any more,' roared Madog, 'or we will be overrun. Men of Wales, follow me.' He stood upright and wielding his shield before him, charged to engage the oncoming defenders.

'What are you waiting for?' screamed Geraint from above, 'your prince is isolated.'

Seconds later the remaining men raced after Madog and both lines clashed in a maelstrom of blood and pain. The English lines held momentarily but within seconds the clash had broken into hundreds of individual battles, man against man in a fight to the death. Bodies fell everywhere as Welsh and English alike were cut apart by swords or impaled on the end of a lance. Pikes cleaved open skulls and faces were smashed in by heavy boots as the fallen were dealt with ruthlessly. Archers from both sides sought their targets but the moving sea of people offered little chance of accuracy.

Up on the battlements, Geraint's men faced the English archers who had cost the attackers so many lives but though their bolts continued to wreak havoc amongst the Welsh, the time needed to reload the crossbows meant Geraint's men were soon amongst them and the threat was ruthlessly wiped out with no quarter considered.

Down below, the smoke from the burning oil stung the eyes of everyone and control was difficult to maintain especially with the Welsh army who were little more than civilians with a few weeks' training.

Despite their smaller numbers the English fought well and Welshmen fell in their dozens at the hands of the trained soldiers. Geraint looked down in horror and realised the day did not go well. He could not see Madog and knew if the Prince had fallen, the army would lack leadership and the battle could be lost. Geraint considered returning to the courtyard but before he had the chance to make any decisions, a cheer echoed around the castle and he heard the sound of horses galloping across the secured drawbridge.

Tarian led his command under the captured portcullis, and the cavalry jumped any dead defenders littering the way as they raced toward the fight raging in the upper ward. Within moments the battle turned and the defenders ran to seek whatever cover they could for simple foot soldiers were no match against cavalry.

Tarian dismounted and stormed through the fight, hacking at any defenders with his sword and using his shield to knock others to the floor.

'Where's the Prince?' he roared. 'Has anyone seen Madog?'

'He is there, my lord,' came the reply, and Tarian could see the young man locked in fierce combat with a huge man clad in full chainmail armour and a tabard emblazoned with the emblem of Edward.

The English knight swung his sword furiously, deflecting any counter with the ease of a man well-practised and the Prince was being forced backward. Tarian could see that Madog was being overwhelmed by the strength and expertise of the larger man, and it was obvious he would soon be overcome.

'Who is that man?' roared Tarian.

'He is Stephan du Clerk,' came an answer, 'Knight of Edward and commander of this castle in the absence of the Castellan.'

'Madog can't beat a seasoned knight,' shouted Tarian, 'he is too inexperienced.' With a terrifying roar, he tried to fight his way to the Prince but found his path blocked by defenders and burning carts. At risk of losing his own life, Tarian fought like a devil, smiting anyone in his path, friend or foe, but his progress was slow and by the time he cleared the way, both men had disappeared. Madog was on his own.

Smoke bellowed everywhere within the castle walls and men fought blindly, desperate to cling onto their lives but finally the defenders realised the day was lost and a horn echoed around the inner ward.

The English soldiers backed off, gasping in exhaustion as they withdrew to safety. Those who could, reformed into a small but tightly defended position against a wall, their weapons levelled toward the Welsh. The attackers were no less tired and when they realised the English were giving ground, they reformed into lines, facing their opponents across the courtyard.

'What are we waiting for?' screamed a voice. 'Their race is run, kill them all, every last one.'

'Hold your arms,' roared Tarian, 'that horn was their signal to withdraw. We will give them opportunity to surrender.' Geraint appeared at the side of Tarian, his face blackened from the smoke and his side bleeding from a glancing blow from a crossbow bolt.

'What do you think?' asked Geraint. 'Their numbers are decimated and one more assault will see them crushed.'

'The men smell victory,' said Tarian, 'but the battle is won, I see no need for further bloodshed.'

Across the courtyard, over thirty defenders stared defiantly over a wall of shields. Tarian could see their exhausted faces, each staring back at him with hatred, many smeared with blood from the brutal battle.

'My lord, the men demand we end this once and for all,' said a sergeant at arms, 'too many of us have died to let even one of them live.'

'I know the feeling of the men,' said Tarian, 'but there is nothing to be gained from their deaths.'

'Finish them,' screamed a voice from the ranks, 'kill the English scum.'

'Hold your tongues,' roared Tarian, 'this is a matter of honour.'

'You are not our leader old man,' came the answer. 'Let Madog decide.'

'Where is he?' asked Geraint quietly.

'I fear he has fallen,' said Tarian, 'the last I saw he was being bettered by an armoured knight. There is no way he could have prevailed.'

'You underestimate him,' said Geraint, 'I have trained with him for years and the man is a terrier when cornered. Don't write him off until you see his corpse.'

All around the castle the individual battles had ended and shattered men stared at each other across the blood-stained dirt.

'Well,' shouted the voice, 'where is our leader?'

All around them the men started chanting and within seconds, the chant became a roar.

'Madog, Madog, Madog...'

Geraint turned to Tarian.

'We should go and find him, whatever his fate.'

'There is no need,' said Tarian quietly, 'my fears were unfounded. It appears our young prince is more than a match for even the best Edward can send.' He looked over Geraint's shoulder and his comrade turned to see Madog walking slowly through the smoke toward them. His left arm held across his chest, bleeding from an open wound while his other dragged his sword behind him. His helm was gone and Geraint could see the Prince was on the verge of collapse.

'Madog,' gasped Geraint quietly and stepped forward to help but Tarian grabbed his shoulder.

'Leave him,' he said, 'the next few moments could be the making of the man.'

Slowly the cheering subsided and silence fell as the Prince walked into the centre of the ward, passing his two friends without as much as eye contact. Finally he stood before his fellow men. He looked around slowly, making eye contact with as many as he could before turning to face the remnants of the English force.

'What would you have us do, my lord?' asked the sergeant who moments earlier had demanded their deaths.

Madog limped forward and stood alone before the defending shield wall, exposed within easy reach of any well-aimed English spear.

'Men of England,' he said eventually, 'you have fought well but your day is done. Lay down your arms and your lives will be granted. Resist further and I will not be able to control those who want you dead. Take heart in your defence, for it was indeed admirable in the face of a superior army, but let it end now. Surrender your weapons.'

'How do we know you tell the truth, Welshman?' shouted a man from behind a shield.

'You have my word,' said Madog, 'and my word is my bond.'

'And who's word is so strong that it can hold the sword arm of so many?'

'My name is Madog,' came the reply, 'Madog ap Llewellyn,' he paused and glanced back at his men before adding, 'and I am the Prince of Wales.'

The English soldier stared at the young man but moments later, stepped slowly forward through the shield wall and drew his sword. He looked around at his scared and exhausted comrades before turning the blade around and offering it to Madog, hilt first.

'Our fight is done, Prince,' he said eventually, 'the castle is yours.'

As the rest of the defenders' weapons were thrown forward to land at Madog's feet, the Welsh army erupted into celebration. The walls of Caernarfon castle echoed with the sounds of cheering and Tarian had to shout into Geraint's ear to make himself heard.

'We did it, Geraint,' he shouted, 'we actually took a castle in Edward's ring of steel.'

'We achieved more than that, Tarian,' answered Geraint. 'Today we helped turn a young man into a prince and if God is on our side, one day he will make a fine king.'

Chapter Twenty-two

Brycheniog

For three days Garyn and his captors rode hard and finally arrived at Brecon castle late at night. As they rode through the gates, a servant ran to take his master's horse and Gerald dismounted to greet the castle steward. For several minutes the two men talked quietly until finally Gerald returned across the courtyard.

'Is there a problem?' asked Hywel, when the Englishman returned.

'Not so much a problem,' said Gerald, 'though there have been unexpected developments.'

'What developments?' asked Hywel. 'I hope the abbot is not trying to recant our agreement, I have his signature on a legal document.'

'Fret not about the reward, Hywel,' said Gerald, 'your money is safe.'

'Is my son harmed?' said Garyn quietly. 'For if he is, I swear I will take my revenge on every soul within this castle.'

'Brave yet meaningless words,' said Gerald, 'and I am too tired to engage in verbal jousting. The boy is alive but for how long, I can't say.'

'Why not? Surely my return is the price for his and his mother's freedom?'

249

'That was my understanding,' said Gerald, 'but it all depended on the health of the abbot. If he lived, they were to be set free upon your return. If he died, or if you did not return, then their lives were forfeit.'

'So is he dead or not?' asked Garyn.

'He is neither dead nor alive,' said Gerald, 'it would seem he is between both worlds and has been for some time.'

'What do you mean?'

'He lies unconscious in a permanent sleep. His skin burns to the touch and though he has been well bled, the apothecary says he could fall either side. Only time will tell.'

'I don't see why you can't just let us all go,' said Garyn, 'or at least the woman and her son. What gain is there to be had by carrying out this unjust act?'

'Every gain,' said Gerald, 'you see, a castle is a very busy place and gossip flies faster than an arrow in such a place. Despite our best intentions to keep certain things confidential, it seems walls have ears and soon everyone knows everyone else's business.'

'Why is that relevant?'

'Because when men such as I hold positions of power, they oft have to make threats of justice and should any indiscretion be carried out then it is essential the threat is taken to its conclusion. What message would it send my people if I was to just cancel the proclamation by the abbot? It would surely undermine my authority and the peasants would expect such mercies all the time. No, I'm sorry but the deal stays. All you can do is hope he regains consciousness and thereby enables their release.'

'But that could take weeks.'

'It could, and during that time you will be held as the outlaw you are. I will tell you now, Garyn ap Thomas, your stay will not be pleasant and the longer the abbot clings to life, the more you will pray for your own death.'

'Your heart is as black as his,' said Garyn.

'A matter of perspective,' said the knight and turned to two nearby guards.

'Seize him,' he said, 'and throw him into the dungeon.' He turned and stared up at Garyn with a sickly smile before adding, 'and there's no need to be gentle.'

The two soldiers pulled Garyn from his horse and laid into him with fists and boots. Gerald and Hywel looked on in silence before Gerald called a halt.

'Enough,' he said. 'Take him away and serve him not with bread or water until tomorrow night.' He knelt down beside Garyn's body and whispered into his ear. 'You belong to me now, Welshman, welcome home.'

—

As the soldiers dragged Garyn's beaten body away, Gerald turned to Hywel.

'You have served us well,' he said, 'and have earned your reward. Will you stay the night and rest from the quest?'

'With respect, my lord, I would be gone as soon as possible. There is a tavern on the road back and I will take my rest there so if it is all right with you, I will just take what's owed.'

'Remind me of the amount,' said Gerald.

'Three hundred gold coins,' said Hywel.

'And you make no claim on the Roman sword?'

'I do not, for though it seems it kindles a fire within your breast, I have no interest in such baubles or indeed the legends that raise it above its station.'

'Such legends can conquer kingdoms,' said Gerald.

'Perhaps so, but this one is a mere tale for the bedsides of children.'

'So be it,' said Gerald and summoned the steward.

'Go to my treasury and secure three hundred gold coins. Place them in a satchel and return them to this man before he leaves.'

'Yes, my lord,' said the steward and walked away toward one of the towers.

'I will not see you again,' said Gerald, 'and trust you will keep our dealings these past few weeks amongst ourselves.'

'I will,' said Hywel, 'for the whole thing leaves a sour taste in my mouth.'

'Then be gone, Hywel of Builth,' said Gerald, 'and spend my coins wisely.'

'I will,' said Hywel and watched as the knight disappeared into the shadows.

–

Half an hour later, Hywel rode back through the gates and headed north toward his hometown. Though it would be too far to travel in one night he knew he could rest at the Black Boar tavern on the way. He rode for an hour through the darkness and was about to cross a bridge when a man called out in the dark.

'Hold there, traveller,' said the voice, 'we would know your name and your business.'

Hywel's hand sought his sword hilt, as he strained to see who addressed him.

'My name is Hywel of Builth,' he said, 'and if you are brigands, I can assure you that by robbing me you will bring down the wrath of the Sheriff himself upon your heads. There will be no hiding place.'

'We are not brigands,' said the voice, 'on the contrary, we serve Edward.'

Hywel breathed a sigh of relief.

'Then we are comrades in arms,' he said. 'Who is your liege?'

A man stepped into the moonlight and Hywel could see he was dressed in the manner of a paid soldier.

'Our master is familiar to you,' said the soldier, 'and goes by the name of Gerald of Essex.'

Hywel's eyes narrowed.

'I have left his presence not two hours since,' he said. 'Are you on his business?'

'We are,' said the soldier, 'the business of retrieving the gold you stole from him.'

Hywel breathed deeply, knowing he had been tricked.

'I stole nothing,' he growled, 'and any monies on my person were well earned and the subject of a legal document.'

'That may be the case,' sighed the soldier, 'but such things are for my betters to decide. Now, hand over that satchel.'

'Never,' said Hywel drawing his sword, 'I would die first.'

'Your decision,' said the soldier and gave a signal with his hand. Seconds later, two crossbow bolts flew through the darkness and thudded into Hywel's chest. Hywel cried out and fell backward from his horse, smashing his head into the wooden handrail before plummeting to the river below.

'After him,' shouted the soldier, 'and make sure he is dead.'

Four other soldiers clambered down the bank and into the river, each with knife drawn to finish the liegeman off.

'Where is he?' shouted one.

'He must be here somewhere,' came the answer in the darkness.

Up above, the first soldier retrieved the satchel of gold coins and tied the victim's horse to his own. After several minutes his comrades returned.

'Was the deed done?' he asked.

'He was nowhere to be found,' said one of the men, 'but the strikes were good and there was no way he could have survived.'

'I agree,' said the first man, 'but if anyone asks, you found him and slit his throat, agreed?'

'Agreed,' said the men and remounted their horses.

'Let's get back,' said the first soldier, 'for this is indeed a night for foul deeds.' He spurred his horse back the way he had come, closely followed by the other four riders.

–

A hundred yards downstream, Hywel groaned and dragged himself through the mud, gasping with pain as the bolts lodged in his torso ripped against his flesh. He managed to crawl a few yards before finally collapsing once more, knowing full well he was dying.

–

The following morning, the sun had hardly cleared the horizon when a young girl tasked with collecting water for her family came across the body and cried out in fear. John the miller heard his daughter's scream and ran toward her.

'What is it, girl?' he asked.

'Look,' she said, pointing at the body, 'there is a dead man in our field.'

John dropped his tools and ran to kneel beside the body. Carefully he turned it over and was shocked to see the eyes flickering open.

'Child, fetch help,' shouted the miller, 'he is still alive.'

The girl ran back toward a nearby village and John tried to make Hywel as comfortable as possible.

'Hang on stranger,' said John, 'the girl will get help and we can get you to a physician. Perhaps he can help you.'

'Too late,' gasped Hywel, 'I need to tell you something.'

'Save your strength, man,' said John, 'it may make a difference.'

'No,' gasped Hywel, 'I can feel myself going. Listen to me, this is important. I want you to take a message. Will you do that?'

'What sort of message?' asked John.

'It matters not, only that this is my dying wish. Will you honour it?'

John paused before answering.

'Aye I will,' he said, 'tell me the message stranger and I swear it will be delivered.'

As Hywel gasped out the last words of his life, John listened carefully, his eyes widening at the implications. Finally Hywel gasped his last breath and his body slumped in John's arms.

'Father, the men are getting a cart,' came a shout, 'they will be here momentarily.'

'It is too late,' said John standing up. 'He has gone.'

The girl's hand flew to her mouth and stared at the corpse as John walked past her and headed back toward his house. For a few moments he stayed inside before reappearing carrying a saddle and a bag of rations.

'Where are you going?' asked the girl. 'Mother has gone to market.'

'Aye, I am aware of that,' said John, 'but I have an errand to run. Tell your mother I will be back in a few days.'

'But can't you tell her yourself? She will be back before noon.'

'No, child. I have a message to deliver that will not wait.'

Ten minutes later he rode to the gate with nothing more than a waxed cape, a bag of bread, and a sack of oats for the horse.

'Where shall I say you are going?' asked the girl.

'I'm not sure,' said John, 'just tell her I have gone north. More than that, I do not know myself. Fare well, child.' He bent down to kiss her before spurring his horse to gallop over the bridge.

'Fare ye well, father,' said the girl quietly and waved at his retreating back, 'travel safely.'

Chapter Twenty-three

The hills of north Wales

Madog, Tarian and Geraint sat silently astride their horses, their fur-lined cloaks pulled tightly around their necks against the biting autumn winds. Behind them, over five thousand men at arms held their cloaks just as tight, each wondering whether they would be alive by the time night fell.

On the other side of the valley, an army of similar size faced Madog, each just as nervous as the morning mist burned away and they could see the forces before them.

'There he is,' said Madog, 'let's get this done.'

It had been ten days since the capture of Caernarfon and in that time the Welsh had buried their dead, sent the wounded to nearby villages to recover and rebuilt the palisades against any counterattack. What had been unexpected was the increased influx of men from all over north Wales who had flocked to his banner as word of the victory spread.

Eventually his army stood ten thousand strong and whilst half were stationed in and around Caernarfon, the rest were backing him up as he faced down another threat to his claim.

Madog urged his horse forward and both armies walked slowly toward each other, halting when there were only twenty-five paces between them.

'Hwyl, Cynan,' said Madog, 'well met.'

'Madog ap Llewellyn,' said Cynan, 'I have heard a lot about you. It is good to put a face to a name.'

'Your successes precede you,' said Madog, 'and I hear you have laid waste to many English properties, as well as Castell du Bere. An impressive haul.'

'Not as great as Caernarfon,' said Cynan, 'but just as satisfying.'

'Indeed,' said Madog and lifted his gaze to stare toward the army at Cynan's back.

'You field a strong force,' he said, 'and any man would think you are expecting trouble.'

'I always expect trouble,' said Cynan, 'that is why I have lived so long.'

'Enough of the jousting, Cynan,' said Madog, 'why have you brought your army northward into lands under my jurisdiction.'

'I'm sorry,' said Cynan, 'but I was not aware that Gwynedd was now under the control of a minor lord, and one so young at that.'

'You know of my claim, Cynan,' said Madog with an edge in his voice. 'I can prove lineage back to Llewellyn himself and as such, lay claim to his crown.'

'A bold statement,' said Cynan, 'but one which I cannot support.'

'So do you ride here to confront me?' asked Madog. 'Are we to see Welsh slay Welsh this day?'

'I hope it won't come to that,' said Cynan, 'but if that becomes the case, then so be it.'

'We are on the verge of greatness, Cynan,' said Madog, 'and though I know you do indeed lead a formidable army, this is not the time for a challenge. Join with me and between us we can drive the English from these lands. When they are once again free, then we can discuss who it is that rules and who it is that serves.'

'But if we are victorious,' said Cynan, 'the people will remember only one name, yours.' He paused before continuing. 'I am not a stupid man, Madog, and indeed recognise your lineage but this is not a time for the heroics of a young man. A chance to make history lies on the horizon but it will take experience to lead us there. Entrust me with your armies and I will bring you the freedom we all crave. You can live the life of a Prince and hold courts to your heart's content but I will rule this land as Lord Protector on the promise that when I die, my son will become prince.'

'I cannot allow that,' said Madog, 'my lineage is true and I will see it honoured.'

Cynan shook his head.

'You are a stubborn man, Madog, and while we stand here arguing like washer women, Edward gathers his forces along the border and waits for an opportune moment to invade. Cast away your pride and cede control while we still have a chance.'

'I will not,' said Madog, 'and all these men behind you know there is only one true prince.'

'Then prove it,' shouted Cynan, 'present the Sword of Macsen and I will kneel before you and swear my fealty.'

Madog stared at Cynan but did not respond.

'Well?' shouted Cynan. 'Where is the symbol of unity we all crave. Present it here before your fellow countrymen.'

'I can't,' said Madog quietly.

'Sorry,' shouted Cynan, 'I didn't hear that, speak up.'

'I can't present the sword,' said Madog, 'for I do not have it.'

A murmur rippled through both armies.

'I thought as much,' said Cynan quietly, 'and as you cannot provide a reason to join with you, then I guess we are against you.' He turned to leave but Madog called out.

'Wait,' he said, 'you are right.'

Cynan turned to face him.

'What do you mean?' he asked.

'I promised the sword,' said Madog, 'and have failed in that task. That much is true and the dream of Macsen has not been realised. But look behind me, Cynan, look at what was born from that dream. Ten thousand men have left their homes in search of freedom, each willing to lay down their lives in its pursuit. A castle lies in ruins not ten miles from here and English occupiers spur their horses toward the border, fearful for their lives. I may not have the sword once held by Macsen, but we do not need it, it is already here.'

'Where?' shouted Cynan, looking around mockingly. 'I see no Sword of Liberty.'

'Don't you?' asked Madog. 'I do.' He walked over to the front rank of his army and picked out an armoured soldier. 'Give me your sword,' said Madog and the soldier handed over his weapon. Madog turned and walked back a few paces toward Cynan before stopping.

'You wanted a Sword of Liberty, Cynan, well here it is.' He drove the sword into the ground and paused before returning to his lines. This time he picked out a pikeman and relieved him of his weapon.

'This too is the liberty sword,' he shouted, driving the haft of the pike into the earth. He reached back and took a pitchfork from the hands of a dishevelled old man. 'And this,' shouted Madog angrily. 'You want a sign of unity, Cynan, then here they are, ten thousand of them, and I for one would rather fight alongside the poorest man with nought but courage than alongside any man with a bejewelled sword and a false heart.'

For a few moments there was silence and Cynan was about to respond when something happened that stopped him short. Further down Madog's line, a soldier stepped forward and drove his own sword into the ground.

'I have a Liberty Sword,' he shouted.

'As do I,' shouted another soldier stepping forward and copying the actions of his comrade. Within seconds, hundreds of men stepped forward to repeat the deed and those behind the front ranks raised their voices in support.

Geraint held his breath and waited to see how Cynan would react but his heart missed a beat when the unexpected happened, one of Cynan's men stepped from their own lines.

'My heart is no less Welsh than yours,' he shouted, 'and I say we fight together.' He drove his sword into the ground before him. 'This is a Sword of Liberty.'

'As is this,' shouted another as he copied his comrade.

Once again, hundreds of men were caught up in the fervour until finally the noise fell away and Madog faced Cynan once more.

'Well,' said Cynan, 'I'll say this for you, boy, you certainly know how to make a point.' He held out his arm and Madog grasped his forearm firmly.

'So do we have an alliance?' asked Madog.

'I'm still unsure about your claim,' said Cynan, 'but I will not fight against you. Together we will rid these lands of the stain of Longshanks and when that is done, then and only then will we discuss sovereignty. Agreed?'

'Agreed,' said Madog and as they grasped each other's arms in comradeship, the two armies closed in on each other, not as enemies but as comrades.

Geraint and Tarian looked at the thousands of men around them, each of them brothers committed to the cause.

'It is as big an army as I have seen,' said Tarian, 'and I feel that at last we will match anything that Longshanks may throw at us.'

'I agree,' said Geraint, 'the time is upon us, Tarian, let the liberation begin.'

Chapter Twenty-four

Caernarfon Castle

Geraint was sleeping in a cot in one corner of the great hall in Caernarfon castle. The past few days had been momentous but now the real work started as they tried to forge the different factions throughout Wales into a united movement. Cynan had withdrawn his troops southward, but had agreed to meet again with Madog along with all the other lords of Wales at the next full moon to discuss the next steps in the campaign.

The hour was late when he felt a hand on his shoulder shaking him awake.

'My lord, your presence is requested,' said a page.

'Is there a problem?' asked Geraint.

'I know not, my lord, I was just sent to wake you.'

'Where is he?' asked Geraint sitting up and yawning.

'He is in his quarters,' said the Page, 'along with some other men.'

'Tell him I will be there directly,' said Geraint. He walked over to a table and placed his hands in the bowl of water placed there by one of Madog's servants. He splashed cold water on his face before drying off, donning his clothes and fastening his sword belt.

When done he left the hall and crossed the courtyard, now free from corpses and screaming men, though the walls were still blackened from the fires. He entered the tower, climbing the staircase to Madog's quarters where a guard opened the door before him.

'You are expected, my lord,' said the guard as Geraint walked into a room lit by dozens of candles and a roaring fire.

Before him he could see several men, Madog, Tarian and two others whom he had never seen before. One was dressed as a noble while the other was obviously little more than a serf.

'Geraint, thank you for coming,' said Madog, 'we have grave news.'

Geraint accepted the offered tankard of warm ale and looked around in confusion, waiting for someone to explain what was happening.

'Geraint,' said Tarian, 'this man is Meirion ap Rhys and he is a noble from the south. Think of him as my counterpart and it is through him we speak to our fellows and those who would support us.'

'A dangerous role,' said Geraint.

'Yet a fulfilling one,' said Meirion, 'and I have seen acorns of ambition grow into oaks of reality in just a few short months.'

'We live in momentous times,' said Geraint. 'So what's all this about?'

'Geraint,' said Tarian, 'we have news of the where-abouts of the Sword of Macsen.'

'I thought this was a dream put aside,' said Geraint.

'Indeed it was,' said Madog, 'but it now lays in the hands of the English.'

'Does it matter anymore?'

'Perhaps not but you should know that the Englishman who has the sword is a knight called Gerald of Essex, Castellan of Brecon Castle and Sheriff of Brycheniog.'

'My hometown,' said Geraint with interest.

'We know,' said Madog. 'This man here is called John Miller and he hails from a village just outside Brycheniog.' The peasant nodded toward Geraint in deference. 'John came to me with a tale recounting the whereabouts of the sword,' continued Madog. 'At first I paid him little heed but he also said that the Castellan had tricked the leader of the Blaidd into handing over the artefact. This raised my interest for I know the Wolves had been tasked with finding the sword and as only a few of us were aware of this fact, it added strength to the miller's story.'

'Anyway,' said Tarian, stepping into the conversation, 'Madog called me in to verify the tale and as only one man knows the true identity of the Blaidd leader, I contacted Meirion to confirm his story or discard it as mere rumour. When he heard the name for himself, Meirion knew the miller told the truth. It appears the leader of the Blaidd managed to locate the sword but had it wrest from his possession at the last minute. It now lays in the bowels of Brecon castle.'

'Am I to assume you are concerned that it may fall into the hands of Cynan?'

'No,' said Madog, 'that is no longer of consequence but when I heard the name of the man arrested, it jogged a memory and recalled the tales you shared about your time in the Holy Land and the effort your brother made to free you from captivity.'

'What about them?' asked Geraint.

Madog glanced at Tarian before continuing.

'Geraint, the leader of the Blaidd is a man called Garyn ap Thomas and he hails from Brycheniog.'

Geraint's eyes narrowed as he looked around the room.

'There have probably been many men with that name from the town over the years,' he said slowly.

'Granted,' said Madog, 'but Meirion came to know him well over the years and on occasion they shared stories about their past.' He turned to the fixer. 'Meirion, perhaps you could take it from here.'

'Geraint,' said Meirion, 'you will understand that the man I know who leads the Blaidd had to be very careful about hiding his true identity, however, it is true that we became friends and he once told me a little of his past life and I recall he once had a brother. I forget the name but I do remember he said his brother sailed on a quest across the sea and never returned. He also said his father was a blacksmith in Brycheniog.'

'That means nothing,' said Geraint defensively.

'In isolation perhaps,' said Meirion, 'but there was one more thing that I remember, something so strange that I never forgot it.'

'Which was?'

'He also said his brother had a Muslim bride called Misha.'

Geraint stared in astonishment.

'Then the tale must be true,' he said quietly, 'my brother is alive but how can this be? When I returned from the new world, I returned to Brycheniog to find my wife had been killed and my brother had been branded an outlaw. I was told he fled the town and was never seen again. I tried to find him but the trail went cold and I assumed he had died from illness or a hangman's noose. Surely after all these years I would have heard from him?'

'Considering the risks of his new life, he went to great efforts to conceal his identity, as indeed do all the Blaidd,' said Meirion, 'so it is little wonder that the trail went cold.'

Geraint's mind was spinning.

'But if what you say is true, then the man held within Brecon castle is my brother and if he is indeed held by Gerald of Essex, then his life is truly at risk.'

'But why would that be?' asked Madog. 'Perhaps Gerald intends just ransoming him back. Indeed, we could send a message to the knight offering terms.'

'It would be a waste of time,' said Geraint. 'Gerald of Essex is a crooked man with close links to the abbot of Brycheniog and an eviler man has never walked these lands. No, if Garyn is in their hands then his life can be measured in days, if not hours.'

'My lord, if I may,' said John Miller stepping forward.

'Speak,' said Madog.

'My lord, as the man lay dying in my arms, he said many things but one of them made no sense.'

'Spit it out,' said Geraint.

'My lord, he said while the abbot lives, then the lives of the prisoners are safe but when he dies, as he soon will, then the prisoners will be buried the same day.'

'Prisoners,' asked Geraint, 'there are more of them?'

'Yes, my lord. Garyn's son and his ex-wife.'

'Garyn had a son,' gasped Geraint, 'no wonder he went back, the abbot must have used that fact against him.'

'John,' said Tarian, 'you say the abbot will soon be dead, why do you think this?'

'Because it is well known he is very ill and our church has been asked to pray for him.'

Geraint turned to Madog.

'My lord, I have no way of knowing if this is true or a tale of coincidences but I cannot risk it, I have to get down there and see for myself.'

'Geraint,' said Madog, 'everything I have become I owe to you, and the coming campaign will need you at its core, but if by allowing you to go it repays even a tenth of the debt I owe you, then go with my blessing.'

'Thank you, my lord,' said Geraint. 'I will leave immediately.'

'Do you need a guard?'

'No, my lord, I will travel quicker alone and besides, a column of soldiers will only attract attention. If I need military strength, I will approach Cynan in your name.'

'Good idea,' said Madog, 'then travel well, Geraint, and I will pray to god you find your brother alive. Get your things together and I will have your horse prepared.'

Geraint grasped the Prince's arm in gratitude before running from the room.

—

An hour later he rode his horse through the repaired eastern gate of the town walls but as he turned to take the road southward a rider approached out of the darkness.

'Who goes there?' asked Geraint, his hand reaching for his sword.

'Hold your arm, Geraint,' said a familiar voice, 'I trust it will be needed before this thing is over.'

'Tarian,' said Geraint in surprise, as his friend approached, 'what are you doing here?'

'You didn't think I would leave you to go alone, did you?' he asked.

'But who will advise the Prince in your absence?'

'The Prince is no longer a boy, Geraint, he will manage fine.'

Geraint paused but realised his friend was right.

'There is no way of knowing how this will turn out, Tarian, and this Gerald is a treacherous man. The chances are we could die on this task.'

'Then it will be a task no different to any other,' said Tarian.

Silence fell between them.

'So,' said Tarian eventually, 'am I welcome or not?'

'You are,' said Geraint grasping his friend's arm.

'Good,. because I was coming anyway. Now, let's go and get your brother.'

The two men spurred their horses southward while behind them, a young prince sat alone in a candlelit room, poring over charts and drawings of castles, making plans on how to break Edward's ring of steel.

–

In the east an English king stood in his bedchamber, staring out over the city below.

'Come in,' said Edward, as a knock came on the door.

Nicholas Fermbaud entered the room.

'My lord,' he said quietly, 'the army is finally ready, we await your command.'

'Good,' said Edward. 'Send word to my squire, ready my armour and prepare my horse. Tomorrow at first light we ride into Wales and crush this rebellion once and for all. This Madog ap Llewellyn may have experienced some minor victories but he has raised my ire and if he thinks he can call himself Prince then he can think again. Let the word be spread throughout Wales, Fermbaud, tell our beleaguered castellans to take heart and hold out a while longer for help is at hand. Longshanks is coming.

In the south, Garyn lay beaten on the stone floor of a wet dungeon, hoping against hope that his worst enemy didn't die anytime soon. As he lay on the floor a rivulet of his own blood flowed slowly past him, the result of his most recent beating. His hand crept forward and using his finger to form the words in the blood, he wrote the name of the son he never knew he had.

Thomas

Author's Note

As usual this book is loosely based around facts from the time but it has to be said, the work is a fictional tale so any inaccuracies were probably necessary for the story to progress.

Madog ap Llewellyn

Although our story refers to a young man called Madog who takes on the might of the English army, the real Madog was much older and proved a serious threat against Longshanks during the Welsh revolt from 1294–1295. He was a minor noble from Ynys Mon and claimed the title Prince of Wales during the revolt.

The Ring of Steel

There was indeed a concentrated building programme of castles throughout Wales during this time and while some of these were built by others, Edward I was responsible for creating probably the greatest of them all, namely Caernarfon, Conwy, Beaumaris and Harlech. Along with his other castles in Wales, they were collectively referred to as the Ring of Steel and were considered impregnable by all who saw them.

The Siege of Castell du Bere

In or around 1294, Castell du Bere fell to a Welsh force of rebels. Little is known about the siege except for the fact that the castle seemed to have fallen very quickly and as its position protects it from any large concentration of siege engines, one can only speculate that there was some other reason for its downfall. After its destruction it was never rebuilt and Edward himself felt the castle was a grievous loss to his defences.

Cynan ap Maredudd

Cynan was a Welsh warlord who fought against the English throughout Wales. He had many victories to his name and some speculate that he was responsible for the fall of Castell Du Bere.

Caernarfon Castle

Due to the spiralling costs of Edward's campaigns in Scotland and France, Edward withdrew funding for the completion of Caernarfon castle in the mid-1280s. This meant that part of the castle walls was unfinished and it is believed that Madog took advantage of this during the assault in 1294.

Caernarfon Town

Before Madog could reach the castle, he had to breach the town walls. This in itself was a formidable task as it was well fortified and occupied mainly by English immigrants. It is recorded that on the day of the attack, the people of the town were enjoying a summer fair and may have been caught unawares. A terrible slaughter was carried out in the town and many of the walls were damaged along with the port. The Sheriff of Ynys Mon was apparently captured in the town and hung as a traitor.

Segontium

Segontium is a Roman fort on a nearby hill. It is believed that Edward selected the location of the castle, not only for its tactical location but also its proximity to the fort, perhaps for spiritual or mystical reasons.

Siege engines

There were many different types and designs of catapults and probably some that we are not even aware of. However, the two mentioned in the story seemed extremely popular at the time. Trebuchets were particularly good at longer distance, especially with heavier loads, while mangonels, a smaller version, were far more accurate. It is interesting to note that similar to a scene from our story above, there is a documented record regarding the use of a trebuchet during the siege of Auberoche in 1334 by the French, where an English messenger was hurled over the walls of the castle with his messages tied around his neck.

The Dream of Macsen Wledig

The Mabinogion, a famous Welsh book from the Middle
Ages, recalls the dream of Macsen Wledig and it is believed
that Macsen refers to the emperor Magnus Clemens
Maximus who died in AD 388. Ellen Lleyddog, otherwise
known as Ellen of the Hosts, wed the emperor and eventually became known as St Helen of Caernarfon. Many
tales record the emperor as staying and eventually dying
in Wales.

The Sword of Macsen

We can only wonder whether the emperor was buried
with his gladius but if he was, then we can probably say it
lies alongside him still.

More from the author

The Blood of Kings
A Land Divided
A Wounded Realm
Rebellion's Forge
Warrior Princess
The Blade Bearer

The Brotherhood
Templar Steel
Templar Stone
Templar Blood
Templar Fury

Novels
Savage Eden
The Last Citadel
Vampire

Audiobooks
Blood of the Cross
The Last Citadel
A Land Divided
A Wounded Realm
Rebellion's Forge
Warrior Princess